P9-DEQ-461

"You're certain these are all the sales you've made?"

"Yes."

She pointed to each name, but Ewan averted his gaze. Three sales.

"This man, Arnold Pickling, needed a screw to hold the chain on his arrastra. Do you know what an arrastra is, Mr. Burke? Mr. Pickling told me all about them."

Irritation built in his gut. "I know what an arrastra is, Miss Sattler." Sighing, he rubbed his hand down his face. "I used one before I built up the mine."

The mine. The years of defending his claim, of mining gold along the creek in the beginning, battling the rain and the snow. Of building the store, the kitchen and his office. The fight to make a living. The desire to be more than a failure to his father.

What if he lost it all?

Miss Sattler placed her hand on his forearm, jarring him out of his thoughts. "Everything will work out, Mr. Burke."

Slowly he met her gaze. "Thank you," he murmured.

She smiled. A nice smile. Genuine. Warm. For all her faults, Miss Sattler wasn't malicious. He'd do well to respect her, even if her personality grated on his patience.

Janette Foreman is a former high-school English teacher turned stay-at-home mom with a passion for the written word. Through her romances, she hopes people see themselves as having worth in God's eyes. When she sneaks in time for hobbies, she reads, quilts, makes cloth dolls and draws. She makes her home in the northern Midwest with her amazing husband, polydactyl cat, bird-hunting dog and the most adorable baby twin boys on the planet.

Books by Janette Foreman

Love Inspired Historical

Last Chance Wife

Visit the Author Profile page at Harlequin.com.

JANETTE FOREMAN

Last Chance Wife

⬥ **HARLEQUIN**® LOVE INSPIRED® HISTORICAL

If you purchased this book without a cover you should be aware
that this book is stolen property. It was reported as "unsold and
destroyed" to the publisher, and neither the author nor the
publisher has received any payment for this "stripped book."

Recycling programs
for this product may
not exist in your area.

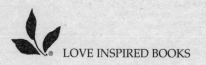

LOVE INSPIRED BOOKS

ISBN-13: 978-1-335-36969-7

Last Chance Wife

Copyright © 2018 by Janette Foreman

All rights reserved. Except for use in any review, the reproduction
or utilization of this work in whole or in part in any form by any
electronic, mechanical or other means, now known or hereafter
invented, including xerography, photocopying and recording, or in
any information storage or retrieval system, is forbidden without
the written permission of the editorial office, Love Inspired Books,
195 Broadway, New York, NY 10007 U.S.A.

This is a work of fiction. Names, characters, places and incidents are
either the product of the author's imagination or are used fictitiously, and
any resemblance to actual persons, living or dead, business establishments,
events or locales is entirely coincidental.

This edition published by arrangement with Love Inspired Books.

® and TM are trademarks of Love Inspired Books, used under license.
Trademarks indicated with ® are registered in the United States Patent
and Trademark Office, the Canadian Intellectual Property Office and in
other countries.

www.Harlequin.com

Printed in U.S.A.

As every man hath received the gift,
even so minister the same one to another,
as good stewards of the manifold grace of God.
—*1 Peter* 4:10

This book is dedicated to Karen Turgeon, my second grade teacher. Because of you, I found my love for stories. Thank you for your continued support and love.

Chapter One

Deadwood, Dakota Territory
September 1878

"In case of trouble, call upon Mr. Ewan Burke at the Golden Star Mine in Deadwood."

Clutching the crinkled note Aunt Mildred had given her, Winifred Sattler raised her gaze to the town in which she'd found herself stranded. Dust curled up as the stagecoach drove away, tinting the air with a dirty dose of failure that caked her lungs. Surely that was what stung her eyes and clouded her vision.

The dust. Not the failure.

Stuffing the note back into her pocket, Winifred wove on foot up the cramped street through a tangle of men, vegetable carts, wagons and horses. Her glance bounced between the wooden buildings and the gaping holes in the road, then scaled the hills on either side of the narrow gulch where the town rested. A slight breeze made the mining town stink of dirt, unlike the sweet aroma of pine that permeated the canyon she had ridden through to get here, and the metallic pounding of stamp mills had begun to give her a headache.

But Winifred would *not* lose hope. She couldn't. Sure, she'd spent the last of her dowry traveling from Denver to Spearfish to marry Mr. Ansell. Then her remaining cash had barely covered the fifteen-mile trip to Deadwood when the mail-order match had turned disastrous.

All she needed now was money to get home. Then she could eat a little humble pie before Uncle Wilbur and devise a new plan. Place new mail-order bride advertisements in the newspapers. Send out more letters to the prospects she would gain. Pray the dear old man hadn't been serious about marrying her off to one of his colleagues if she—again—returned unmarried.

At least this time the mail-order disaster was entirely *not* her fault.

As she focused ahead, a sign for the Golden Star Mine caught her attention—barely. Small and brown, it blended with its natural surroundings. Winifred approached the tall wooden building that scaled the hillside in stair-step fashion and knocked on the door. The entrance certainly didn't feel inviting. How much prettier it would be with flowers or a hedge. Did the slat siding need to be a weathered, natural brown? Wouldn't it be nicer painted white?

Lost in her design ideas, she almost didn't hear the door open.

"Ma'am, may I help you?" A man stared down at her, blocking the entrance. His suit seemed a bit threadbare, though meticulously pressed. Sandy blond hair was combed up off his forehead—which pinched at the sight of her—and gray eyes narrowed in suspicion. "The shop is closed for the night. Might be closed for the rest of the week."

She dug for the note in her pocket. "Are you Mr. Burke?"

His forehead wrinkled further. "Yes…"

Winifred released her breath. "Oh, good. I'm Winifred Sattler. Wilbur Dawson's niece? Nice to meet you." She wedged her way inside before he could protest against it.

She found herself in a quaint, cozy store lit by a lantern on the corner counter. Shelves of merchandise lined the walls, the entire space smaller than Aunt and Uncle's airy sitting room. Except she had thought this to be a gold mine. Why had the man attached a store?

When Winifred turned to Mr. Burke, who didn't appear much older than she, she noted the confidence in his stance, the square rigidity of his shoulders. Strong. Masculine. He crossed his arms and waited for her explanation, so she hastened to give one. "I apologize for my abrupt visit, but my aunt gave me your name in case I ran into trouble, and I must say, I have certainly run into trouble. You would not believe—"

"Hold on." Mr. Burke sliced through her words. "I'm sorry. Who are you?"

"Winifred Sattler, sir." She stood straighter, hoping she didn't look too frazzled after riding the coach so long. She'd left Denver over a week ago, roomed in Deadwood last night, and traveled to Spearfish this morning…only to turn around and come back to Deadwood tonight when prospects in Spearfish turned sour. If Mr. Burke didn't help her, what options would she have? "I'm Wilbur Dawson's niece."

His eyes narrowed further as he looked her over.

She moved one polished black boot against the other, touched her bonnet lined with forget-me-nots. "Lovely place you have here."

Mr. Burke frowned deeper. "Wilbur Dawson...from Denver?"

"Yes. He works closely with your father, Peter Burke. At least that's my understanding."

"Miss Dawson—"

"Sattler."

"Miss Sattler, please understand my confusion." The poor man obviously grappled to keep up. "I was not expecting you. What sort of trouble are you in?"

She opened her mouth to answer, then thought better of it. "I'd rather not say." Best to figure out her next move before sharing her embarrassing mail-order blunder with a stranger. "I can assure you it's nothing illegal. I simply found myself in Deadwood without a place to stay or funds with which to seek lodging or get home." She lifted her face with her brightest smile. "That's where I hope you'll come in. Might you have a place for me to spend a few nights? Any place would do, really. Or I can be gone in the morning if you need me to be—"

"Please." The man held up his hand, signaling for her to stop. "I do have a place available for a few nights. If you need it."

"Oh, I do. I do." She wanted to clap, to shout to the ceiling in triumph—but decided it might be too much for her benefactor to handle.

Mr. Burke locked the front door, turned down the lantern, then lit a small candle. Without a word, he led the way down a long hallway, casting shadows along the wall with his flame.

She followed close, her footsteps light. Removing her bonnet so it hung down her back, she watched the surety with which he carried himself. "So, why will your shop be closed for the week?"

"My clerk quit this afternoon."

Quit? Winifred quickened her steps. "You mean you have a job opening? I'd love to have it. Temporarily, of course."

Mr. Burke glanced back at her. "Why would I hire temporary help, Miss Sattler?"

"To get you through the week, naturally." She shrugged. "Or longer, if needed."

Hopefully her request wasn't too forceful. A temporary clerk job would help her purchase a stagecoach ticket home. When she'd chosen to accept Mr. Ansell's romantic—albeit hasty—proposal, she hadn't gained Uncle's approval. Only after much discussion had he and Aunt let her go…with the understanding that she would pay her own way. Which, of course, meant finding her own way home, too.

Mr. Burke seemed to consider her offer. "Unfortunately, there are other factors I must take into account, but I'll give you my answer in the morning." He led her to a door and knocked. "Cassandra?"

The door opened swiftly, revealing a wiry woman whose brown skin glowed in the candlelight. "Yes, Mr. Burke?"

"This is Miss Winifred Sattler, who is to share your room tonight." The man motioned for Winifred to step closer. "And this is Cassandra Washington."

"But everyone calls me Granna Cass." With a grandmotherly smile, the woman guided Winifred inside. "Everyone except Ewan. He can't stand to call people by their nicknames."

Winifred glanced back at Mr. Burke, who joined them inside before shutting the door.

"Thank you for letting me stay here." Heat blasted Winifred as she entered a kitchen, complete with stove and preparation table. Various cooking tools hung along the walls, and in the back corner, a section had been partitioned off for what appeared to be Granna Cass's sleeping quarters.

"Come on in, child." Leaving Winifred's side, the woman zipped back to the table, where several small pails sat side by side. "Ewan, help yourself to soup on the stove while I finish the lunch pails. Miss Sattler, fill them with me while I get to know you."

Mr. Burke crossed to the stove and ladled soup into a bowl, his movements efficient and sure. Winifred rushed to the woman's side and followed her lead as she constructed sandwiches and wrapped them in paper. "Pardon me, but did you say lunch?"

"For the night-shift workers." Granna Cass set one sandwich into a pail and had a second one half made before Winifred finished her first. "Miss Winnie, tell me your story."

"My story?" Winifred couldn't help but glance at Mr. Burke as she placed a chunk of corned beef between two slices of bread.

Turning from the stove with his soup, he met her gaze. In the stronger light, his hair had a coppery tint. Hardened lines etched his facial features, like he always had something on his mind and didn't stop to laugh and joke very often. Such a sad way to live. He seemed so stern, like he couldn't be bothered with charity work—which had basically become her situation, at this point.

Her cheeks began to warm. "What do you want to know?"

The elderly woman chuckled. "Whatever you want to tell me."

That wouldn't be much, then, at least not with Mr. Burke staring at her like that. "I was born in Kansas and moved to Denver with my aunt and uncle when I was six."

"Ah, chasing gold?" Granna Cass's skilled hands moved like lightning. "Ewan's family works in Colorado. His brother has a successful gold mine, doesn't he?"

Mr. Burke cleared his throat, then sipped his soup, not commenting further.

Winifred slipped another sandwich into a pail. "My uncle invests in entrepreneurs. We moved to Denver so he could find businesses to help." Mr. Burke's gaze narrowed again. Her chest tightened at his obvious disapproval of her. Sure, she'd shown up unannounced tonight, but was that any reason to glare at her so harshly?

"Miss Winnie, you'd better have some of that soup, too. Not much left. The boys already had their supper." Granna Cass moved to the large pot perched on the stove.

"The boys?"

"The miners." Mr. Burke's voice held a guarded edge. "Many of my men eat here during the shift change. It's a benefit I will not compromise."

Winifred blinked as she tried to make sense of his

defensive explanation. Did he expect her to disapprove of his offering food to his employees?

No sooner had she slipped a sandwich into the pail than a commotion like a thundering herd approached the kitchen door.

"There they are," said Granna Cass. "Right on time."

In quick motion, the kitchen door flew open. Men barreled inside, their boots clomping along the hard floor. Dirt clung to their clothes. Winifred pushed against the wall as they encircled the table like wolves surrounding prey. They plucked their pails from the table with big hands and acknowledged Mr. Burke's presence with a solemn nod before trudging back out, circling wide rather than getting too close to their employer.

One man inspected the contents of his pail. "Corned beef again, Granna Cass?"

"Yes, sir." The woman shot him a knowing smile, propping a fist on her hip and raising her graying eyebrows. "Just like every day before."

The man looked like he wanted to say more, but he glanced at Mr. Burke and seemed to decide against it, then gave Granna Cass a cautious smile and left with the others.

When the door shut and silence took over the room again, Winifred thought about what the miner had said. "Does he not like corned beef?"

"Those boys, I tell you." Granna Cass shook her head and handed Winifred a bowl of soup. "Always wanting something more. Last week, that same boy asked if we could have mutton in the sandwiches. *Mut-*

ton. Sure, I'd love to fix it for them, mutton, goose, fish…"

"Why don't you?" Winifred licked a bit of soup off her spoon, and her eyes widened at the explosion of flavor cascading over her tongue.

"Because this is a business," Mr. Burke cut in. "Funds are limited. Cassandra, that reminds me, I have an investor coming tomorrow, if you can add an extra serving to your noon meal." Mr. Burke placed his bowl and spoon on the table. "I'm heading out. Thank you for supper." He turned his stare on Winifred again. "I'll give you my answer on the clerk position in the morning."

Winifred forced a nod. "Of course."

Mr. Burke left, his footfalls fading down the hall.

She took another bite. "You're quite the cook, Granna Cass." But even as the delicious soup coated her throat, she wrinkled her nose and glanced at the door. "Mr. Burke strikes me as the pragmatic type."

"Which tells me you're not." Granna Cass didn't hide the grin spreading her brown cheeks. "Yes, Ewan Burke is the pragmatic type. But underneath that practical exterior, he's got one of the warmest hearts I've ever known. You'll see."

Winifred doubted it. "I'm afraid I'm only in town long enough to earn coach fare back home." She'd leave Deadwood long before she could witness whatever Granna Cass believed about Mr. Burke.

Funny how a man could be handsome and yet as stuffy as a freshly starched collar.

Not that she cared how handsome he was. Or about the striking sense in his eyes. Her only interaction with this man would center on her temporary arrangement and nothing more.

After putting away the sandwich materials, Granna Cass made up a narrow sleeping pallet at the foot of her bed inside the secluded nook. "I know it's not much," she said, tossing a blanket over the thin mattress, "but it seems to work until we find the women decent housing."

"The women?" Winifred untied her bonnet ribbons from beneath her chin.

Granna Cass paused. "Ewan didn't tell you about the women?"

Winifred raised her brows. "No..."

"Then I'll wait to say anything else." Granna Cass moved back to the preparation table, to the mounds of dough she'd allowed to rise there. "It's Ewan's mission, so I'll let him explain. Point is, I hope your stay is comfortable, however long it may be."

Mission? What did she mean? But Winifred's question faded as she watched Granna Cass rotate her wiry arms and push the heels of her hands through the dough. "Want help?"

"No, no, this job relaxes me before I go to sleep. Gets me in the right mood for tomorrow. Do you do anything before bed, Miss Winnie?"

"Usually I read, but I left my books at the station with my trunks." She would get them tomorrow, provided she still had a place to stay.

The elderly woman smiled and tossed her a newspaper. "This is all the reading material I've got, but you're welcome to it."

Winifred smiled. "Thank you. For everything."

"Don't thank me. Thank Mr. Burke. He's the one allowing you to stay."

True. She would thank Mr. Burke in the morning. Telling herself not to think of her empty future, she finished removing her bonnet and tossed it beside her pallet. She frowned as she stared down at it, the bonnet with the golden sash and blue forget-me-nots she'd promised to wear for Mr. Ansell. After today, she'd likely burn the wretched thing, for all the good it had done her.

As she slipped beneath her thin blanket, the reality of her situation pricked her eyes, causing the newspaper print to blur. She had been so certain of Mr. Ansell. Ever since her parents died, she'd dreamed of having a love like theirs, a sacrificial, deep, abiding love that no one else would understand. With suitor after suitor, she had developed a better idea of what that love would look like, sound like, feel like—and Mr. Ansell had fed her all the right sentiments to make her believe he shared her dream and could make it come true.

All she wanted was to be cherished for who she was. That wasn't too extravagant to ask for, was it?

Now, because she'd fallen for the wrong man—a man who had proven unworthy of her trust, much less her love—she'd stranded herself in a foreign place, forced to pick up the splinters of her heart alone.

She would send a letter to Uncle and explain everything. Of course, she'd have to find a way to convince him not to marry her off as soon as she returned to Denver. She'd tried his approach before, allowing his cronies to court her, but soon learned investor businessmen were as dull as they came. When she married, she wanted a man of passion. And she wanted him to love her for who she was, not for the connection to her uncle she could offer. That's why mail ordering seemed so ideal. She could travel to a new place, meet new people and be a part of something bigger than herself.

Winifred lowered her eyes. At least, at first, that's what drew her to the idea of courtship through the mail. But now, after six failed attempts, she wondered if it wasn't merely adventurous to take this path toward marriage but, in fact, downright foolhardy.

Losing her appetite to read, she picked up the newspaper to toss it away—when two small words caught her eye: "Wife Wanted."

Frowning, she set the newspaper back on her pallet and scanned the short ad.

Wife Wanted: Mr. Businessman seeks wife. Needn't be beautiful; must be practical.

Winifred dropped her head and groaned into her blankets.

Now she'd heard everything. This was what seeking a wife had come to—stating truth, yes, but bluntly. No romance there, not even an attempt to promise love or affection should a woman be desperate enough to answer such an ad.

An idea struck her, and she reached into her nearby valise for a pencil and stationery. For his honest request, this man deserved an honest reply. Not that she would send it. But maybe writing the silly thing would ease her frustrations about today's events. She thumbed through her envelopes for the perfect one to seal away her pretend response. In her boredom during the coach ride from Cheyenne to Deadwood, she had resorted to sketching sprawling images across her envelopes, leaving just enough space on each one for the recipient address and the stamp.

Settling on one with a hummingbird in flight above a half dozen flowers, she smiled and tucked the rest away in her valise. Then, using the newspaper as a hard surface, she laid out her pretty floral stationery and penciled her reply. This was exactly what she needed in order to forget Mr. Ansell.

"Dear Mr. Businessman…"

If there had been a way to fail at gaining an investor, Ewan Burke had surely found it.

Judging by the firm line etched across Mr. Richard Johns's forehead, anyway. A line that only deepened the farther he read through Ewan's report.

Ewan rubbed a hand down his mouth, pausing on his shaven chin. He glanced at his office clock. Nearly five. The investor had read through the plans twice but still hadn't relayed his thoughts.

"Mr. Johns…" Prompting seemed like the way to go. "May I answer any questions?"

"Yes," the man responded in a gravelly voice, eyes still glued to the stack of papers. "When do you plan on turning a profit?"

"Very soon, sir." Not as soon as he would like, but he had built this mine from nothing, and he counted any growth as progress. "I have worked out the numbers and estimated our growth over the next few quarters, and—"

"And you'll still be no closer to making this into a prospering business." The older man sighed and lifted off his spectacles. "Look, Mr. Burke. Your enthusiasm for the Golden Star Mine is admirable. And the business is new yet. But I don't invest in charity cases. If you want my funds, then this company needs to prove it will make me money soon—not in some fairy-tale future. Understand?"

Pursing his lips, Ewan stifled his own sigh. "Of course, Mr. Johns. I agree."

"There, now. I'd best be off." The investor plunked the stack of papers on Ewan's desk in a ruffled heap and stood.

Ewan hastened to meet him at the door, then escorted him out of the office and down the flight of stairs leading to the Golden Star's main level. Only the light slapping of their shoes on the stairs filled the silence between them. Resisting the urge to cling to the banister, Ewan opened the door at the base for the middle-aged man to exit through first. *Kindness, regardless of affliction.* Of course his mother's relentless teaching reverberated through him now, when tossing the investor out on his rotund rump sounded like the more tempting option.

From the moment Ewan received Father's letter announcing his colleague's trip to Deadwood to invest in Black Hills gold, he had spent countless hours preparing for this meeting. He'd meticulously compared the average growth of his gold production with others', based on the year the Golden Star was a simple placer mine by the creek and the six months that followed, when it'd become a drift mine carved into the mountainside.

His business wasn't perfect, but it was just beginning, and he'd been confident that his report showed how the Golden Star was poised to thrive, if it could only gain the support it needed to pass through these growing pains. But now after this rejection, Ewan had to fight the sinking feeling clawing at his stomach as he shut the stairwell door and followed the investor to the front of the office building. Bidding farewell to Mr. Johns might very well mean bidding farewell to his own dreams of making something of himself.

Ewan opened the next door, the one that connected the Golden Star's offices with its tiny general store. He crossed the shop floor in haste. "Thank you for coming. I wish you safe travels back to Denver." He turned to Mr. Johns with his hand outstretched.

The man slipped his knobby hand into Ewan's politely, but nothing cordial appeared in his pointed stare. "Your father told me I wouldn't be disappointed." He pulled their hands closer to his body, causing Ewan to lean in. "I hate going back empty-handed."

Ewan kept his stare calm and confident. "My father is never wrong, Mr. Johns. When will business bring you back to Deadwood?"

"In December."

"Ah." He broadened his smile to keep from wincing. "Three months." Not much time to begin showing a profit—but then again, judging by his ledger, he didn't really have a choice.

Yes, his growth had been slowly climbing over the past six months, but a series of recent setbacks had put a weighty strain on his finances. Damaged and missing equipment, broken-down machinery…even production was suffering because a few of his employees had quit. According to a conversation Ewan had had with one of them, the man had learned how fledgling the business truly was and had felt it was too risky to stay. Ewan had tried explaining that every business started this way, that all they needed was time—and funds—to blossom. But apparently the man hadn't expected the business's financial state to be so precarious, and his worry about shutting down had spread to the others.

Like gangrene through a wounded body.

Just how many others had been infected, Ewan didn't know. To be sure, only a few had quit, so he prayed the concerns had stopped with them.

Mr. Johns's investment would give them a boost. And they certainly needed one. As much as Ewan hated to admit it, the Golden Star could only tread water so long, and he needed to get the mine over this financial hump before his employees' worries came to fruition.

"Come back when you're in town, Mr. Johns," Ewan said, "and I'll show you the improvements we've made."

"And the money." The man emphasized the M word like the chop of a guillotine.

"Of course, sir. How nice to meet you."

Mr. Johns grunted as he shut the outside door behind him and was gone.

Feet stuck to the rug, Ewan stared at the door's paned glass, not focusing on the smattering of dust collecting there, nor on the booming gold town that lay beyond his establishment.

He had three months to get the Golden Star Mine earning more than it spent. Three. Plenty of gold existed in the mountain to do that very thing. The problem was extracting it and refining it to sell. Every penny he'd made already went straight back into the business—buying equipment, digging the mine and constructing the main building, which held offices, a small kitchen and meager housing for a few employees. But in order to grow—and cover those unexpected recent expenses—the business required more money than what his current profits could cover. He still needed extra hand drills, black powder and miners to reach more gold. And what good was more gold if he didn't purchase more stamps for his stamp mill to process it? Those were what he needed in order to produce the growth Mr. Johns wanted to see.

And aside from producing growth, he needed room in his business to offer employment options for disheartened men who no one else would hire, or when women arrived from the Gem Theater and other desperate situations with nowhere else to turn. Those situations didn't happen often, but when they did, he refused to turn the downtrodden away.

Point being, Ewan *needed* to prove to Mr. Johns that the Golden Star wasn't too much of a risk. That *he* wasn't too much of a risk.

Raking his fingers through his hair, Ewan turned away. Just then, the door to the rest of the office building opened and Cassandra slipped through, holding the empty bags she always carried when she visited the venders downtown who sold vegetables from their carts.

"Good morning," she said with all the warmth of the grandmother she'd become to him. "I'm off to fetch ingredients for the noon meal. I'll be sure to buy extra for your investor guest."

Ewan exhaled. "No need. He left."

She paused in her trek across the shop. "Left? So soon?"

"He doesn't want anything to do with us until we're more profitable. He'll be back in three months' time to see if we've changed enough to justify his interest."

Cassandra tilted her head, a knowing look crossing her gaze. "That's not much time."

"I know." Ewan allowed his focus to trail to the clerk counter, where Lucinda Pratt had stood since nearly their opening—until she surprised him yesterday with her resignation, due to a marriage proposal from some gentleman she barely knew. They were riding off to Montana Territory at that very moment to start their new life together. The store was only a small part of his business, but it brought in some money. Money he would have to do without until he found a replacement for her.

"Never underestimate what God can accomplish." Eyes glittering, Cassandra continued toward the door as if the matter were settled. Then she spun back again. "Oh, I almost forgot. Here's yesterday's paper, which you never had the chance to read." She deposited the copy of *The Black Hills Daily Times* on the counter. "By the way, I saw your mail-order bride advertisement inside."

A teasing lilt to her voice coated the comment. Ewan felt his spine straighten. "What's wrong with it?"

"For one thing, it doesn't include your name."

"Advertisements can be expensive. Every word costs. The rest of the content was essential—including my name was not. If someone responds, I'll gladly send her my name." The letter would get to him regardless. The postmaster, Sol Star, knew of his pseudonym, much to Ewan's chagrin. Sadly, he couldn't even hide his marital struggle from the postmaster.

Mr. Businessman. How prosaic, even for him. Finding a mail-order bride hadn't been his first choice, but after feeling the shame of being left at the altar, Ewan had moved out of Denver to start over in the wilds of Wyoming Territory and then Dakota. Problem was, once his string of moves had led him to Deadwood to finally set down roots and claim his mine, wifely prospects practically shrank to nil.

Sometimes a man had to swallow his pride if he wanted to achieve a greater goal—to succeed in his personal life as well as his professional to make his father proud.

"Is the high cost also the reason behind your brief, oh-so-endearing description of your ideal bride?" Rustling the newspaper, Cassandra cut through Ewan's thoughts, bringing the advertisement closer to read. "'Needn't be beautiful; must be practical.'" She dropped the paper and eyed him.

Ewan fidgeted. When read like that, it did sound a bit harsh. "It's the truth. I know what my match should be like—staid and sensible. The vivacious, effervescent type is not for me."

He'd tried that kind of romance once before. Never again.

"Well, love finds people in the strangest places sometimes. If the Lord has a bride for you, you'll find each other somehow—even if it's by newspaper." Her eyes glittered brighter, like his situation amused her. "I'm off. I hope you find your no-nonsense wife." The door shut behind her, and again, Ewan stood on the shop rug, staring through the dusty windowpanes, at a complete loss for words.

What a day. First, he hadn't gained the investor he needed. Second, his store had no clerk. Third, Lucinda, a woman he'd vowed to keep from prostitution, had moved on with life too prematurely. She was throwing herself into marriage with the same impetuosity she'd shown when she'd come to town to answer an ad for singers for a local theater, never guessing that the ad was a scam and the "theater" was nothing more than a brothel. Would this latest plan of hers, this whirlwind wedding, end in disaster as well? And what of his own marriage prospects? His fourth problem today was that he had to seek a wife through the local paper, where his only options were uncouth like Calamity Jane, or at the very least, were pining insatiably for adventure. They'd never be in a male-heavy, primitive mining town otherwise.

A world of good either of those types would do him. But what other choice did he have? He'd come to Deadwood with one intention—to prove himself as capable as Samuel. If everything his twin brother touched could turn to gold, then Ewan should have the same power. Yet, so far in his twenty-nine years, he had no success to show for himself. No wife and no thriving business, and he was an ongoing disappointment to his father.

Getting an investment from Mr. Johns, and placing this newspaper ad for a wife, was his chance at redemption.

"I wanted to thank you again for this opportunity, Mr. Burke."

Ewan forced a smile at Miss Sattler as he shut his

office door, leaving them both in the hallway. "And again, you are welcome. Now, follow me. I'll show you around the store."

He moved down the flight of stairs with Miss Sattler close behind him. "It's amazing how things work out when you look for the silver lining," she began. "And when you take the Lord's providence into account. Even though I'm in a foreign town, I've wanted for nothing. I've had a roof over my head and food to sustain me, and everyone has been so friendly."

She laughed, and Ewan shot her a polite smile. But inwardly, he fought reservations. Had he been too hasty in hiring her? All she needed was temporary work—and judging by her frilly attire and what he knew of her uncle, she'd be perfectly looked after once she returned home. She was bound to be headed back there soon—which was all to the good. Ewan wanted to keep the position open for someone truly in need. That was one reason he had a store in the first place—to employ souls in desperation. He'd created a couple other jobs for the same purpose: clerical work, helping Cassandra. Though none paid as well as the store.

Lucinda had appeared at his mine with no family and nowhere to turn, besides living on the street or returning to the brothel that had entrapped her in the first place. There were plenty more like her, just gathering the courage to ask for help. Miss Sattler didn't have those problems. Well dressed, educated. Had a wealthy family. Her uncle would no doubt snatch Miss Sattler from trouble if she ever found herself there.

But as much as he'd rather place Miss Sattler in a less prominent job, he couldn't very well shut down the store until another woman came to him for help.

Could be weeks. Months. And he needed the supplemental income.

"Miss Sattler." He interrupted her explanation. "You can stay with Cassandra as long as there is room. I have to warn you, though, I have visitors from time to time. They receive precedence. If one comes to stay, I'll let Cassandra decide if there is still space for you, too."

"Oh, yes, of course." She nodded, her red earrings swinging back and forth. She wore her brown hair in a fashionable chignon with pearl combs that somehow made her grayish-blue eyes brighter.

He was staring. Tearing his attention away and back to the door at the base of the stairs, he opened it for Miss Sattler. "I want to ensure you understand that this employment is temporary. If someone comes in seeking permanent employment, I need to be able to offer it."

Nodding, she paused in the doorway. "Understood, Mr. Burke. I'm just glad you're giving me a chance at all."

Her eyes held the same earnest, warm expression they had when she'd appeared in his shop last night. Normally that kind of thing didn't move him, at least not from privileged women like Miss Sattler, but his desperation to keep his store open tipped the scales in her favor. And he couldn't very well permit a woman with no ready funds to search for other lodging when he had the space.

She chattered as they made their way down the corridor, allowing Ewan to observe her unabashedly. While he had never personally met her uncle, he knew the man had a shrewd reputation when it came to his investments in gold. And an investor was exactly what Ewan needed. Had Wilbur Dawson heard about the Golden Star? Perhaps Miss Sattler had been sent to look the place over, covertly, and then report back her findings.

Or maybe Father had sent her. No telling with that man. He might want to pry into the business to see if the mine's progress relayed in Ewan's letters home was true—or he might want to lure Ewan into an advantageous marriage. Advantageous for Father, of course. Not that Ewan would fall for that maneuver again. He would find a wife on his own. Someone like Miss Sattler would never suit. Not with her obvious tendency to dream, to flit from one topic to the next without much depth. He wasn't interested in a relationship with someone who couldn't maintain a serious conversation, couldn't shoulder the weight of the business as his partner.

And he certainly wasn't interested in someone who reminded him of the woman who left him at the altar seven years ago.

"Here we are." At the corridor's end, he pushed open the shop door for Miss Sattler to enter ahead of him. "We sell mining supplies and a few staple items, as well as other general merchandise. To the outside eye, it might seem strange to sell staple items alongside mining supplies—but the more merchandise I have to offer, the more money I can potentially make."

Even though she had seen the store before, Miss Sattler floated to the middle of the room to take it all in, as if it were a palace and she a princess presiding over its splendor. Her light blue dress brushed the floor as she turned a slow circle and gazed at each shelf—

which might as well have contained priceless jewels, judging by the smile spreading her mouth.

She met his gaze. "It's beautiful."

His brow rose a little. *Beautiful* wasn't a word he'd ever associated with the shop. Efficient, yes. Reliable, certainly. But beautiful?

"I expect you here by nine sharp every morning," he explained, getting the conversation back on track. "You may take a half-hour break to eat lunch with Cassandra at noon, and then it's back to the shop. No dallying in the kitchen when you should be working."

Miss Sattler gave a definitive nod. "Of course."

"Close the shop at five thirty, and not before. A key hangs beneath the sales counter. Do what you'd like before and after work hours, as long as it's legal, safe and will keep your reputation and mine in a positive light."

"Naturally." She grinned. "This will be so wonderful, Mr. Burke. I can't express to you how thankful I am for your help."

Though it wouldn't stop her from trying. Ewan mustered another tight-lipped smile. "Just run the store as if you're working for the Lord and not for man. Then we'll get along fine." He strode to the door leading outside. "I have an errand to run. Will you be all right on your own?"

"Oh, yes." She splayed her hands across the clean counter as if it, too, were made of gold. "I have everything I need."

Ewan suppressed a sigh. Truly, Miss Sattler was turning out to be as silly and overemotional as they came. But thankfully, this arrangement would only be temporary.

He shut the door and crossed the wooden walkway

shielded by tall ponderosa pines. Stepping into sunlight, he shook his head to clear his thoughts. That woman was something else.

And seemed to hold a secret. He'd suspected it from the moment she walked into the store last night. Why else had she circumvented questions about her situation? Something had brought her to Deadwood, without money or resources beyond a couple of trunks and a scrap of paper bearing his name. Perhaps she really was gathering information to bring back to her investor uncle. While Ewan hoped she'd send home a favorable report, he really didn't like the idea of being scrutinized. Or lied to.

No matter the reason for Miss Sattler's visit, however, he couldn't let her distract him. He had a three-month deadline to think of. And thinking about her twirling in his shop, with those big eyes, already distracted him.

Clearing his throat, Ewan stepped inside the Deadwood post office, which appeared empty. Most people wouldn't come until tomorrow—the stagecoach only picked up mail and dropped it off once every three weeks, creating an incredibly long line of patrons on that day. No way would he ever stand in line like that. Nothing was that important. But he did have two letters to post today. One for Mr. Johns and one for Father. His note of thanks for the investor wasn't much, but he hoped the small courtesy would be enough to solidify a positive memory in the man's mind. His letter home explained the outcome of his meeting, so Father didn't solely hear Mr. Johns's impressions.

"Good morning, Mr. Star." Ewan dropped his envelopes on the counter. "I would like these to leave on the coach tomorrow, if you please."

"Morning, Ewan." Mr. Star smiled, his words tinged with a slight Bavarian accent. "Denver. Are you writing home?"

"Yes, sir." Ewan worked to hide his lack of confidence. He needed his father to hear his side before he heard Mr. Johns's report, to understand why his son had failed to snag the investor he'd practically handed to him. To know Ewan would do everything in his power to remedy that.

"Oh, and I have a letter for you, too."

"You do?" Ewan frowned, leaning forward slightly on the countertop. "But the mail doesn't come until tomorrow."

"This one's local. I'll fetch it." Mr. Star left the front desk and ambled to the back room.

Ewan drummed his fingers on the countertop. Who would send him a letter? Hopefully not Mac Glouster, owner of the Sphinx, the mine north of Ewan's claim. He'd been trying to convince Ewan to sell out to him practically since the Golden Star began its operations. And it had better not be from that California capitalist who had been buying up claims around the area as of late. Graham Young might have bought the Glittering Nugget, the mine directly to the Golden Star's south—for a pretty penny, too—but that didn't mean Ewan would give in to the pressure. Selling would be shortsighted. He was certain that his land carried great wealth, and he refused to get a mere portion of money, no matter how sizable, if it meant giving up the land.

Besides the wealth, the Golden Star Mine had become home. He had labored to build it to this level, despite the numerous letters from Father telling him to leave the venture and come work for his brother in a stable Colorado mine. Selling out now would solidify his reputation within the family and the mining community as the unsuccessful twin, the poor, unfortunate fodder for gossip.

"Here you are." The postmaster reentered, waving the envelope in his hand. "Looks like you've garnered interest of the female variety. Look at all that frilly sketching on the envelope."

An answer to his advertisement. Not a capitalist inquiry. He was pleased but also surprised—he hadn't expected a response so soon. Ewan snatched up the envelope, his gaze following the pencil rendering of a bird as he turned to leave. He stopped and looked back. Where were his manners? "Thank you, Star."

"Sure thing. Hope it's good news." The postmaster grinned knowingly, and Ewan pretended not to notice.

As he strolled back to the mine, his attention wandered over the sketch—a hummingbird among flowers, clear as day. Though he couldn't deny the frivolity of embellishing envelopes, he also could not ignore the fact that the artist had talent. And oddly, part of him felt a little special that whoever wrote him back would send something this time-consuming.

A wagon rolled by and dust swirled through his path. He ran his thumb under the letter's seal to break it, then extracted the note.

Dear Mr. Businessman,

    I am not actually responding to your letter in particular but to bride letters in general. To be clear, I am not looking to begin a relation-

ship with you. I have experienced enough letter writing with other men to imagine what was
going through your mind when you wrote your
advertisement, and I confess I'm tired of men
having ulterior motives while seeking a bride.
I am convinced that most use letter writing as
a coward's way to find a wife. For once, I wish
men would think about the feelings they are creating within a woman and stop acting like it's a
simple game of pursuit that could either end or
carry on with little consequence. When I find
someone to marry, it won't be through letters.
It'll be in person—and to someone I trust.
Sincerely yours,
Thoroughly Disgruntled

Ewan blinked a few times. Frowned. Turned the
paper over, then back again. Was this some sort of
joke? He checked inside the envelope again, just in
case he'd missed another portion that explained the
whole thing had been a tease.

Nothing.

Scowling, he stepped into the Golden Star store.
Someone had actually paid postage to mock his attempts to find a wife. Unbelievable. Did no one have
common decency anymore?

"Mr. Burke?" Miss Sattler's voice came from the
corner, where she pulled things out from behind the
counter. "Do you know where the ledger is? I need to
record a sale—"

"I don't know." In fact, he wasn't certain he'd even
heard her question fully. He stalked between the table

displays to the door at the back, pushed through it and marched down the hall and up the steps to his office.

The nerve of some people.

Taking a seat at his pinewood desk, he read through the letter again. But as he did, his frown softened. *Kindness, regardless of affliction.* Forcing himself to see the writer's words through the lenses his mother gave him, he recognized a distinctly different tone than what he had been aware of before.

"I wish men would think about the feelings they are creating within a woman and stop acting like it's a simple game of pursuit that could either end or carry on with little consequence."

She sounded hurt, not prideful. As if she'd been taken advantage of by someone careless.

Ewan had known far too many women who had been used by men for their own pleasures, whether physically or emotionally. The women's feelings had never been considered or valued in the slightest. Men like that cared only for themselves. And he had determined never to be one of them.

Swiping a clean sheet of paper from his desk drawer, along with a pencil, he formulated a reply.

Chapter Two

Two days down. Winifred had been on Mr. Burke's payroll for two days without much mishap…though without obvious success, either. Mr. Burke spent hours in his office. Days for Winifred were spent alone in the store with only the very occasional customer, then nights were spent in Granna Cass's kitchen. The hours rolled by with little action, and it had begun to drive her mad.

Sleep proved difficult due to the pounding of stamp mills rumbling the ground. So last night she'd spent a couple of extra hours awake by Granna Cass's fire composing a letter to send home to Aunt and Uncle. While she didn't shy away from explaining her situation, she did use plenty of graceful language to avoid the ugly particulars.

Now, in the minutes before work began for the day, she walked to the post office using the directions Mr. Burke had given her, letter in hand.

Inside the post office, her heels echoed in the empty room. The man behind the counter glanced up, his thinning hair parted and slicked to one side. A little sign on the counter stated "Sol Star—Postmaster."

"Mornin', ma'am." She detected a slight accent, though she couldn't quite guess at the origin. "Here to pick up your mail?"

"No, I'm afraid I don't have a box." Smiling, she approached the counter with her small valise hanging around her elbow. "I came to post a letter."

The man leaned on the counter, regarding her. "No box? Would you like to open one?"

"Oh, thank you, but I'm only planning to be in town temporarily. Any correspondence I might happen to get can be directed to the Golden Star Mine."

She opened her bag and withdrew the letter she'd written to Uncle Wilbur. Hopefully it would keep him from panicking and hastily marrying her off. And if she were blessed, maybe her honeyed words would convince him to send the money she needed to get home, so she wouldn't have to take advantage of Mr. Burke's kindness. Her employer had been good to hire her, but he'd made it clear her presence was a bit of a bother.

"You do know," the postmaster began, "that the mail came through yesterday."

Blinking, she waited for him to continue, her envelope poised above the counter. When he didn't, she furrowed her brow, grappling to understand his implication. "Oh?"

The postmaster looked at her like she should understand. Clearly, he thought she had missed something by not coming in the day prior, but what could it be? She certainly had no reason to watch for the arrival of any mail. No one even knew she was here. "That's fine. I'm not expecting anything."

"Right. But, ma'am, it means the letter you're sending won't leave this office for another three weeks."

"Three weeks?" Her hand holding her letter dropped to the countertop. "The mail only comes through every three weeks? Is that common up here?"

Mr. Star nodded. "Basically, yes. It goes by coach, not train. Hopefully you're not expecting an urgent reply."

She was. If it took three weeks for the letter to *leave* Deadwood, who knew how much longer it would take to reach Uncle Wilbur in Denver? If she were fortunate enough for him to send funds, and send them immediately, his reply still wouldn't reach her for another three weeks—unless, of course, he missed the deadline, and then it would be three weeks after that. The weeks stretched out before her, pressed down upon her, and her heart began to crumble beneath the weight. At this rate, it would be impossible to receive enough money to leave Mr. Burke's employment any faster than if she earned the stagecoach fare herself.

She glanced at her envelope and tapped it lightly on the counter. "Then I might not send this." No need to tell Aunt and Uncle about her situation if she'd likely be on the stage before the letter reached home.

The postmaster pressed his lips together beneath his wide, dark mustache. "Perhaps a telegram would be better?"

Winifred raised her gaze to his. "A telegram? Oh, yes, that would be splendid." But her brow pinched as the man reached for a form on which to write the note. "I'll have to pay for it later. I don't have enough for a telegram yet, but I do have a job, so once I—"

"Sorry, ma'am." The man slid a form across the counter. "Gotta have the payment first. Too many transient folks in town, you understand."

"Oh… How much is a telegram per word?"

When he told her the exorbitant amount, Winifred shifted, her pulse increasing. It would take her a long time to earn that much. And once she did, would it be wise to spend it on a telegram, or simply save it for a coach ticket?

Then again, there was still the chance that Uncle would send money once he heard about her predicament, and it might arrive before she had a chance to earn fare—which would likely please Mr. Burke. "Thank you, then. I'll return when I have the correct amount."

"That sounds fine." His gaze settled on her letter and froze, brows drawing together. "Can I see that?"

He reached for her letter, but she withdrew her hand. "No, remember? I won't be sending it."

"I'm not going to send the letter." Mr. Star chuckled. "I just want to see the artwork on your envelope."

This one contained a sketch of a buffalo in the prairie grass. She'd spotted a herd near the trail and had drawn one from the safety of the stagecoach.

She handed over the letter. When she'd used her envelopes as her canvas, she'd had Aunt Mildred in mind. The dear woman asked her not to stop drawing just because she traveled off to become a wife. The art had been for her, not only to prove that Winifred hadn't stopped, but also to help Aunt see the beautiful land Winifred had planned to call home.

All for naught now. She'd have to give the sketches to her dear aunt in person when she returned home, humiliated and still unmarried, yet again. Which was why she'd wasted one of her envelopes to seal up the letter to "Mr. Businessman"—a letter that would never leave her valise in all her days.

"An envelope very similar to this came through the other day." The postmaster turned the envelope over, following the scrawling sketch. "Ah, yes, see here? The initials embedded in the drawing itself. WS."

Her eyes widened. She'd thought the initials were hidden quite well in the drawing. And wait—how did the postmaster know...

"Are you Miss Thoroughly Disgruntled?" The man's gaze twinkled, meeting hers. "This buffalo is quite nice."

"I beg your pardon?" Winifred felt the blood drain from her face, along with her ability to understand complete sentences. Surely he hadn't just called her...

"The advertisement reply to Mr. Businessman," Mr. Star prompted. "Your letter had no return address, so when he mailed a response, I kept it in the back in case you came in—though I wasn't sure how I'd know you, without a name or description. Handy thing, having those drawings as a calling card. I couldn't believe he had the gall to call you that on the envelope. Though I suppose you must've kept your name a secret or he would've used it. But 'Miss Thoroughly Disgruntled'?"

He let out a deep belly chuckle, and Winifred had to catch herself on the counter to keep her knees from giving out beneath her.

"I think you have me confused with someone else."

No way could he have meant her. The advertisement, a reply…they had to be coincidental. Her letter still lay secured in her valise. Though she couldn't exactly explain away how he'd guessed the nickname she'd signed to the letter or how he knew her initials were in the sketch.

"You did respond to an advertisement for a wife, didn't you?" He cocked his head to the side. "The envelope that came through looked just like this, except it was of a hummingbird. Wait one moment."

The man left the counter and went into a back room. Alone, Winifred plopped her valise on the counter and unhooked the buckles. It didn't make sense. Everything he said described *her* response to the ad. But it *couldn't* be hers. The envelope remained in her bag.

She riffled through her tangled contents. "Come on, come on…" Heart beating wildly, she yanked out her stack of envelopes and flipped through them. Empty. Every single one, and no sign of the one with the hummingbird.

"Here we are." The postmaster returned with a letter, and she prayed it would be hers. But no, she could see the envelope's crisp whiteness from a distance, void of her rambling sketches. As he set the envelope on the counter, he grinned as if he'd found himself involved in a most creative and intriguing plot. "Your mystery suitor replied immediately. Same day, actually. I've never seen someone so eager. And what providence to be in the same town, so your mail reaches each other so quickly. Do you want to know who he is?"

"No." Winifred's stomach flipped. "I—I need to get to work now. We'll be opening soon."

"Of course."

He scooted the envelope closer, and she jumped back. *Silly, it's not a rattlesnake.* With a shaking hand, she dragged the envelope to the edge of the counter and dropped it into her bag.

"You said you work at the Golden Star Mine?"

"Yes, in the store."

A strange smile lifted his lips, one she didn't know how to read. Then he cleared his throat. "If I come across a letter for you, I'll direct it there. Your name, ma'am?"

"Winifred Sattler." Why, oh, why couldn't she disguise the tremor in her voice?

Muttering a farewell, she took to the street, weaving through passersby and breathing in dust without really noticing it as she returned to the Golden Star Mine. With every step, her heart plummeted farther into her gut. The realization that *somehow* her letter had been mailed washed over her again and again until all she wanted to do was sink into a mine shaft and disappear forever.

What had he thought of her? While the poor man had used an unfortunately phrased ad to seek a wife, that did not mean he deserved to be barraged with the bitter sentiments of a jaded woman. The valise bounced against her hip as she walked, almost like it begged her to look inside at his reply.

Why had he written her back? To berate her, lash out at her careless words? No one spoke to strangers in such a forthright way, least of all through formal written correspondence.

At least she hadn't used her real name, so he couldn't hunt her down in person. As her feet hit the long wooden walkway that led to the shop's door, she glanced at the sky and groaned. "Lord, please help me know what to do now."

"Miss Sattler?"

Having just stepped over the threshold, Winifred gasped at the sound of her name. She hid her bag behind her as if she'd been caught with pilfered goods. Mr. Burke stood at the counter. He raised one brow at her jittery response, so she forced a smile. No reason to look guilty in front of her employer. She'd done nothing wrong. He acted suspicious of her enough as it was—the last thing she needed was for him to think she'd been up to something.

Ewan felt the smooth wooden counter beneath his fingertips, hoping the action would calm his irritation. *Kindness, regardless of affliction.*

Miss Sattler scrambled into the store in a manner not unlike a little whirlwind. Commonplace behavior for her, it seemed. "I'm not late, am I?"

He glanced at the small clock perched on a shelf. "No, you're on time."

"Oh." Miss Sattler relaxed her shoulders and made her way to the counter, then slipped her bag beneath it, out of sight. "I had to…run an errand."

Did a blush color her cheeks? She was permitted to run errands in her free time, so why the embarrassment? And why had she paused in her explanation? "Miss Sattler, I need to discuss something very important with you."

Miss Sattler brushed a loose strand of brown hair behind her ear and exhaled, like she needed to calm herself before listening to what Ewan had to say.

Ewan stepped away from the counter. "Please explain to me what you've done with my store."

Miss Sattler stared at him, wide-eyed. "What do you mean?"

Did she honestly not know, or was she pretending? "You moved things." He strolled into the room, touching merchandise as he went. "The potatoes, the dry goods, the shovels…"

Miss Sattler hastened to open the curtains in the front windows. "You walked through here last night as I rearranged and didn't say a word about it, so I figured it was fine."

He flicked her a glare. Had he really been that preoccupied? "I wouldn't give permission to move my merchandise. You're supposed to watch the store, take customers' money. Not fiddle with design."

"I was bored. I needed something to do."

Ewan almost laughed. "Then mop the floors or dust the shelves." He gestured toward the mop and broom propped in the corner behind the counter. "There is plenty you could do, but do not touch my arrangement again under any circumstance."

"All right, I'm sorry." Throwing up her hands, she yanked the broom from behind the counter, giving vent to her obviously building nerves. "Although I fail to see why it's a problem."

"It's a problem because this store needs to be in pristine condition. It's the public face of the mine." *And, right now, a major source of income to keep the whole business afloat.*

"My point exactly." She paused midsweep to look at him, maintaining eye contact surprisingly well. "People like things that are new and fresh. Isn't it dull to go into a store that always looks exactly the same? And the current arrangement didn't make sense, so I fixed it."

Ewan narrowed his eyes. "Didn't make sense?" He'd put a lot of thought into where things went. "Tell me, have you decorated a store with success in the past?"

"Really, Mr. Burke, the shovels by the onion bulbs?" Her thin hand gestured at the basket near the door.

He folded his arms in return. "That makes perfect sense."

"No, shovels should be with other mining supplies."

"*Or* with gardening supplies, where I put them, next to the onion bulbs."

She didn't reply—only lowered her brows and stared at him. What emotion was that? Confusion or defiance?

Ewan crossed the floor toward her, his shoulders feeling square and severe, like he'd been carved from wood. "Just...*ask* next time. In fact, there shouldn't be a next time. I can't allow this kind of whimsical nonsense to affect my business. It is my name on the line, not yours."

"Will switching a couple baskets and crates tarnish your reputation, Mr. Burke?"

Ewan cocked his head and watched as fire ignited Miss Sattler's cheeks while she focused on sweeping. Had he been too harsh? Might've been, to coax such sarcastic responses from her.

Kindness, regardless of affliction.

Turning away, Ewan ran a hand over his hair and then down over his mouth. When he faced her again, he worked to keep his voice lowered. "I apologize for speaking so harshly. I overreacted."

Miss Sattler stopped her sweeping and looked up.

Exhaling, he reached the counter, facing her on the opposite side. "I don't know why I feel compelled to tell you this, but it seems you need to understand what I'm up against—why every aspect of this business is crucially important to me. The Golden Star Mine sits on prime real estate. Our water rights are coveted by every mining camp downstream, and while our gold production isn't where it should be yet, our current findings promise quite the delivery."

He paused, formulating his next sentence. Miss Sattler watched him with wide, interested eyes, nudging him to continue.

"Right now, the store is a major source of income. A potentially *steady* source of income, when we don't know what the yields will be in the mine from one day to the next. There are many other shops in town offering the same things, so nothing really makes us stand out—all we can do is offer good quality, fair prices and a pleasant shopping experience. Which means having all the goods right where people know they can find them. I must have complete control over what happens. I can't afford to let anyone else handle it."

Miss Sattler set aside her broom. "Why do you need the store to supplement your mine's earnings?"

An innocent question, but it stung just the same. "I need capital to expand this mine into what it should be, but so far all of our proceeds go back into the business simply to stay afloat. There are veins in the mountain I'm sure will lead to large quantities of gold, but I don't have enough resources yet to mine or process it. More machinery is needed, both inside the mine and out, and more drifts need to be driven. I'm currently seeking an investor to help me over this hurdle."

"Yes, you met with one the other day. It must be easy to find an investor in this town."

He gave her an ironic smile. "Only easy if you want him to buy you out completely, or at the very least become a majority shareholder." He shook his head. "No, I need someone who wants a small share rather than control of the whole operation. Someone who can offer capital and gain a profit but not dip his greedy fingers in too deeply and change all I've worked hard to create."

She nodded as if she understood, then tipped her head to one side. "So, where will you find one of those? In Denver? Might your father know someone?"

"Yes—my father spoke with a business friend, the one interested enough to visit."

"See, there you go!" She flashed him a bright smile. "Who was it? Perhaps I know of him."

"Mr. Richard Johns."

"Oh, yes, he's a good friend of my uncle's, too." But then her smile faded. "You don't seem too excited about his visit."

"He wasn't ready to invest at this time. I…have some work to do before he's interested." What that work would entail, Ewan wasn't sure. How would he yield the proceeds Mr. Johns sought if he didn't have the capital to make it happen? "He'll be back in three months to see the mine again. Hopefully I'll be able to impress him then." If only Ewan's voice didn't sound so heavy. He didn't really want to be this vulnerable.

Miss Sattler stood a little straighter. "Mr. Johns was here that day?" She pursed her lips in what appeared to be disappointment. "If only I'd known. I could've caught a ride with him and repaid him for the fare when I reached home. Or at least had him carry a message to my uncle so that he could wire me the fare."

"Is fare money all that keeps you here?"

"Basically."

"Why don't you let me pay for a ticket?"

She shook her head. "Thank you, but with mail the way it is, it would take months to pay you back. Besides, I don't want to owe anyone anything. A quick repayment is one thing, like getting fare from an investor living in the same town as my family. But I'm not interested in accepting seemingly innocent gifts from men."

Seemingly innocent gifts from men? How should he respond to that? "I can assure you, Miss Sattler, my offer to pay your fare is purely platonic. I have no romantic or other interest in you."

Her brows jumped. "Oh—no, not *you*, specifically. I only meant in principle—"

Now *his* cheeks burned. Ewan dragged a finger along his collar. "Let's get back to business. I want to show you how to calculate sales and keep track of them in the ledger."

"No need." Miss Sattler seemed to weather the change in subject easily, reaching for the ledger beneath the counter. "I have already calculated the sales I've had since my first day."

"You have?" Frowning, he flipped open the book as soon as she placed it on the countertop. From his angle, the ledger lay upside down, but just as she'd said, Ewan found her numbers scrawled in the appropriate columns.

Unfortunately, she'd listed only three entries.

He scrunched his nose. "You're certain these are all the sales you've made?"

"Yes."

She pointed to each name, but Ewan averted his gaze. Three sales. The store used to make so much more money than that. What had happened? He carried quality merchandise and had competitive prices. Nothing more could be done.

"This man, Thomas Thornton, came in looking for a new gold pan because he'd lost his when it fell from his pack," she said. "I helped him find the right size for the spot in Whitewood Creek where he headed next. And this man, Arnold Pickling, needed a screw to hold the chain on his arrastra. I wasn't sure we'd find one, but we did, with a little digging! Do you know what an arrastra is, Mr. Burke? Mr. Pickling told me all about them. They're contraptions used to crush ore if you don't have a stamp mill. It's a ring in the ground made of stone—"

Irritation built in his gut. "I know what an arrastra is, Miss Sattler." Sighing, he rubbed his hand down his face. "I used one before I built up the mine."

The mine. The years of defending his claim, of mining gold along the creek in the beginning, battling the rain and the snow. Of driving drifts into the mountainside and finding veins of ore running deep, like lifeblood. Of building the store, the kitchen and his office. The cash he'd sunk into this place to get gold dust in return. The fight to make an honest living in an occupation many looked down upon. The desire to be more than a failure to his father.

What if he lost it all?

Miss Sattler reached across the counter and placed her hand on his forearm, jarring him out of his thoughts. "Everything will work out, Mr. Burke."

Slowly he met her gaze, but otherwise he didn't move. Had her gesture offended him or scared him frozen, he had no idea. But flecks of softness hovered around his hardened heart, coaxing him not to worry so much.

"Thank you. Except it's going to take more than encouraging words to save the mine," he murmured, then thought better of it. "That doesn't mean I'll allow you to rearrange my store."

She smiled. A nice smile, if he were honest. Genuine. Warm. For all her faults, Miss Sattler wasn't malicious. He'd do well to respect her, even if he didn't agree with her methods, even if her personality grated on his patience.

"I mean it." He leveled a gaze at her, unable to ignore the gray-blue in her eyes. "No more moving the store around. Is that clear?"

She didn't answer immediately.

"I won't give up until you acquiesce."

Finally, she nodded. "I promise."

"Good."

Miss Sattler might have promised not to meddle—but as Ewan withdrew his arm from beneath her hand, he couldn't help but wonder if she'd hold to that agreement.

Chapter Three

Dear Thoroughly Disgruntled,

Your sentiments are indeed valid. And, if I'm honest, similar to my own. If I had any other choice, I would seek a wife in a less popularized fashion. Believe me, I would much rather carry on stimulating conversation with a woman in person than run through the correspondence rigmarole of how-do-you-dos and the listing of personal facts on paper as if we were reduced to a mere checklist rather than actual hearts and souls.

A checklist gets the job done, sure, but where's the true connection in it?

All this to say I appreciate your blunt reply. Except please allow me to correct your belief about my stance on romance. Like you, I despise the game of pursuit, but I get the feeling from your letter that you accuse me of using such a game to play women falsely. And to that, I strongly object. Honesty is what I offered in my advertisement. Romance can either be a game or be straightforward, and I intend to cultivate the latter with my future wife. As a general rule, I find it easier to have faith in people who give straight answers.

If you'd like to write again, I'd welcome the camaraderie—as friends, of course.
Sincerely yours,
Mr. Businessman

By the light of the fireplace, Winifred stared at the crisp page. She'd already read the letter three times, and yet she had to read it a fourth. The hand lettering struck her. So quickly penciled and slanted to the right, it almost looked like Greek script. Or hieroglyphics. Yet she could read it without hesitation, as if the message were coded only for her.

She dropped her head to her pillow and sighed, listening to the fire across the room crackle and pop over its kindling. Oh, how afraid she'd been to open this letter. He could've easily shredded her feelings by lambasting her for the rude tone her letter had employed. Instead he'd engaged her in conversation. He'd been kind in the face of her skepticism, which was something she hardly ever was—and that grace moved her.

"I suppose if my letter had to go to anyone," she whispered to the page, "I'm glad it went to you."

After all, she wasn't ready for another romantic relationship, and nothing in this letter suggested that as a possibility, anyway. He'd invited her friendly correspondence. But would she write? Part of her scoffed at writing a stranger for no definitive purpose. But another part of her felt touched by his openhanded offering.

It would be nice to have a friend, especially now in this foreign place.

Except, how did she know it was truly openhanded, asking nothing in return? Mr. Businessman certainly didn't sound like he had a hidden reason for writing her, especially since they'd both been clear about not wanting to create a romantic exchange out of this… but how was she to be certain? Perhaps he had ulterior motives, like so many other men she'd met through letter writing.

Lord, I don't know who to trust. Which way should I go?

For now, she felt no rush to respond. She folded the note and slipped it back in the clean white envelope and placed it into her valise.

"Is that another letter you want sent?" Granna Cass stood at the preparation table, up to her wrists in dough. "Forgot to tell you I mailed one for you the other day."

Winifred's head shot up. "That was you?"

The woman punched the dough and flipped it, a poof of flour billowing upward. "Mail only comes through every three weeks. I had to post a letter to my son—he lives in Virginia—so I figured I'd mail yours, too. Otherwise it could've been weeks before it left town."

Releasing a breath, she felt her cheeks blanch. "Where did you find my letter?"

"Sitting on the floor by the pallet. Beautiful drawing on the envelope. Did you do it?"

"Yes."

"Wish I could draw like that. But these skinny fingers know nothing but how to make bread." Laughing, she reached into her flour sack and sprinkled more over the doughy mound. "A letter home to your aunt and uncle, was it? Didn't take time to read the address."

How should she answer? Could she tell Granna Cass she'd never meant to send that letter, that the recipient hadn't known Winifred existed until her letter appeared in his mailbox? A barrage of questions from the dear old woman wouldn't entirely be—

The kitchen door burst open.

Though fully clothed in her polonaise and skirt, minus her overbodice, Winifred tugged her blanket up to shield herself. Hidden from view behind the partition, she craned her neck to find Mr. Burke in the doorway, frowning, his eyes darkened and skin creased between his brows.

"Cassandra, grab your supplies. There's been an accident."

"Oh, no…" Granna Cass dropped the dough and wiped her hands on her apron. Murmuring a prayer, she yanked a bag from beneath her bed and followed Mr. Burke.

An accident? Winifred dropped her blanket and scrambled from her pallet. Grabbing her overbodice from the top of the trunk and tugging it over her arms, she dashed across the kitchen, air still humid from the evening's meal of roasted potatoes and breaded chicken.

In the darkened hallway, she scurried toward the sharp turn at the end, where the faint light from Mr. Burke's candle flickered on the wall. The side door opened and closed, leaving her in silence and darkness.

Breathing a prayer for the injured, Winifred pushed open the door and rushed outside.

Night had fallen and crickets chirped in the nearby brush, a sound quickly swallowed by the clamor of Deadwood's stamp mills. Loose shale scraped beneath her shoes as she hastened to catch up with the others, who marched directly toward the mountain. Having been employed for only a few days, she hadn't yet ventured out to see the rest of the grounds. Now, in the moonlight, buildings loomed around her in shadowy shapes. Brilliant stars spilled over the top of the mountainside, and somewhere she thought she heard the faint trickling of creek water.

"I'm not sure exactly what happened," Mr. Burke said to Granna Cass as Winifred drew close enough to hear. "I sent Jacobson to fetch the doctor, but I'll need your help before he arrives."

"What were they doing?" the woman asked.

"I don't know, except that a timber support frame came loose. I don't know if it hit McAllister or if the falling debris did the job."

Winifred hastened to keep up as the two reached a rocky outcropping along the mountain's edge. Leading out of the mountain, a track like a railroad connected to one of the large buildings she'd passed. Rocks slipped beneath her feet as she climbed, moonlight acting as the only light to guide her steps. At the mouth of the tunnel entrance, Mr. Burke paused to pluck a lantern from a hook and proceeded to light it with his candle.

Then he noticed her.

"Miss Sattler, what are you doing here?"

The surprise in his voice caught her off guard

enough to make her stumble on a railroad tie. She steadied herself before she fell flat, then stood and brushed her hands off on her skirt. "I—"

"You can't be here." He stepped into the moonlight, his piercing eyes pleading with her. "It's too dangerous."

She glanced around him. Blackness swallowed the long tunnel, save for where the lantern dangled from Mr. Burke's hand. At a short distance, Granna Cass waited.

"But you're taking Granna Cass. Surely I can be of some help, too."

"It's a long way in, and if you get lost without a light, it could be days before you're found. I'm taking Cassandra because she's aided before in accidents while we wait for the doctor."

"Hun—" Granna Cass's voice drifted from within the tunnel. "Go on back to the kitchen and tend the fire. That will help us. I left in such a hurry—I'd hate for anything to happen because I wasn't thinking straight."

Winifred met Mr. Burke's eyes again. Even with much of his face in shadow, he shook her resolve. As her boss, he had the right to ask her to leave, regardless of her eagerness to help. Turning away, she tried not to let her shoulders droop, but they did a little anyway. She made her way down the rocky outcropping and then across the grass in silence.

"Hey, lady?"

Winifred jumped at the voice in the darkness. A male voice. Whirling, she spotted a man standing in front of a building, the one attached to the mountain by railway.

"Were you just at the mountain?" he called to her. Hidden mostly in the shadow of the building, only the man's crazy hair caught fragments of moonlight.

She stepped closer, making out a thin, wiry frame. "Yes, sir."

The man looked up at the mountain. "What's goin' on up there? Stepped outside and saw all the commotion."

He must work inside that building. "There was an injury. I don't know how serious or what happened, exactly."

"Injury, huh?" The man shook his head, his body going rigid. He stepped backward, then forward, like an uncomfortable shuffle. "I knew it. Just knew it. Lady, I tell 'im, and I tell 'im. Don't matter."

"Tell who?"

"The boss."

A chilling breeze snaked by, causing Winifred to wrap her arms around herself. The man didn't make sense. She wished she could see his face.

"What's your name?" The man folded his arms. "I never seen you 'round here before."

"I'm new. Winifred Sattler. Just working in the store for a short while." She tipped her head to one side, squinting as if it would help her see him better. "Who are you?"

"Charlie Danielson." He jutted a thumb over his shoulder. "I manage the night stamp-mill crew."

The stamp mill. That's what the building housed. "Sounds interesting. I—"

"Yeah, if the job's around long enough. No tellin' nowadays."

The man's words killed off Winifred's intended reply. She frowned. "Why do you say that?"

"We're losin' the business, ma'am, like blood from a gunshot wound." He shrugged in a helpless fashion. "Ain't right holdin' on to us like this. Keepin' us from findin' other work. Leadin' us on like he can save the company."

Winifred's brows drew together. "He can save it, though…can't he?"

"Ma'am—" the man shook his head "—he's been fightin' a losin' battle for this mine since it began. And even though I tell 'im so, he's too stubborn to give in."

Winifred's thoughts flashed back to their conversation at the store, when Mr. Burke had opened up about the Golden Star needing an investor. How protective he'd been. And the wounded look he displayed when they examined the ledger, like his worth was wrapped up in those three tiny sales.

And now, an accident had compromised one of his men.

"Mr. Burke carries the weight of this mine on his shoulders, Mr. Danielson." Straightening her spine, she stuck out her chin. "He cares about the well-being of those who work here. I, for one, am glad he's sticking to his vision."

Nodding farewell, she continued her trek to the office building.

Mr. Burke was a tough man who didn't smile. But now she knew meanness wasn't the reason for his stalwart behavior. Fear was. Fear of losing everything he had labored so long to build. And he deserved his dream.

He seemed to work hard to keep this place afloat,

despite the doubt that had crept into some of the staff. She could only imagine the pressure. Her constant push to find a husband seemed like the closest experience she had to relate. The failed mail-order attempts, the downcast glances of Aunt and Uncle's society friends. Mr. Ansell's comment that because she'd been six times ordered but never a bride, there must be something wrong with her and that no one else would ever want her.

If Mr. Burke felt anywhere near how she felt, then he needed encouragement. The *mine* needed encouragement. She understood his persistence, his refusal to give up or give in to despair. What woman who had accepted six proposals wouldn't?

Winifred didn't know what needed to be done, but she determined to help Mr. Burke find more success than she had. Her mind buzzed with ways to help—provided she didn't rearrange the potatoes and gold pans while at it.

Ewan's footsteps clipped down the corridor toward the kitchen. Dawn had come much too early after a late night inside the mine, but with help from everyone, they were able to secure the timber support beams lining the damaged drift and get McAllister to safety.

First thing after a few meager hours of sleep, Ewan had bathed, but the stench of sweat and soot still lingered somewhat—a constant reminder of how yesterday could've been so much worse. He'd thanked God over and over for His mercy on McAllister's life.

But what baffled him was why the timber frame had collapsed in the first place. Nothing like that had ever happened at the Golden Star. He used high-quality wood, never willing to skimp on something so essential, and held his miners to a high standard of safety, which they had always seemed to follow.

Perhaps he simply needed to check in more often, maybe inspect their work at closer intervals for a while to ensure the utmost safety.

But for now, he had a new order of business. Stepping into the kitchen, he located Miss Sattler.

She stood at the preparation table filling lunch pails for the day shift. Her trim, plum-colored gown brushed the hardwood floor as she worked, her brown hair piled on her head in a confusing puzzle of twists and curls and pins. The ways of women—in both appearance and behavior—baffled him, and yet, he couldn't help but appreciate their efforts. This woman's in particular. A realization that had taken him by surprise last night.

"Morning, Ewan." Cassandra wiped her hands on a towel. "Breakfast is in the oven still but won't be long."

"Not a problem. I'll be back for breakfast. For now, I'm actually here to collect Miss Sattler."

The young woman's head shot up. A sandwich hung in her clutches above a pail as if time had stopped. "Me?"

"Yes, you." He motioned toward the door. "I am giving you a tour of the grounds this morning."

Miss Sattler stared at him. Flicked her gaze to Cassandra and back. "You are?"

Good grief. Did he have to spell it out? If her current behavior held any indication, he'd be surprised if she didn't venture out on her own at some point in the near future to explore the claim: both the outbuildings and the mine itself. And if he was any judge of

her character, he'd expect her to approach the dangerous passages with glowing enthusiasm and no cau-
tion whatsoever. So, rather than finding himself in
the middle of a fiasco later, he'd take control of the
situation now.

"If you'll be employed here for a while, then it's
time you learned how the mine operates. We'll look
around at the beginning of the morning shift, so we
cause the least amount of disturbance."

He could have sworn the twinkle in her eyes bright-
ened a hundredfold. Dropping the sandwich in the
pail, she applauded the outing, then scooted across
the room to join him.

"I'm so excited about this," she said as they made
their way down the corridor. "I've wanted to look
around." Suddenly, her hand landed on his arm. "How
is the worker from the accident? Is he going to be all
right?"

Unbidden warmth traveled through him. "He should
be fine. He is at the doctor's now, but I was told this
morning he might be able to go home this afternoon.
Regardless, he'll be out of work several days to re-
cover."

At the very least, thankfully, Miss Sattler had followed orders last night. Her response to danger had
been rash and reckless…and heartwarming. Before
she'd even known what the situation would hold, she'd
been eager to help. But he hadn't wanted to worry
about her getting injured, too, in the midst of all the
chaos. Surprising how much her well-being suddenly
meant to him.

To begin the tour, he led her up the mountainside.
"First things first, these are some of the employees

you'll need to know about. Gerald Foster watches the grounds. He lives in his own apartment off the kitchen. He might be an old man, but he has impeccable aim. We've never had troubles here, but having him around is a security that helps me sleep at night."

"Can't be too careful," Miss Sattler agreed.

"Exactly. Then there's Marcus Lieberman, who manages the day shift of the stamp mills, while Charlie Danielson manages the night shift. And of course, you know Cassandra."

"Yes."

"You'll also want to know a few terms." He indicated the opening of the mine as they reached it. "This entrance is called an adit or a portal. Inside, the horizontal tunnels are called drifts. The vertical tunnels are shafts."

"Adits, drifts and shafts," Winifred repeated. "Got it. Do we get to go inside?"

"Yes, but stick close." A chill ran through him as he lifted his lantern from a spike driven into the wall. Safety first, especially after yesterday. Miss Sattler should be perfectly safe by his side…but yesterday, he'd thought his men were safe inside the mine, as well. At least the men knew their way around, however. "I meant what I said about how easily you could get lost in a maze of drifts. Do not venture off on your own for any reason."

He lit his lantern, and they traveled into the darkness, the dank chill familiar to him. Water dripped nearby. Rubble scraped beneath his feet as he followed the rails embedded in the walkway. Soon, the familiar *ching-ching-ching* of miners' chisels and hammers reached Ewan's ears.

"So, the mine covers much of the inside of this mountain?" Miss Sattler's voice sounded close and small in the tight space.

"Yes. I'll show you one stope, and then we'll go back outside."

"What is a stope?"

"An excavation room." Ewan paused at the entrance to the stope and waited for his employee to join him before lifting his lantern.

He heard her sharp intake of breath as she stared upward into the cavernous room several stories high. The closest miners didn't pay them too much mind, just glanced their direction before continuing to drive their chisels into the rocky walls with long-handled hammers.

"Truly amazing." Miss Sattler shook her head and stepped closer.

Ewan glanced at the woman beside him, now close enough to brush shoulders. The wonder on her face sent a surge of pride through his chest. "I gather you've never been inside a mine before?"

"No, never. Uncle talks about them sometimes, but this is the first I've seen." She shifted her gaze until it collided with his. "It's very impressive, Mr. Burke."

Lantern light flickered against the wisps of her brown hair. It made a far prettier picture than one would ever expect to find inside a dark, dirty mine.

The squeak of metal on metal rose above the sound of hammers against chisels. Ewan broke his stare and guided his light toward the sound. Leaving the stope, a mule pulled a large cart, and alongside, a man walked the rail line.

Ewan stepped out of the way, gently tugging on

Miss Sattler's elbow. The miner eyed him, then Miss Sattler, before halting his cart and mule beside them. His thick, graying beard shone beneath his crinkled good eye and black eye patch. "Miss Sattler, this is Lars Brennan. He ensures that all the ore reaches the stamping mill."

The man removed his cloth hat. "Howdy, ma'am."

Miss Sattler smiled back as she dipped her chin. Ewan watched for any indication that Lars's eye patch might scare her, but she looked boldly into his face as if she saw nothing wrong. "That sounds like an important job," she said. "How much ore is that, Mr. Brennan?"

"This cartload right here's about a ton."

The amount made the woman laugh with surprise. "A ton? Really?"

"And he does sixteen of them by the end of each day." Ewan clapped Lars on the shoulder. "Not a cart less."

The man glanced between Ewan and Miss Sattler, rubbing his fingers against his gray hair before sticking his hat back on his head. Fidgeted a little.

"Feel free to continue on your way." Miss Sattler ushered him forward, still smiling. "Thank you for meeting me."

Lars grunted, like he wasn't really sure what to say, then continued down the track with his mule and one-ton cart of ore.

As soon as Lars turned the corner, Miss Sattler whirled to Ewan. "The ore goes to the stamp mill from here?"

"Yes, ma'am."

"Can we go there next?"

Thankful for the dark, Ewan forced down the grin appearing on his mouth. Business as usual. This wasn't a little romp to waste time for fun's sake. He'd only offered to show Miss Sattler these places so she wouldn't put herself in danger by venturing to them on her own. "Yes. The stamp mill next, and then back to the store to open for the day."

They made their way out of the mine. At the base of the mountainside, Ewan helped Miss Sattler off the final slippery crush of shale, then ushered her toward the stamp mill.

"I assume you noticed Mr. Brennan's eye injury." He glanced her way.

She nodded, her eyes glowing with compassion as she fell in line beside him. "What happened?"

"He worked for a mine in Lead City, the town three miles from here. At the time, he worked on a two-man crew chiseling ore. A flying shard of rock blinded him in one eye."

"The poor man." Miss Sattler shook her head. "Then how did he come to work here? Seems like an eye injury could prevent a man from working for a mine."

"Well, he came looking for work, and it was clear he didn't have many prospects otherwise. And honestly, pulling a cart doesn't require both eyes, so it seemed like the perfect job."

"It certainly does." Miss Sattler squeezed his arm and offered a smile. "And how very thoughtful of you to offer it to him."

The effects of her smile lingered as they reached the stamp mill—continuing to trip up his heart. Why did her admiration suddenly mean something to him?

Could it have something to do with the woman herself, or was he simply desperate for approval?

Hopefully, the latter. As much as he hated that option, it was better than the first. Hadn't he told himself not to care for the store clerk walking beside him? A woman like her had the potential to capture his heart if he wasn't watching close enough. And risking his heart meant risking the chance that she would then stomp on it before he knew what happened.

At least she wouldn't be staying long. If he kept a wary eye, he just might survive this temporary arrangement unscathed.

Chapter Four

Weeds might overrun the surrounding grounds untouched by the miner's pick, but if Winifred had anything to say about it, the front yard of the Golden Star would be immaculate.

Not that any grass grew there, either—but still, even plain old dirt would look nicer than the unruly nest of weeds collecting at the shop entrance. Unable to locate a garden hoe around the premises—save for one she'd have to purchase to use—Winifred found herself crouched near a tangled web of flowering bindweed, plucking it at the source. She tossed handfuls into the growing pile near the wooden walkway leading to the shop door, then started in on another section.

Though the sun had barely risen, she could already feel the heat creeping up the back of her neck. It would be a hot one. Yesterday, the best part of the day had been during these early-morning hours, seeing the claim with Mr. Burke. The only strange matter had been her sudden sense of interest in the man himself. As they trekked from place to place, she had come to see a side of him beyond being *the boss*. A piece of his personality had peeked through his well-crafted exterior, and she liked what she saw. If only he didn't spend so much time being a curmudgeon.

Even his employees seemed to distance themselves from him. She saw it in the young miner's face when he'd asked about variety in their meals, and she'd witnessed it in Mr. Danielson's doubt and Mr. Brennan's discomfort. It seemed Mr. Burke's preoccupation with saving the mine had overshadowed his ability to be cheerful and approachable.

Then, the rest of the day hit. She sat in the shop, practically bored to tears. Mr. Burke had made it sound like the store was an important source of income, so the fact that it hadn't made much money as of late concerned her. If no one stopped to visit again today— well, she didn't want to think about it. Hence, the weed pulling. She needed *something* to distract her. Something productive but not irritating to Mr. Burke. Because if she slowed down, her thoughts would begin to wander.

If they strayed too far, she would start thinking of her broken mail-order dreams.

Dreams of a life with Mr. Ansell, for example. Her heart had been foolish to trust that man. She saw it now—the deceit she'd blinded herself to before. She blamed herself for not being more cautious, more suspicious of the gaps in his story. But really, how could she have guessed that he was not a bachelor, as he'd implied, but a married man with children who was seeking a new wife to replace his current spouse?

Even more horrifying than his behavior and his lack of respect for his wife and for the marriage vows he had taken, was the idea that he'd expected Winifred to go along with it. He'd known she was spending the last of her money to come to Spearfish and seemed to have thought that, alone and without resources, she would simply give in to his plans to leave his wife in order to marry her.

Of course, he had said nothing about those plans until he had her alone and far from home. In his letters, the scoundrel had been discreet about his family. He'd been secretive about his own circumstances, filling letters with questions for her, instead. Seemed attentive at the time, but really he'd been diverting the attention away from his own twisted life. He hadn't even wanted to exchange cabinet cards, though she had offered more than once—wanting to see a picture of the man she planned to marry. That made sense now, considering he probably didn't have a likeness of himself without his wife and children. And he probably didn't want Winifred's floating around, in case it fell from his pocket at home. It wouldn't do, after all, to have his wife find out his plans before he had her replacement on hand.

Winifred heaved a sigh, yanking harder on nearby weeds. "Thank You, Lord, for preserving me," she whispered.

The weeds pulled up fast. If only she could so easily tear Mr. Ansell's words from her memory and the embarrassment from her stained heart. The words he'd spat at her in anger after she'd rejected him and boarded the stage to Deadwood. *"Six times ordered but never a bride. No one will ever want you now."*

The shop door squeaked open on the hinges she needed to oil. Footsteps sounded on the walkway. Slow, confident, deliberate. They could only belong to one man. What was Mr. Burke doing here at this early hour? But when Winifred looked up, Mr. Burke was exiting the store with two suited men behind him. She squared her shoulders. Here early, *and* conducting a meeting?

Mr. Burke stopped beside her, the brim of his hat shading his face from the morning light. "Farewell, gentlemen."

"Farewell," one said over his shoulder, though his voice sounded tight. The other didn't say anything, only shot Mr. Burke a narrowed look before they headed toward downtown Deadwood.

Winifred tipped her head back to look up at her boss. "Who were they?"

Mr. Burke stared after them. "Graham Young and his partner, Terrance Michaels."

Capitalists from California. She remembered him mentioning them before—a duo of cousins who'd bought up several establishments in the area. "I gather they wanted to buy us out?"

"Yes, and they were most displeased to hear me say that my business is my business and will remain so." Dropping his gaze to hers, he cocked his head to one side. "What are you doing?"

She would ignore his lack of courtesy. "I thought I'd pull weeds while I waited for customers to arrive."

The man blinked. "Then you plan to help customers in sweaty clothes?"

"No, I—I…" The question caught her off guard. *Mr. Burke* caught her off guard. Just when she thought she knew what he'd say next, he surprised her by coming up with something even more exacting. "I wanted to work when the temperature is coolest—which is now."

"Except, why are you working in the yard at all?"

She stood, brushing off her hands. "The weeds are atrocious. I figured as long as I worked at the store, I'd make the place look a little nicer."

"Miss Sattler." The man's eyes caught hers, a piercing crystallized gray. "I hired you as the clerk, not the gardener."

His statement made her eyebrows raise. "Then you should hire one of those, too, because no one's going to shop at a place that looks like rubbish." Sales attested to that fact. Wiping her hands on the apron she'd borrowed from Granna Cass, Winifred bypassed Mr. Burke and made her way to the store.

For someone so concerned with the success of his shop, Mr. Burke would do well to consider the tactics that attracted customers.

As her heels clicked over the wooden surface of the walk, she couldn't help but string together a list of other things she wished to say—like how an occasional motivating word would go a long way in benefitting his staff, making this place wonderful and thriving instead of dull and stringent. And that life was too short to waste himself acting like a starched shirt.

The boss fed and housed his employees, took in strangers, and hired people who didn't have a chance anywhere else. So, obviously kindness existed in his heart. He only needed to show it.

A hollow spot in her heart ached for encouragement from Mr. Burke, but she kept her mouth shut. So far, she had created havoc nearly every time she stood in his presence. Enough damage had been done for one morning.

* * *

Ewan watched Miss Sattler disappear inside the store, her skirts nearly getting caught in the closing door. She had the gall to accept a position at his store, then talk to him like she had ownership of the place? Turning, he strode from the walkway and headed for the post office, forcing that young woman from his mind—as well as the two men he'd met with this morning.

Graham Young and Terrance Michaels were his gold-mining neighbors in most directions, save to the north, which was a plot owned by the Sphinx Mine. After the pair of cousins cornered him last night on his way home, Ewan had reluctantly agreed to meet them for a discussion early today. But he'd been quick to turn down their offer to buy. Or *swindle* might really be the best descriptor.

Their offer had been extremely low, and most importantly, the cousins cared very little about what would happen to the Golden Star's current workers. Not only would Ewan be a failure for selling out, he'd also jeopardize the future of his employees. Some of them, like Lars Brennan, wouldn't easily find work elsewhere. And Young and Michaels certainly wouldn't have employment options for women in dire straits, like Lucinda Pratt. If Ewan gave up control of the Golden Star, they would have no employer available to help them escape their circumstances.

Not a choice he'd be willing to make.

Sol Star looked up as Ewan stepped into the post office. "Howdy, Burke. What can I do for you?"

Ewan approached the counter, suddenly noticing a

little sweat slicking his palms. "I wondered if I'd received any more local mail."

The postmaster grinned, the devious goat. "I'll see what I can find." He wasn't in the back long before he returned with two envelopes. "Looks like your popularity is growing, my friend."

He passed the two envelopes over the counter's surface, each addressed to "Mr. Businessman" in two distinctly feminine scripts.

Two crisp, white envelopes, unblemished and…undecorated.

"They're not from Miss Thoroughly Disgruntled." Star offered an apologetic shrug.

Did Ewan wear his disappointment so obviously? "No, of course not." He swiped up the envelopes and slipped them into the pocket inside his coat. "I figured as much. She didn't suit me anyway."

She'd made herself very clear about not wanting to become romantically involved. Furthermore, he was silly for being disappointed in her lack of a reply. Had he really expected the woman to choose him, a complete stranger, as a safe place to lay her burdens? She'd said she didn't trust letter writing. He'd be foolish to think she would consider friendship and correspondence with him.

He'd gone and gotten attached to the first woman who responded to his ad. That was all. A natural response. Didn't mean she was more special than the rest.

Surprising, though, how sad the envelopes looked without a cheery sketch overtop.

Ewan lightly slapped the counter, announcing his

departure and breaking his mental wallowing. "See you around, Star."

"Hey, Burke?"

Ewan turned. "What?"

Star scratched at his head, then smoothed down his hair, brows crinkled above brown eyes. "This mail-order deal—how long will your identity stay a secret?"

"Until I find someone I trust."

The postmaster hesitated, his brows crinkling further. "So…you're gonna build mutual trust…by hiding portions of yourselves?"

The man had a point—but he also didn't understand the nature of the mail-order correspondence. "A name shouldn't matter, Star. Two people should find attraction through discourse and common interests. Not in their names."

His name didn't mean much here, but back in Denver, it'd been enough for Marilee to agree to marry him, as wished for by their fathers in a business agreement. She hadn't needed anything else on which to base her decision—which became an indicator of exactly how strong her commitment to the match would be. When a bigger name showed interest, she left Ewan behind.

Ewan exited the post office with a full mind. Was he doing the right thing by trying to locate a wife through the paper? Seemed so ludicrous, if one really thought about it. Choosing a life partner by mail.

Unfortunately, he'd become desperate enough to do it. He needed a wife and a business for his life to be in order. If he failed at his business, then failed—again—in getting married, he wouldn't be able to look his father in the eye.

He could still hear his father's muttering, *"Why can't you be more like your brother, Samuel?"*

His boots clomped over the wooden walkway leading to his store. Pausing, he took notice of the bare dirt where Miss Sattler had cleared away the weeds. Pivoting his gaze, he examined the rest of the yard and all its snarled, neglected vegetation.

It really did look horrible.

He shouldn't have been so short with the woman. Among all her other well-meaning, idealistic behavior, she'd had a point about the yard. She'd seen a problem and had tried her best to fix it.

Crouching to his knees, Ewan wrapped his fingers around a weed and tugged.

It pulled free, the weak root trailing beneath it in the breeze. He dropped it beside him as the start of a pile, then moved on to another unwanted plant. As he worked, the door to the shop creaked open. Miss Sattler poked her head out, eyeing him with an unreadable expression. He met her gaze for a moment before dropping his back to the work at hand.

Slowly, the door shut and he heard Miss Sattler's heels scuff lightly across the boardwalk. She lowered herself beside him and reached for a nearby weed.

They worked in silence for a while. Ewan couldn't help but glance at her a few times as the breeze threaded through her light brown hair. Her hands, petite with slender fingers, yanked weeds from the ground like she was made of steel instead of flesh and bone. What a curious combination of vigor and idealism she was. A mystery he couldn't quite grasp, no matter how hard he tried.

"Miss Sattler, how did you come to be in Deadwood without a place to stay?"

Her glance shot to his but immediately dropped. "It's like I told you when I arrived—I ran into some trouble in Spearfish and need to get home but only had funds to get this far."

"See, that's the part I don't understand." He leaned a forearm on his bent knee. "What were you doing all the way in Spearfish when your family lives in Denver?"

"Just visiting." She uprooted a couple small ones.

Did she hide something? "Family? Friends?"

A look of pure annoyance darkened her blue-gray eyes. "I thought I had an opportunity to move to Spearfish, but the position ended up far different from what I was led to believe. I had no choice but to leave right away."

As her words sank in, his shoulders began to sag. Her story sounded all too familiar. "Sorry to hear that," he murmured. "I've seen enough girls duped into believing one thing that turned into something else entirely."

She lifted her head, and he swore he could see questions in her eyes—hoping for him to understand, yet fearing he would discover whatever secret she kept and be disgusted by her poor choices.

"I don't know what deceitful activities go on in Spearfish, but the Gem Theater is our culprit here. One of them, at least." Ewan added a handful of weeds to the growing pile between them, the scent of dirt and vegetation lingering on his fingers. "Last year, the owner advertised back east that his variety theater needed women entertainers to sing and dance. Paid for their one-way ticket and said he would make them stars. Except when they arrived, they were forced to join his brothel instead."

A gasp escaped Miss Sattler. "How awful!"

"Yep. Join up or live on the streets. Most don't come with enough money to get home." He pressed his lips tightly before continuing. "Or they don't have a home to go back to. Which is why they took the job in the first place." Lucinda Pratt had been among those unfortunate ones.

"The dilemma I faced in Spearfish was not quite that drastic."

He met her gaze, and though her face had blanched from the topic of conversation, she maintained eye contact.

"I came because I chose to, because I thought an opportunity...of a different nature...awaited me." Her voice came out a near whisper. "It wasn't what I thought, so I left, thankful that I had money enough to pay for part of the journey and for the information about you my aunt had given me. But no harm befell me, and I always remained in control of my choices and actions." For just an instant, her gaze wavered. "It's nothing like what those women encountered, but all the same, I beg you not to ask about it."

Silence hung between them as he collected his bearings. He hadn't expected this level of intimate conversation with Miss Sattler, and frankly, he wasn't prepared for the way his heart began to stir. "Of course. I won't bring it up again."

Dipping her chin, she went back to pulling weeds. He followed suit. It was none of his business what

sorts of events had taken place in Miss Sattler's past.
If she'd wanted to share, she would have.

"All the same," he continued, "I'm glad you're all
right and that you are on your way home. No woman
deserves to be taken advantage of or deceived."

She remained quiet. When he lifted his focus, he
found her staring at him. Wide-eyed and brow slightly
pinched. So vulnerable. What sort of hurts lived in her
past? The breeze caught wisps of her hair again and
brushed them across her forehead and cheeks. His gaze
traveled her face, and his chest swelled at his sudden
awareness of their silent communication, connecting
his heart to hers in a way he hadn't felt in years.

Since Marilee.

Terrible news. Very terrible news. Talkative, lively
girls drew him in like a bee to honey, but they were
bad for him. Oh, were they bad for him. He didn't
need, couldn't afford, a distraction—not for his business and not for his heart…and as much as he hated
to admit it, Miss Sattler had the potential to become
a distraction for both.

"Mr. Burke," she whispered, "how pleasant your
mine would be if you showed your workers this side
of you instead."

The trance surrounding him dropped. "Pardon?"
He blinked, listening to her words again in his mind.
"What do you mean, instead? Instead of what?"

"Instead of being so grouchy all the time." She offered a small smile, but he didn't see the mirth in
her comment. And here he'd started to enjoy himself.
She tucked a strand behind her ear. "Maybe then your
workers would have more faith in the company."

Her statement walloped him like a hammer. He drew back. "More faith in the company?"

Miss Sattler's brow began to crease again. "Yes, doubt and discouragement are written all over their faces. Mr. Brennan, Mr. Danielson—"

"Danielson is a worrier and a complainer. Don't take anything he says seriously." Ewan got to his feet. He'd have to talk to that man tonight about curbing his speech, the way he spouted off the doubts and fears spurred by his insecurities as if they were gold-plated truth. "Faith in my company." He scoffed, tugging at his vest beneath his coat. "Danielson is a gossip and enjoys the excitement of spreading rumors. Does that interest you, too?"

"No, I—"

"Then hear me, Miss Sattler. I care about my workers. And they respect me in return."

"Respect you?" She, too, scrambled to her feet. "Or are they skittish around you? Which is the more accurate picture, Mr. Burke?"

Her fists landed on her hips to match her glare. But he could match it, too. "What a ridiculous assumption. You make me out to be a tyrant? I tore myself up over that accident the other night. These people are my responsibility. No one else's. I would give my life for each one."

"Then *smile* once in a while!" Miss Sattler stamped her foot on the boardwalk. Actually stamped it. "Laugh. Tell them you care. Encourage them to continue working as hard as you do. You're only as strong as your weakest link, and if you don't change something, weak links will start popping up all over the place."

He narrowed his eyes, her words cutting through him in ways he didn't understand. "Don't yell at me like that—" But Miss Sattler cut off his statement by whirling on her heel and marching back inside the store, shutting the door a little too hard behind her.

Jaw clenched, he stared at the door. Gripped and released his fingers. How dare she? Miss Sattler had been here all of a week. No way did she understand how his operation worked or how he felt toward his workers better than he did, himself. Or how they felt toward him.

But beneath his singed pride, her words continued to burn. A few of his men had already quit because of doubt. He'd hoped the urgency of that issue had passed. But what if it hadn't?

The question continued to barrage him throughout the day as he took care of paperwork in his office. Then again as he made rounds through the mine and outbuildings to check production. This time, he closely watched his workers' reactions to him, and they were exactly as Miss Sattler had implied. How had he missed it before? They followed his orders, certainly, but many acted stiff and guarded, leading him to believe they showed respect out of fear, not admiration.

Why would they fear him? He'd never given them a reason to think he would be cruel—but doubt that the mine would stay open…he saw that fear in nearly everyone's eyes. Again. Their zeal to continue pushing forward waned, and he had no idea how to fix it.

"Mr. Burke?" Winifred slid sideways through the closing side door, somehow managing to keep the pie from toppling out of her hands. "Please—wait for me."

As the afternoon heat faded from the air, Mr. Burke turned to face her. His hat shielded his face from the sun, casting intriguing shadows across his sharp features.

No. Not intriguing. Interesting? No.

Winifred slowed when she reached him, lifting her chin so she could look into his face. *Angular.* Yes, uninterestingly, not-at-all-intriguingly angular shadows ran across his sharp features. And she mustn't get started on how his suit coat, simple as it was, hung on his confident shoulders like it'd been made for his very curvature.

Honestly, she shouldn't be thinking about it. Any of it. Bad enough that she'd felt a connection this morning with him while pulling weeds that caused her mind to stick on him throughout the day. The hushed tone of his voice, his passion for the well-being of women. These surprising aspects of his personality overwhelmed her, moved her. And when he'd promised not to ask about her experience in Spearfish with Mr. Ansell, protecting her privacy in such an earnest way... he'd made her feel welcomed here, like she might find her sense of purpose in this place—something she had never found while growing up in the luxury of Aunt and Uncle's privileged lifestyle.

Then, of course, she'd had to ruin their openhearted conversation.

Now, the gray of Mr. Burke's eyes took in her pie before glancing at her and then the door. His ever-permanent seriousness materialized in a frown. "What are you doing?"

That was apparently the question of the week.

Winifred cleared her throat. "Granna Cass said you

were visiting Mr. McAllister tonight, so she wanted me to bring this along. She would have come herself, but it's nearly dinnertime, and she has to feed the miners." And since the time was nearly five o'clock, Winifred hadn't needed to close the store too terribly early to fill in.

"Well, here." He extended his hands. "Let me save you a trip and take it myself."

"Oh, no, I couldn't allow you to do that." She tucked the dessert closer to her middle, feeling a bit slighted that he might not want her along…proving how she really had hurt him earlier today. "I promised Granna Cass I wouldn't let this pie out of my sight." A smile wavered on her lips, hoping it would draw a truce. "I couldn't help Mr. McAllister the night of his injury— I'd like to offer at least this small gesture."

Mr. Burke seemed to consider it. Then he nodded his understanding, and with an inclination of his head, they turned toward the trail he'd been walking a few minutes ago.

Sunlight winked through the evergreen boughs as her feet shuffled over a blanket of fallen pinecones and brown needles. She stumbled on a root but righted herself before anything could happen to the pie. Her heeled shoes weren't exactly suited to hiking.

The trail seemed nearly nonexistent. Winifred followed Mr. Burke past ferns and through wildflowers as he led her farther from the claim. The scent of creek water mixing with soil caught her senses.

"Are you sure you know where you're going?" She sidestepped a spray of lovely white flowers that reminded her of dainty lace.

"Of course I know." A hint of irritation circled in

his tone. Irritation probably left over from that morning's spat.

Winifred cringed. "About this morning… I'm sorry for sounding like I was accusing you of not caring about your workers."

"You didn't *sound* like you accused me. You *did* accuse me."

"That wasn't my intention." She hastened to keep up with the man's long strides. Couldn't he slow down? "I didn't mean to hurt your feelings."

He didn't answer.

She exhaled. "It's just that I seem to cause trouble every time I'm with you, and—oh!"

Her heel caught in a snarl of underbrush and down she went. The pie flew from her fingers, landing somewhere in the flowers just before Winifred's torso made impact with the ground.

The sudden collision stole her breath, stung her joints. Blinking, she was still trying to fathom what had happened when Mr. Burke rustled through the flowers toward her and two hands hoisted her to her feet.

"Are you all right?" This time no irritation hung in his tone. Without warning, he plucked a pine needle from her hair and brushed dirt from her shoulders and arms.

Winifred swallowed. He was so intent on the process of tidying her up, she doubted he realized how close he stood. Hadn't kept *her* from noticing. "I'm fine."

He made a final dusting over her shoulders and swiped a strand of hair from her face, then he finally froze. Stared at her, slightly slack jawed. A trace of something burning and tentative sparked in his gaze. A gaze she could lose herself in…

Mr. Burke squeezed his eyes shut and stepped back. "We'd better check on that pie."

Ducking her head, Winifred found capacity in her lungs again, then made a move to walk forward. But when she took a step, her right ankle wobbled beneath her on shifting ground. Or deep mud. Whatever it was, she sank in clear to the sole of her shoe. Except when she looked down, she realized she hadn't sunk in at all. Worse than that—she had completely broken off the right heel of her shoe instead.

"Fiddlesticks." Bending, she swiped her broken heel off the ground and held it up for Mr. Burke to see. "See what I mean? Trouble. Everywhere I go."

The man pressed his lips together. A corner of his mouth turned upward, and he pressed his lips firmer.

Winifred narrowed her eyes. "Mr. Burke…are you trying not to laugh at me?"

"Never." His mouth wobbled a bit more before he finally released a chuckle. A genuine, bona fide chuckle—which had a nice ring to it. "All right, fine. I tried not to laugh. Didn't work so well." Still chuckling under his breath, he walked away from her and knelt in the flowers. "Good news. The pie survived."

Exhaling her relief, she covered her face with one hand. "Thankfully! I did *not* want to walk home and tell Granna Cass that I ruined her pie."

"Like you ruined your shoe."

His grin was widening now. So much so, she might have wished to wipe it from his face if the sight hadn't been so unfairly appealing. Fighting her own grin, she feigned disgust and shoved his shoulder as she passed him on an uneven gait. "Come on, quit wasting time. And for that laugh, you get to carry the pie the rest of the way."

"Mmm…not sure that's a good idea." Plants rustled as he caught up with her, his movements easy now. "If I'm in charge of food, McAllister may not have a pie by the time we reach his cabin. What kind is this?"

"Rhubarb." She glanced his direction, saw his eyes still glittering and brushed more loose hair from her forehead. "Granna Cass says there's a wild patch growing just beyond the office building."

Bringing the pie close to his nose, he inhaled. "One of my favorite flavors."

"I don't care much for it." She kept her weight on the ball of her right foot, hopefully not hobbling so noticeably. "Too sour for my taste."

"I suppose you like the really sweet, fruity flavors, like raspberry or strawberry."

"*With* ice cream, of course. What girl doesn't like sweet things?"

Her foot landed on a stone, causing her to lose her balance again. But this time, she caught herself before tumbling to the ground.

"Do you need me to carry you the rest of the way?" His voice came from behind. "Because if you sprain your ankle, you'll be left without a leg to stand on."

"*Au contraire*, I'd still have at least one leg."

He laughed.

Winifred whipped around. The sound of that laugh—not just a chuckle this time but a real, sustained laugh with his head thrown back—was like water running over rocks, filling her heart with warmth.

Her heartbeat stalled. Ewan Burke had a sense of humor after all.

He stumbled closer, his laughter fading as he rubbed one eye. Then her gaze caught his, and his smile softened. How was this the same man she'd worked alongside this entire week? Her breath came shallowly as she lifted her chin, gaze moving around his face. Mere inches separated them in the seclusion of the forest. A strong desire built within her to connect, to continue what they'd begun while pulling weeds. She reached out and touched her fingers to his where they hung limp at his side.

But as the heat of his skin permeated hers, he drew away.

Inhaling, he dropped his gaze to the ground. A myriad of emotions crossed his face as he stepped back and ran his trembling hand over his forehead. Emotions Winifred couldn't decipher. Even with a good three feet between them now, she could still feel the memory of his fingers. She should say something. Anything. But her tongue stuck to the roof of her mouth. Her left hand clutched her broken heel tighter as the shadows clouded his features.

"Mr. Burke, I—"

"Don't." Holding up his hand to silence her, he brushed past and continued down the trail, pie in the crook of his arm. "Perhaps you'd better go back to the mine."

Jaw slack, she watched him go. Her right hand grasped her arm above the elbow as the muscles tightened along her spine. "I didn't mean—"

Turning, he met her gaze with a wintry cold that made her shiver. "Go on. We won't speak of this again.

See to the shop, and I'll see to the workers, just like before, and that's it between us. Understand?"

Had she so gravely misunderstood their connection? Her eyes began to sting. "I'm sorry."

The muscles moved along his jaw, something akin to hurt hanging around him.

Swallowing hard against the lump forming in her throat, she turned and hobbled back to the office building.

Unfortunately, she wasn't able to last two minutes in Granna Cass's presence before the old woman dropped two fists on her narrow hips and eyed Winifred with a motherly look. "What happened?"

Winifred sank into a chair at the preparation table, surrounded by the scent of fresh bread and corned beef as the cook made sandwiches. "I don't want to talk about it." In fact, she scarcely knew what words could describe the evening. Had she been looking to make Mr. Burke her friend? More than that? All she knew was that he'd awakened something inside her. Dared her to believe she could be appreciated. Cherished. Could be important enough not to be tossed aside. And she hadn't wanted to let go of it.

Until, of course, he made it clear he was only interested in tolerating her at a distance.

One of Granna Cass's gray eyebrows popped up. "You're back mighty fast for having delivered a pie all the way to McAllister's."

"I... I broke the heel off my shoe. After that, Mr. Burke took the pie the rest of the way. He—we—felt it best I head back."

With the woman's brow raised like that, Winifred gathered she hadn't been all that convincing. She halfheartedly waved the shoe in question, wishing that was the whole of the issue. But it wasn't, and she couldn't very well explain the rest of the evening in detail. Mortification would swallow her whole.

Winifred exhaled, the reality of her behavior hitting her full force again. What had she been thinking? He'd *laughed*, that was all. But somehow, knowing he could tease and laugh as well as care about the deeper things in life had her heart tangled in knots. Her response had happened so fast, she hadn't known how to stop it.

"You two ain't getting along so well." Granna Cass wrapped a sandwich and dropped it in a pail. "I can tell something happened between you two out there in the woods."

Releasing a soft groan, Winifred dropped her forehead onto her hands on the table. "Things have been rocky between Mr. Burke and me from the start."

"Don't want to tell me what happened, fine. None of my business anyhow. But it sure is God's business, and He knows exactly what happened out there. You can go to Him with your concerns about it."

As tears burned her eyes, Winifred didn't lift her head off the table. Instead, she listened to the fire crackling in the hearth. "Sometimes I wonder if God's tired of hearing about my faults by now. I have so many."

"Never." The final sandwich landed in the pail with a light clang. "God made you, just like He made each star in the sky. He can't get tired of your worries and troubles. It's not in His nature."

Winifred lifted her head, finally able to blink the tears back. "Thank you, Granna Cass. I'll pray to Him about it."

Suddenly, she had the desire to share her frustration…with one other person. Mr. Businessman might not be looking to her as a wife, but that was fine. He'd warmly opened the invitation for her to send him her frustrations, so that's exactly what she would do. She'd never meet the man anyway. What did it matter if she wrote him once, maybe twice more?

She left the table and sat down on her pallet behind the bedroom partition. From her valise, she swiped up a clean sheet of stationery.

Dear Mr. Businessman,

You certainly sound like a sincere man. I want to believe you don't play games when it comes to romance. I would like to accept your offer of correspondence—though I'll admit the largest motivator is that I'm desperately in need of a sympathetic friend right now.

Do you ever feel like you're trying so hard but getting nowhere? That nothing you do in life is significant enough? That you're not appreciated? Sometimes I feel like I could disappear—move to some far-off land—and only a few people would miss me. Do you ever feel that way? Thank you for allowing me to put my thoughts on paper and send them to you. I know I don't know you from Adam, but for some reason, as I struggle with these doubts and questions, you're the only place where I want to turn. Even if you throw this letter straight into the wastebasket, I still appreciate the chance to explain my feelings. Sometimes I realize how alone I am in the world.

Sincerely yours,
Thoroughly Disgruntled
PS You may call me TD for short, if you feel the
urge to respond. Don't feel obligated to, however.

She should feel guilty about sending such an emotional letter to a man she didn't know. How many times
in the past had she opened her heart to potential hus-
bands through letters? To be sure, in those cases she
had thought that her openness would lay the foundation for a life together. She hadn't stopped to consider
that her suitors, in turn, had shared far less. But this
time seemed different. Mr. Businessman had no intention of courting her, so she didn't worry about being
vulnerable.

An incredibly freeing realization.

She looked up as Granna Cass peeked her head
around the partition. "Honey child, I've been thinking. If you're so intent on gettin' home, why are you
trying so hard to improve things around here? I heard
about the rearranged merchandise and the weeded
front yard."

Winifred didn't answer right away. "I suppose I
wanted to help Mr. Burke save the mine."

A light laugh found its way out of the cook. "Bless
your heart, but there is nothing you can do to save or
lose this mine for Mr. Burke." Granna Cass sat on her
bed opposite Winifred, her voice soft but strong. "Let
him handle those problems. You worry about getting
enough money for the fare you need."

"I may not be able to wait that long. I think I've
outstayed my welcome."

"Nah." Granna Cass cupped the side of Winifred's

face. "I'm telling you, Miss Winnie, don't worry about pleasing Ewan. He's got his own plans to think about. If you really want to make a difference here, then help the workers. Give them a word of encouragement. Make a difference in their lives and let yourself decide that you don't care a hill of beans what Ewan has to say about it."

Easier said than done. But Granna Cass had a point. Winifred didn't have to focus on helping Mr. Burke directly. She could focus on the hardworking miners. That would keep her out of the boss's way, and maybe with God's help, it would even be enough to make her feel needed.

Chapter Five

On the edge of his desk, Ewan tapped the corner of Thoroughly Disgruntled's second letter, still unopened.

Of course, he'd wanted to open it from the moment he left the post office this morning, but self-control kept him from doing so until he was safe in the privacy of his office. Now that he was here, though, a bit of hesitancy kept him from breaking the seal. He'd told himself this letter wouldn't come, after all. He'd finally convinced himself that one heartfelt note would be all he'd have to remember her by. Quite possibly, he'd built the mystery woman up unrealistically in his head, simply because her first letter had made such an impression. He'd wanted to become better acquainted with a woman who spoke her mind and shared her feelings so frankly. But maybe that wasn't who she was after all, and the second letter would be nothing like the first.

Which was ludicrous, really, because Ewan wasn't an idealistic person. He was rational enough not to put people on pedestals. Wasn't he?

Enough dawdling. He slipped his thumb beneath the seal.

He unfolded the letter and started to read—and found himself poring over every word, drinking them in. When the note ended, he read it a second time before locating a pencil and paper to respond.

TD. She wanted him to call her TD. Obviously, she didn't know of his aversion to nicknames. Then again, "Thoroughly Disgruntled" was so long—and really not a good indicator of who this woman seemed to be at her core. So, maybe just this once, *once*, he would use a nickname. She deserved at least that.

Dear TD,

You are not alone. Trust me. There are many times I feel alone in the world, too. My father had high expectations for me growing up, wanted me to reach a certain level of success. But sadly, I have disappointed the dear man time and time again. None of my efforts back home seemed to make a difference. Deadwood became my last resort. I love it here; I love what I do. But until I make my business successful and find a wife with whom to start a family, I won't be seen as capable in the eyes of my father. And I want those things. So believe me when I say I know how it feels to be alone, to have no one to turn to. Thank you for turning to me. Honestly. I hope you don't mind if I return the favor and send you a few of my own frustrations on occasion. Suppose I'll sign off for now, but before I do, I wanted to make sure you knew there was one more person who would miss you if you disappeared to a far-off place…

Ewan paused, pencil poised above the paper. Did that sound too personal? He hadn't realized he would write it until the words were already scrawled across the page.

Oh, dear. He meant it, too. That was the scary part. It was much too early in their correspondence to be so forthright. In fact, he shouldn't be saying things like that at all. She wasn't one of his matrimonial prospects.

Frowning, he scoured his thoughts to find a way to smooth over his sentiments. TD had no idea she'd encouraged him this afternoon, and he wanted to express his gratitude—but without frightening her away.

At least, it's been nice to talk to someone. Wish me the best while finding a wife.
Sincerely yours,
Mr. Businessman

It wasn't Shakespeare, but it would have to do.

Now he had to focus on saving his business. In a way, now wasn't the time to find a wife, not with his professional future so unsteady. But he was lonely. And his father had never forgiven him for losing Marilee. He'd never really forgiven himself, either. Not that he missed Marilee or wanted her back, after seeing her true nature. But he did wish for companionship. Nights in his creaky house had become a little too empty as of late. Having someone to share his burden would be of some comfort.

Too bad TD wasn't interested. Already, she'd struck

a chord in him he hadn't been able to replicate with any of the other mail-order responders. They each sounded fine in their own right, but their letters were *too* straightforward. Too dry, emotionless. Just the specific details—name, age, current situation, children, if any. It was all rather cold sounding, and not at all what he'd expected when he requested a serious wife. One could still be warm while being serious, couldn't one?

In any case, it was too challenging to fall for women hiding behind their facts.

As Ewan pulled out his ledger, his thoughts moved to Miss Sattler. He might not feel anything for most of the women who'd responded to his advertisement, but he'd felt an uncanny connection with Miss Sattler a week ago in the forest, similar to his attraction for TD. But that was a grave problem. His parched heart drank up her charm and enthusiasm so quickly, he hadn't realized it until he was in over his head.

A tangle of beauty and vim and sweetness—that's what she was. A dangerous combination that lured him in unsuspectingly and then chopped him off at the knees. Oh, that draw had been powerful. Women like her—women who jumped from fancy to fancy—were his weakness. For a moment out on that path, with her so close, he'd allowed himself to become distracted, but that must end. He had to remain on the lookout for a sensible wife.

As well as focusing on preparing the mine for Mr. Johns's return.

A knock sounded at his door.

"Come in."

When the door opened, Mr. Marcus Lieberman appeared, dusty from his dark, haphazard hair to the tips of his clunky boots. "Mr. Burke?"

Ewan sat forward. The manager of his stamp mill was one of his hardest workers. He never left the site during business hours for anything short of an emergency. "Is everything all right?"

"Well…" The man fidgeted, his eyes hesitant. "That gal you brought through the mill last week?"

Ewan's muscled tensed. "Yes?"

Marcus scratched his dirty fingers against his hair. "She's, uh…introducing herself to all the workers."

Ewan's brows shot upward. "She's what?"

"She's at the mill, and she's shaking everybody's hand. Kinda in the way, too."

Closing his eyes against a developing headache, Ewan pushed back from his desk. "Of course she is."

This wasn't what he needed right now. He led the way down the stairs, shoes clamoring a quick rhythm that echoed off the walls. He pushed through the door at the base of the stairwell and marched down the hall to the side door leading outside.

Breaking into the sunshine and crossing the field, he ignored the soot filling his lungs and the incessant sound of stamp mills pounding in his chest. When he told that woman not to meddle with his store, not to meddle with him, he hadn't realized he'd need to include the miners in the list, too. Of all ridiculous ideas, to go about interfering with men hard at work! He'd take shelf rearrangement any day over her pestering his staff.

A haze of dust met him inside the stamp mill, but with a quick scan he spotted her. Plain as day, Miss Sattler stood on the upper-level platform in a stream of light from one of the high windows. The metal cams churned his stamp batteries up and down like clockwork. Seemingly oblivious to it all, Miss Sattler offered George Bates, his deaf employee, a handshake as if they were attending a church picnic instead of standing in the middle of a working mine operation.

Of course, she had no idea he couldn't hear. She yelled a greeting over the rumbling stamps crushing ore beneath the platform—her skirts precariously close to a battery's spinning power wheel and belt.

Ewan's heart seized, and he hopped the steps to the second level. He caught Miss Sattler's arm, snatching her back toward the stairway—away from the miner, the spinning power wheel and the railing-less edge.

She startled. "Mr. Burke! What are you doing?"

"Getting you out of here." Anger clogged his throat nearly as much as the dust did. Encircling Miss Sattler's upper arm with his hand, he barreled down the stairs and out of the building.

"Mr. Burke—" her voice strained as the mill's grinding faded some "—you're hurting me."

Immediately he released her. Standing in the sunshine, he turned to face her, working to quell the adrenaline coursing through his veins. He hadn't meant to grip her so tightly, but when he imagined what could have happened to her while standing so close to that power wheel...

"Do you have any idea the danger you put yourself in?"

Miss Sattler blinked those wide gray-blue eyes, as if she tried desperately to think of what he meant. "I—"

"My office. Now." He ushered her ahead of him and worked to calm his breathing as they crossed the field and entered the main building. *Kindness, regardless of affliction* echoed in his thoughts, but he pushed the words away. They didn't apply to this situation—not when she had made it clear that only firm, direct orders got through to her at all. But for all that, he'd wait until they got inside. It was high time for a strict conversation, and he didn't feel right about scolding her in the open where any passersby would see.

Once inside his office, he shut the door and crossed to his desk.

"Have a seat, Miss Sattler."

She did so, wringing hands perched on her lap. Too much energy kept him from following suit. Instead, he paced behind his desk like a caged animal, stopping occasionally to look at her small and forlorn person seated across from him.

"The stamp mill is hardly a place for a lady," he began. "I have told you that before. It is incredibly dangerous. That platform has no railing. If you had fallen, you would have landed on an amalgamation table among the mercury and shards of ore, or worse, if the hem of your skirt had caught in the belt on the power wheel, it would have been disastrous."

"I promise I watched where I stood."

"Accidents happen, Miss Sattler." He dropped both hands on his desk and leaned closer to her. "My men don't *try* to get in the way of their dynamite blasts, or *want* to cause the occasional cave-in, but the smallest moment of inattention can lead to frightful consequences. Mining is a dangerous job, and you are not allowed over there. It is a liability, and I can't protect you all the time." Suddenly drained of energy, he sank into his own chair. Breathing deeply, he prayed his headache would cease. "What's worse, you could have put George Bates in danger."

"George Bates?"

"The man you were speaking to when I interrupted. He lost his hearing in a mining explosion years ago in Colorado. Now he works for me in the stamp mill. It's a dangerous job, and everyone has strict orders not to sneak up on him while he works." Ewan rubbed at his temples. "Apparently, I have to reiterate that you belong in the store, where you are employed. You are not to romp around the property like Little Red Riding Cape on her way to Grandmother's house. Do you understand me?"

She didn't answer right away. When he finally glanced up, he saw she still stared at her hands, eyes misting over.

Oh, dear. Hurting her feelings made him feel like an oaf. But rules were rules, and they were there for a reason. "Just do your job and don't interfere in the miners' work, all right?"

Pursing her lips, she nodded and stood. "I understand. I'm sorry."

She left the office, the door closing quietly behind her. Ewan turned his focus back to the paperwork on his desk, but as he picked up his pen, he found it difficult to ignore the niggling guilt rising within his chest. Perhaps he should have let her explain why she'd been among the miners in the first place.

Except it wouldn't have changed his rules. She had endangered herself and George, and he couldn't stomach the idea of allowing another accident to happen.

Folding his hands, he propped his forehead against them and closed his eyes. For a long moment, he didn't think anything—just allowed the worry and stress from the past six months to wash over him. "God," he whispered. "Why isn't anything working as planned? She says she ruins things, but honestly, I can't help but think the ruin comes from me."

His father had been right, back when Marilee left. Standing in his parents' home just after the wedding ceremony debacle, Ewan had met his father's eyes and heard him say, "Son, why does it seem like everything you do comes to ruin?"

"Whatever happens moving forward," he prayed, "please help me not to mess it up."

Winifred reached the store and shut the door behind her, pressing her back against the surface. Tears squeezed from her closed eyes. No, she wouldn't cry. Strong, capable women bowed at the force of the wind—they did not break. She could weather this just like she weathered everything else.

But that was the problem. She hadn't yet learned to weather everything else. Rather than overcoming obstacles, she seemed to just carry them along with her. Her sixth mail-order flop. Being stranded away from home. Feeling so utterly alone. She hadn't triumphed over any of it.

Now something as simple as a reprimand caused her wobbly knees to buckle.

She'd thought she'd finally found a way to boost morale without irritating Mr. Burke, but apparently not. It didn't matter that she'd made her rounds during lunch instead of eating with Granna Cass, or that some of the miners seemed to genuinely enjoy her friendly introduction. Mr. Burke saw what he wanted to see. And he saw her as annoying. Dangerous, even. Someone who was only ever in the way.

Mr. Ansell's words suddenly played through her head, like a terrible song stuck there. What if she was just as incapable of helping others as she was at finding love? What if she would never be appreciated but merely tolerated?

At five o'clock, she stepped out on the front porch and locked the door. Turning, she took a few minutes to gaze at the sun hanging lower in the sky than it had this same time a week and a half ago. Crispness sparked the September air, promising that autumn wasn't too far away. And not long after that, the anticipated visit from Mr. Richard Johns. The future of the Golden Star would then rest in his hands.

These workers seemed so glum, moving from task to task, day to day. Where was the passion for their jobs? She saw that fire in Mr. Burke, and it was a shame his miners didn't share in it.

Releasing a pent-up breath, Winifred rounded the outside of the store to the side door that led directly into the kitchen. When she opened the door, the place already bustled with men. Some at the table, others lining the walls.

Granna Cass spotted her and waved her closer. "Come on, Miss Winnie. Grab those rolls coming out of the oven, please?"

Winifred did as she was told, the sound of the scraping of the baking sheet coming out of the oven barely disguised by the din of male chatter.

As the men ate their meals, she and Granna Cass kept the warm biscuits coming.

"Hey, ma'am?" one of the men said behind her at

the table. "I heard you were walkin' around meeting all the fellas. Why didn't you come meet me?"

A few other men chuckled. Slowly, Winifred turned around, baking sheet balanced in her apron-covered hands. Did he mean to ridicule her? But when she met the young man's eyes, nearly covered by his shock of blond hair, she only detected friendly mirth in their depths.

"Where do you work, sir?" She placed a roll on his plate and another on the plate of the miner beside him.

"Inside the mine."

"Well, now, that's probably why I didn't meet you. I'm not allowed to enter the mine by myself." The pan's heat seeped through the layers of fabric into her fingers. Switching the pan to her left hand, she stuck out her right. "But that won't stop me from meeting you now. Miss Winnie Sattler."

The man's eyes twinkled. He couldn't have been more than nineteen, maybe younger. "Pleased to meet you, Miss Sattler. I'm Adrian Birkeland. This here's my partner, Roger Holloway. And these two blokes are my friends, Rogan Scott and Walter Martin. They're partners, too."

Winifred shook each hand in turn. Rough were their palms, but shining were their eyes, and each one wore a cheerful smile. "Lovely meeting all of you. Now, what do you mean by partners?"

"We work together in the mine," Rogan explained, raking a hand through the gray hair salting his temples. "One of us holds the stake while the other hammers it into the wall."

"We create holes for the black powder," Adrian added. "Then we light a fuse and…"

Laughter died around him, so his explanation trailed off. Winifred looked up with the others to find Mr. Burke in the doorway.

For the past few days, since their walk through the forest, he'd taken his meals in his office. Granna Cass ran the food upstairs after the rest of the company was served and eating. So to see him here, albeit late, with everyone…

"Good evening, all." He stared over the group with his usual stern expression before stepping in farther and accepting a plate from Granna Cass. "Thank you, Cassandra."

The awkward, uncomfortable hush continued to cloud the air as he took a seat on the end. Winifred placed the baking sheet on the stove top and collected a couple of rolls. She crossed to Mr. Burke and placed them on his plate. He sent her a glance of gratitude with a silent nod before lifting his fork. Soon, the miners finished their meals and moved out of the kitchen, some on their way home for the evening, and others to grab their night-shift supplies before coming back for their lunch pails.

After every miner left, Mr. Burke remained, buttering his bread and eating in silence. A stab of pity rushed through Winifred, so she made up a plate of her own and took a seat opposite him.

"I'm probably the last person you want to sit near," she said quietly, "but all the same, no one should eat alone."

Mr. Burke made a wry smile. "I eat alone quite often. It's not so bad, once you grow accustomed to it."

She smiled, but before she could answer, a sudden pounding at the back door made her jump. Winifred looked to Granna Cass, then to Mr. Burke. The pounding came again, this time for a longer stretch. Mr. Burke crossed to open the door, revealing a slight woman in a large coat.

"Please, sir." Her voice came strained. "Please, let me in."

He immediately ushered her inside and shut the door behind her. "Is anyone following you, ma'am?"

"I don't know." She gasped the words out as Granna Cass took one of her arms and helped her into a chair at the table. "I... I just don't know."

Mr. Burke locked the back door and rushed for the one leading to the hallway. "Just the same, I'll ask Gerald to watch the grounds extra closely tonight. Cassandra," he said over his shoulder on his way out, "clean her up."

The door shut behind him, and a chill filled the room in his absence, the untouched portion of his dinner sitting across from Winifred.

"Winnie?" Granna Cass's voice made Winifred jump. The older woman was seated beside the visitor, a hand protectively resting on the woman's shoulder. "Fetch me the washbasin?"

Realizing she sat at the table dumbly, Winifred sprang up, lifting the heavy water bowl from its stand in the corner and shuffling to the table, careful not to spill over the bowl's porcelain lip. Once she placed the bowl on the table between the two women, she finally got a good look at the newcomer's face.

Young—younger than Winifred's twenty-six years. Dark eyes, blond hair. Physically beautiful but with a haunted deprivation in her gaze that made sympathy clench in Winifred's gut. She sank to a chair as

Granna Cass dipped a rag into the water and held it to the young woman's cheek, where a bruise had begun to form.

"Hold this here and try to calm down, missy," the older woman murmured. "You're safe now."

What was she safe from? Or whom? Gooseflesh ran over her arms as Winifred glanced at the outside door, imagining someone barreling in. Would he be armed? What would he do to them? What had he already done to this poor girl?

Mr. Burke reentered the kitchen from the hallway. "Gerald is patrolling the grounds. You'll be safe here tonight." He made his way back to the table and took a seat beside Winifred so he could look the young woman in the eye. He folded his hands on the table. "Ma'am, I am Ewan Burke, and I own the Golden Star Mine. This is Cassandra Washington and Winifred Sattler. We'll make up a bed for you right here, with them, and you can stay as long as you need."

As long as she needed? Winifred had expected him to give the woman the same warning he'd given Winifred when she arrived—that there wouldn't be room for her to stay on a long-term basis.

"What establishment are you running from, ma'am?"

"Bella Union." The woman barely looked up, her chin beginning to tremble. "I started at the Gem, then tried to leave and couldn't find work, so I ended up at Bella Union, and—"

Mr. Burke slid his hand across the table to stop the woman's explanation. She lurched away as if he were a snake, so he drew back. "It's all right. I won't hurt you."

Winifred's heart fell to the pit of her stomach. *The Gem.* Mr. Burke had explained to her what that place was, and now she looked at one of its former employees who wanted out and clearly had nowhere else to turn.

"You will work here," Mr. Burke was saying. "We have plenty of things for you to do, and we will explain them all in the morning after you've had a chance to calm down and take in your surroundings." He stood and scooped an empty bowl from the cupboard before crossing to the pot of soup still warm on the stove. "Here, you will learn skills to support yourself. You can stay as long as needed. This is a safe place."

His movements were sure and confident, yet gentle enough not to scare the woman again. Sitting down, Mr. Burke placed the bowl and a spoon in front of the woman as if he were setting out food for a frightened animal. "We have everything you need. You won't need to worry anymore. What is your name?"

The young woman's chin trembled. "They called me Trixie, but my real name is Delia Richardson."

"Miss Delia Richardson," he said, his voice calm and soothing, "welcome to the Golden Star Mine."

Delia's eyes flickered gratitude, and soon she ate. Slowly at first but picking up speed and interest as she went. The poor dear. While Winifred watched, still trying to fathom the emptiness of such a life, Mr. Burke's hand clasped hers beneath the table.

Startled, she looked up at him. He offered her a small smile. "Why don't you accompany me to the store, Miss Sattler? Cassandra will stay with Miss Richardson and help her settle in."

Unable to find her voice, Winifred nodded and followed him out of the kitchen. Colors from the low sun glowed through the hallway windows as they made their way around the twists and turns that now felt so familiar to her.

"I thought this might be a bit overwhelming for you." His voice still sounded hushed, the same soft tones he'd used with Delia. "Perhaps an explanation is in order."

Before tonight, she'd never quite heard that tone from him, nor seen the gentleness in his actions toward another person, and her heart filled with warmth. Whatever explanation he thought he owed her, she could assure him he did not.

He unlocked the store and stepped in first. Odd— usually he stepped aside like a gentleman.

"Just a minute." Then he swept through the store and checked the front door to make sure it was locked to the outside, and with a rush of appreciation, she realized he had stepped in first to protect her from any threat that might be lying in wait. He came back to where she stood in the doorway and ushered her in. "All clear. I wanted to make certain."

Entering, Winifred took in the shop with new eyes. "Are we in some sort of danger?"

"No, probably not. But one can never be too careful."

He moved to the counter to light the lamp waiting there. Winifred ambled to the window and stared out at the golden sun, bursting into a sunset. She touched the pane with her fingertip. "Is Delia in danger?"

Mr. Burke released a heavy sigh. "I never know. We haven't had any problems in the past, but I don't want us to be caught unawares."

"In the past?" Winifred turned. "You mean there have been others?"

"A few." He leaned a hip against the counter. "That's what I wanted to talk to you about." Low light from the lamp cast those shadows across his face again, and he crossed his arms over his broad chest. "The Golden Star has a reputation in town. When people need a place to turn, they know they're welcomed here."

Winifred turned her body to face him fully. "You mean people like Delia."

"Sometimes, yes. And also people like George and Lars." Mr. Burke shook his head. "It all started so suddenly. I met a woman named Lucinda, who had run away from the Gem and had nowhere to turn. I'd recently completed my office building, so she moved in with Cassandra and began managing my store after that. She actually quit the day I hired you. Others have come and gone, doing office work or helping Cassandra in the kitchen." He smiled faintly for an instant before his face grew serious. "I only tell you this so you're not confused about what's going on. People come here to find a new start, Miss Sattler. When they have learned skills and are confident in using them, they have the chance to move on with their lives somewhere else, where no one knows them and they can begin again."

Her already-warmed heart melted into a pool, and her throat thickened. "So, you save their lives?"

Mr. Burke waved off her question. "They save themselves by choosing to turn toward a new path. Cassandra helps out tremendously. I only supply the building."

One of her brows arched. "You're being modest. I

saw the way you took charge in there. You'll help Delia more than either of us will."

He shrugged a shoulder, obviously unprepared for how to respond to her compliment. Not that she really knew where to go from there, either. Even after all the stern comments he'd said to her since she first came, she had a strong desire despite it all to cross the floor and kiss him for his good deeds tonight.

The thought brought a blush to her cheeks, and she whirled to face the window. *Winnie Sattler, get a hold of yourself. You can't go kissing Mr. Burke just because he did something that moved you. Have you gone mad?*

Or worse, was she that desperate for a solid, good-willed man in her life?

"I admire your courage and servitude." She drew a line along the windowsill. "Most people would be like the characters in the story of the Good Samaritan and walk on by, but you stop to help. More than that, you hang a light in your window so that people in need know they can come to you." She swallowed, fortifying her thoughts. "My father was a man like you. He and my mother owned an orphanage in Kansas. A small one, with maybe ten or twelve children. But they loved their work—loved building a home full of care for children who needed it so badly. Then one night, there was a fire. He managed to get me and the other children out, but my mother—" Pausing, Winifred blinked back the emotion pressing down on her. "My mother was sick. After rounds and rounds of entering that building, in and among flames and smoke, my father still went in for Mother." The golden light outside took on an orange hue above the evergreen trees. "My parents' relationship was like nothing I'd ever seen before or since. A sacrificial love that covered everything."

It was a love she had fervently prayed to have for her own. And every time a mail-order agreement didn't work, she clung to that picture of her parents and set her shoulders, telling herself the next one would be it. The next one would be that sacrificial love she wanted so desperately. But it never was, and she always ended up alone.

"They died together." Tears clogged her words. "Some say in each other's arms."

Two hands touched her shoulders from behind. Turning, she allowed Mr. Burke to put his arms around her as she pushed her face into his chest. Oh, how desperately she wanted not to cry, to be strong, but in the warmth of someone's comfort, she couldn't hold back her tears.

She had been alone for so long. "Aunt and Uncle did their best, but—"

"Shh…" He placed his chin on her head and gathered her closer. "We don't always understand why life happens the way it does. My mother died when I was a child, too. But know you're safe here, that the Golden Star is a second family for you."

He had no idea how true his words were. No matter what had brought her here, Winifred knew she needed this place and these people. And God had orchestrated it all.

But there was still the matter of it not being permanent. They might be her family now, but what would happen when she earned enough money to leave Deadwood and go home? The Golden Star had become more like home to her than anywhere else had since losing her parents.

And what would happen if the mine failed, if Mr. Burke couldn't secure an investor? What if this place was not just gone to her, but soon disappeared completely for everyone who needed it?

Chapter Six

Ewan slipped his folded response into an envelope and sealed it. Flipping it over, he wrote the return address across the front before tossing it into the growing pile of envelopes on the corner of his office desk.

One more rejection for a potential bride. Hopefully the woman wouldn't be too upset.

He stared at his correspondence from the last couple of days. Three rejection letters and one in the "maybe" pile. Actually, he was surprised his advertisement had interested anyone at all, much less four applicants. But their responses had been lacking, enough to drop them from his list of possibilities.

One had assured him she didn't look the slight bit beautiful, quite ugly in fact, and that others could verify it. Even though he'd partially asked for it in the ad, her response left a bad taste in his mouth. He'd politely declined her offer. Another had several children. He loved children, of course, and wanted his own someday, but with his business so precarious right now, exposing so many children to that kind of uncertainty wouldn't be right. This last one, the one he'd just added to the pile, actually came from a cousin of someone in town, looking for an excuse to leave the life of teaching and a handful of other responsibilities she'd apparently acquired in a town east of here. But shirking responsibilities wasn't an enticing quality, either. He wanted his wife to be his full partner in life—someone who would help with the mining business in whatever means necessary.

The fourth prospect had mining experience. So she'd gone in the "maybe" pile.

Sighing, Ewan rubbed his fingers along the bridge of his nose. He'd expected there to be maybe one letter in the bunch that didn't meet his qualifications, but he hadn't expected three-fourths of them to be that way. Finding a wife proved harder than he'd hoped—and more tedious than he'd anticipated.

With a sideways glance toward his right-hand drawer, he imagined the flowery stationery and penciled envelopes that lay inside. Including a new one he hadn't read. The heart of that woman easily outshone all the rest.

Having saved it for last, he opened her latest letter now.

Dear Mr. Businessman,

I suppose if we are both lonely, then corresponding might be a good solution for a while. You can keep me company while I'm getting over a disappointing period in my life, and I can do the same for you. Or help you sift through all those letters you are sure to receive. The right woman is out there. I know you'll find her soon...

A knock at the door interrupted him.

"Mr. Burke?" came the muffled voice behind the door.

Miss Sattler. Another spot of confusion in his life. If only he could figure out what he felt toward her—irritation or attraction. He would prefer indifference. That would be much easier to handle.

"Come in." Ewan dropped the envelope and stationery in his drawer as the door opened wide and Miss Sattler entered. More like bounced, as was her usual way, he'd come to realize.

"You wanted to see me?" She sank into a seat opposite his desk, her smile permanently fixed in place.

"I did." He shifted in his chair. "I spoke with Miss Richardson this morning, and she said she wants to stay with us for quite some time." He folded his hands, waiting for the implication of what he would say to sink in. "So, I'm—"

"You'll be giving her my job?"

Before he responded, he watched for her reaction. She only smiled. "I'd hoped you'd understand," he continued, "since I informed you at the very beginning this might happen. The store clerk is the highest-paying job I have for someone like Miss Richardson, who has no other training, so I'd prefer she have it."

"Certainly." She shook her head as if to tell him not to worry. "I expected as much."

A smile tugged at Ewan's mouth. He admired her generosity—she clearly had no qualms about giving up her position to someone in greater need. "Excellent. Now, as for your position, Miss Sattler, I've decided to hire you as a clerk in my office." Before she could react, he held up his hands. "It's temporary work, too, and I'd only need you a couple hours a day, at most. It pays less than the store, so unfortunately, it'll take you longer to earn that fare."

Despite his warning, her eyes lit at the prospect. "It still sounds wonderful. I already checked downtown, and no one was interested in hiring me for temporary work. Honestly, you've done so much for me, Mr. Burke. I don't know how to thank you."

The tips of Ewan's ears began to burn. "Well, I—"

"And I wanted to express again how much I admire what you're doing for Delia. No doubt she's seen all sorts of horrors, and you've given her a reason to hope again."

He fiddled with the corner of a page on his desk, her words touching him deeply. "Thank you. And please, you're welcome to stay as long as you need. If Cassandra wants you out of the kitchen, let me know and we'll search for accommodations for you."

Her gaze snagged his and seemed to communicate gratitude deeper than her words could provide. His heart began to soften toward her until he realized what a pile of mush he'd become.

Ewan cleared his throat. "But as long as you're on my property, as an employee or a guest if you find other work elsewhere, I still expect you to uphold our reputation. And keep out of the miners' way." He could probably add a dozen more do-nots to that list.

"Thank you, Mr. Burke." She stood, then paused. "Actually, can I just call you Ewan? I've known you for nearly two weeks, and 'Mr. Burke' sounds so formal and distant."

That was the idea—especially when it came to his dealings with Miss Sattler. But Ewan didn't say so aloud. She looked at him with that wide blue-gray expression, so hopeful it could rival a puppy's. Whatever made her so excited to familiarize his name?

He sighed. "Fine. You may call me Ewan."

"And you may call me Winnie."

"'Miss Sattler' is fine."

Her shoulders dropped. "But I thought we were ceasing these formal airs."

"You may." A half smile tugged at his mouth. "I prefer to be professional."

She rolled her eyes yet couldn't contain a grin. "Fine. How about a compromise? Instead of calling me Miss Sattler, just call me Winifred. Yes? It's not one of those nicknames Granna Cass says you hate to use."

Ewan stared at her. What was it about this woman's never-give-up attitude that won him over, even against his better judgment? "Fine. Winifred. Now head out, please. I have a lot to do."

"Isn't that part of my job now?" She didn't even try to hide her laughter. "Helping you with all that work?"

He could already see how he'd regret giving her the office job. "No, you'll start tomorrow. Today, I want you to show Miss Richardson around the store and help her get settled in."

"Well, then, Ewan, thank you again for this opportunity to continue working for you, and I hope the rest of your day goes well." She skirted her chair, her bustled gown swinging as she practically skipped out into the hallway.

"I expect you first thing in the morning," he announced as she shut the door behind her.

Stifling a sigh, he lowered his head into his hands and tried to push back a headache that threatened to begin. He really couldn't afford to think about her right now. Instead, he must focus on the mine. This place had become his goal, his dream, his chance at a new beginning. The thing that would make him successful in his father's eyes. But staring at the workload ahead of him to make this place perform to Mr. Johns's standards, he began to wonder if maybe the investor had been right.

What if he couldn't turn enough of a profit? Or worse, what if he himself really was worthless and doomed to failure?

Oh, he knew he'd been made in the image of God. And he knew God didn't make junk—that's what prompted Ewan to reach out to the downtrodden in the first place. But beyond his creation as a human being, did he hold worth? Would his mark on society be enough to truly make a difference for anyone? He tried so hard, worked so diligently, and what if it wasn't enough to give him the same worth his brother had?

Enough of that train of thought. He scooped up TD's letter and immersed himself in her flowing script and genuine words.

> God has a plan for all His children, Mr. Businessman. Are you a believer? I hope so. Experiencing His steadfast care and comfort is the greatest blessing I can imagine. I draw so much encouragement from Him, and I hope I can extend some of that to you, as well.
>
> I'll be praying for you in the days to come.
> Sincerely yours,
> TD

He would try his best to keep the mine intact, to find a wife who would be a solid business partner. He would become like his brother in every way, and not merely in appearance. Because if he didn't succeed…

Well, he didn't want to find out what would happen.

In the early morning, before even Granna Cass was up, Winifred snuggled beneath her coverlet and stared at the words her mystery friend had written, allowing the warmth of her heart to heat through the rest of her. This was her fourth letter from him, and it was as intoxicating as the first three. Was it possible to be smitten with a man's handwriting? Or perhaps it was the way he worded his sentences. Most realistically, it was the fact that, letter after letter, he felt the same emotions she did and didn't mind sharing them openly with her.

Who was she kidding? *All* of those things made her smitten with Mr. Businessman. Totally and completely smitten.

Which made things a little more complicated.

Sure, she wasn't *in love* with the man. She'd only known him two weeks. She didn't have any plans to suggest herself as his new bride. Though the Golden Star had begun to feel like home, she wasn't long for Deadwood. She belonged in Denver with Aunt and Uncle. Once she made that final amount needed for fare, she'd be gone.

Besides, she couldn't trust another man with her heart any time soon, not after Mr. Ansell—and all the others before him. Not even Mr. Businessman could be completely trusted, and especially not through letters—of course, that didn't keep her heart from betraying her as she reread his note.

Dear TD,

I've not yet found a promising match, but someday I know she'll come along. And to answer your question, yes, I am a believer. You're right about the comfort of God's everlasting love. Thank you for encouraging me. You have no idea the impact you have made. Even in such a short time, you've become a good friend.

As my friend, you have me curious…what are you dreams? What do you hope for your future?

Her hopes and dreams? Winifred sighed. When she finished the letter, right down to his scrawled "Sincerely yours," she dropped the page on her lap. Sentimental heart. It betrayed her, led her in every direction, whichever way fit her present whims. And it often disappointed her.

Love—true, deep, sacrificial love—didn't happen often between a husband and wife. She had seen it in her parents but in no one else. Even Aunt and Uncle had their little silent patches and eye-rolling moments. And if she had any dreams for the future, that would have to be it. A realistic, practical love where she was not merely tolerated but cherished. But a love like that seemed so out of reach. Could a deep, sacrificial love exist for her one day, or was she doomed to chase it forever?

Her vision blurred behind tears, so she folded up the note and turned onto her side.

Mind too full for sleep, she quietly slipped from her

coverlet and dressed in her robe. Delia's pallet lay beside hers, and the woman slept soundly beneath a pile of blankets. For the hundredth time in the past week and a half, Winifred thanked God that Delia had had the courage to leave the dangerous life she'd lived and that she was slowly blossoming here into the woman she was supposed to be.

Grabbing her sketchpad, Winifred stepped over Delia's bed and made her way to the kitchen window. Small, it faced mostly trees, but it seemed as good a spot as any to draw. In the days since she'd been relieved of her duties in the store, she'd spent a few hours each day helping Ewan in his office, filing papers and calculating expenses. Then a few more hours were spent helping Granna Cass in the kitchen. But in her free time, she had begun to revisit her artistic hobby.

Pulling up a chair and sitting, Winifred looked out the window at the trees, listening to the stamp mill's pounding that thrummed through her chest and tapping her pencil against the side of her paper. Her artistic gaze analyzed the angle of the evergreens' boughs, the smoke rising from far-off buildings, the men moving along the road into town and the jagged profile of the mountain in the background.

She lifted her pencil and tried to capture the image. Gliding the pencil lines across the textured surface, she shaded the dark shadows and accented the spots of emerging sunlight. She had barely realized she'd begun before she finished the drawing. As a small sketch, it was something easily accomplished in a matter of minutes and miniscule enough to fit in the palm of her hand.

An idea sparked, and Winifred sat up straight. Why

hadn't she thought of this before? There might indeed be a way to reach the miners, to give them something of herself to cheer and encourage them. Her drawings.

The notion burst through her, sending her heartbeat full steam ahead. She flipped the page and began another sketch of the same landscape, focusing on a cute pair of trees. Little sketches would do the trick. Small enough that she could fit four on a sheet of paper and light enough that she could hand them out during a meal. No one would have trouble holding on to a sketch that size all day before heading home. It could easily fit inside their lunch pails, even. And she wouldn't have to stop with one drawing for each man. She could write Bible verses, words of encouragement, artwork they could take home to their wives...

Purpose drove deep within her, her head spinning so fast, she almost didn't hear Granna Cass and Delia stirring for the day.

Winifred snapped shut her sketchbook and hastened back to the sleeping quarters. "Good morning," she whispered, her usual excitement increased tenfold. "Isn't it just a lovely day?"

Rubbing a sore spot on his shoulder, Ewan crested the stairs and approached his office. After a late night poring over his books and a restless night's sleep, the muscles in his neck and shoulders were feeling the brunt of his efforts to keep the mine afloat. And now for another day of shifting costs. A yawn pushed past his lips as he opened the office door. He wouldn't rest well until he found a solid solution.

"Good morning!"

The greeting nearly sent him out of his skin. Bright

eyed, Winifred stood beside his shelving unit in a stunning yellow gown. Boxes and boxes surrounded her on the floor, and stacks of papers were in her arms as well as lying in heaps along the shelf.

Was he in a nightmare? Blinking, Ewan scanned the room. Minus the accounts he'd studied on his desk yesterday, his office had been immaculate when he'd left for the night.

"What is going on here?"

"I thought you could use a little organization. It's hard to find anything in this office."

Scoffing, he motioned to the piles covering the floor. "Well, sure, it is now."

"Ewan—" she tipped her head to one side "—don't tell me you knew where anything was in this mess."

"Of course I did. And it wasn't a mess."

"Well, I got to thinking this system could use a little help. Have you ever thought of purchasing a cabinet letter file? My uncle has a couple in his office. They're new, and they'd be much better than the system you're using now, I promise. Though, for now, I'm thinking multiple boxes on this shelf could be a good temporary fix." She twirled to face the bookcase. "See, here, I'm putting last year's files in a box labeled '1877.' This year's files are split into several boxes, according to what records are contained within them…"

As she explained her new ideas, Ewan riffled through the papers on his desk. He plopped a large pile off onto another pile and scowled. "Where is my ledger?"

She turned. "This year's ledger?"

"Yes."

"Here, in the box marked 'Current Sales and Expenses.'" She lifted the ledger from a box she'd already shelved and handed it over. "Just put it back when you're done. The system won't work if you don't use it."

Ewan stifled a sigh and took a seat, opening his ledger to where he'd stopped his calculations the night before. "Miss Sattler, I think I need a few minutes alone. Why don't you go down to the kitchen and see if Cassandra needs anything?"

The firm line of her mouth told him she didn't like the idea. But at least she didn't complain. "All right, but please don't move anything while I'm gone. I have everything where I want it."

And he was expected to concentrate in this jungle of papers? He silently prayed this new project wouldn't stretch out over a period of several days.

As soon as she left, he set to work, comparing proceeds to costs and looking for clues. Unfortunately, he'd already cut expenses wherever he could think to do it, and thought up some ways to increase productivity, and *still* his mine wasn't making enough money.

After a series of frustrating calculations, he stood and paced behind his desk—the only place not covered in boxes—surprised he hadn't worn a hole clear through his rug for how many times he'd worried the floor in this manner in the past month.

But what else could he do? He'd tried everything.

God, please help me find a way to impress Mr. Johns. There has to be a way.

A soft knock sounded at the door. He paused and looked up. "Come in."

The door slid open a couple of feet, and Winifred poked her head inside. "Ewan?" He still hadn't grown accustomed to hearing her say his first name. He hadn't had the gumption to call her by her name, either—saying it was like taking down another barrier between them.

He blinked. "You're back soon."

"Actually, it's been an hour," she said, a smile tilting one corner of her mouth.

"Oh." Must've been more preoccupied with his books than he thought. He shuffled papers. "Well, first thing I want from you is to go through this pile of expense reports and see if you find anything else we could possibly cut—"

"Actually, first," she piped up, "Granna Cass has sent your breakfast up with me. Everyone else has eaten."

Breakfast. Yes. In the midst of his meticulous mathematics, he'd completely forgotten about sustenance.

Winifred gently placed a steaming mug of coffee and a heaping plate of eggs and potato slices on the edge of his desk.

Ewan lowered himself into his chair. "Thank you." Though he didn't have much of an appetite, he couldn't mention that after all the work Cassandra had gone to.

He reached for the fork, then realized Winifred still stood beside his desk. "Did—you need to say something else, too?"

Her half smile grew. "She also wanted me to tell you to be anxious for nothing, but in everything by prayer and supplication with thanksgiving let your requests be made known unto God."

A soft chuckle escaped him, the Bible verse unexpectedly filling him with a small sense of peace. "That woman." He shook his head. Cassandra spoke truth through the darkness like a lighthouse in a storm. "I'll be sure to do that."

"So, is that what you're working on this morning?" She stepped into the room again. "Looking for ways to increase the mine's earnings?"

She took a seat as Ewan nodded. "I had figured the numbers weeks ago for my report for Mr. Johns, but since he wants me to turn a profit before he'll invest, I felt I had to revisit those numbers yesterday. I need to cut more expenses if I'm to make more than I spend, but I'm coming up short. I won't compromise on my extra jobs available for people in need—that's my ministry—but I will need to make some difficult decisions about cutting something else."

"What have you cut already?"

"Some food, the amount of candles they take into the mine… I'm not sure what else I can do." Shaking his head, Ewan folded his arms and leaned back in his chair. "I didn't think it'd ever come to this." The mine, his dreams. Vanishing like fog in the sun. "Maybe I should get rid of the evening meal altogether to save costs."

"No." Winifred straightened in her chair. "You can't do that. When I arrived, you were adamant about keeping it."

"Yes, but I'm running out of expenditures to cut."

"It sets you apart from other mines," she explained, her voice unusually calm and rational. "If you take away all of the perks, what's to keep your employees here and not hiring on somewhere else?"

Her question poked at his insecurities. He dropped his gaze to his desk for a moment, racking his brain for a possible solution. "I don't know what else to do, short of firing workers."

"Which you definitely can't do. Fewer employees would give you a lower payroll, but it would also mean lower production. And if you did happen to pick up production again and want to rehire those employees, well..." She shook her head. "What would make them trust you enough to come back after you'd fired them once already?"

Ewan realized he was nibbling the inside of his lip. Ceasing the habit that only showed weakness, he rolled her words over in his mind. "I've looked at this from every angle." Every way he turned was a dead end. Each decision he was tempted to make would only haunt him. Maybe even ruin him.

"Surely there is something." Winifred rested her hands on her knees. She gazed at him with earnestness in her blue-gray eyes. She implored him to believe. "We will find places to cut costs that won't hurt everyone in the end. I know we will. There is always a way to fix things if we think about it long and hard enough."

Ewan sighed and glanced away. "Well, I forgot who I was talking to."

When he looked her way again, a shadow had tainted her gaze. "Ewan, you might think I'm some silly chatterbox who doesn't know the difference between a pickax and a stick of dynamite, but I do. And what I don't know, I learn quickly. You don't know everything about me, and I wish you wouldn't dismiss me so quickly all the time."

"Winifred—" there, he'd said her name "—I apologize. I didn't mean to offend. I do appreciate your optimism, I really do. But bolstering enthusiasm for a project won't be enough to turn things around. It is going to take hard work and a lot of rational decisions. Most of those decisions will be very unpopular to make but necessary for the business to grow."

"Maybe so," she said, tipping her chin upward in a demonstration of her strong-willed demeanor, "but just because difficult decisions must be made on occasion, doesn't mean that is always the case. Sometimes we're looking so hard for one answer we miss the obvious ones right in front of us. Sometimes we need a little faith and ingenuity to go along with that hard work."

"Do you really believe I don't have faith in this mine? How do you think I got this far?" He leaned forward in his chair, too. "My twin was the star of the family. Could do no wrong. Me, I left home at sixteen to make something of myself because I was never good enough in my father's eyes. Came home once, when I was twenty-two, but that didn't work out, so I left again and followed boom after boom. When I heard about gold in the Black Hills, I made my way up here. I've busted my hide, battling snow, wind, frigid temperatures, insects and sweltering summer heat, just to find my way in the world and build this mine up out of nothing. I have never had anything handed to me, Winifred. I worked for everything I've got."

"Then don't give up so easily." Winifred set her jaw and leaned forward on the other side of the desk, mimicking his stance with that stubborn way of hers. "I've seen your books, and I know you're bringing in money. We'll find creative ways to cut expenses, so you can make more than you spend. All right?"

How did she infuse steel-lined delivery with the softness of femininity?

Her gaze locked on his. "I'm not giving up if you're not. There are things we haven't tried yet, I'm certain of it."

While he marveled at her gumption, she straightened and grinned. "Well, then. Are you with me, Ewan Burke?"

Something in the way she said his name made a smile unexpectedly hitch on his lips. "I'm with you, Winifred Sattler."

Rolling her eyes, she reached for the pile of expense reports. "I wish you'd just call me Winnie like everyone else."

A chuckle escaped him as he speared a forkful of eggs.

"4 for 4" MINI-SURVEY

We are prepared to **REWARD** you with 2 FREE books and 2 FREE gifts for completing our MINI SURVEY!

FREE
Value Over
$20!

You'll get...

TWO FREE BOOKS & TWO FREE GIFTS

just for participating in our Mini Survey!

Dear Reader,

IT'S A FACT: if you answer 4 quick questions, we'll send you **4 FREE REWARDS!**

I'm not kidding you. As a leading publisher of women's fiction, we value your opinions… and your time. That's why we are prepared to **reward** you handsomely for completing our mini-survey. In fact, we have 4 Free Rewards for you, including 2 free books and 2 free gifts.

As you may have guessed, that's why our mini-survey is called **"4 for 4".** Answer 4 questions and get 4 Free Rewards. It's that simple!

Thank you for participating in our survey,

Pam Powers

To get your 4 FREE REWARDS:
Complete the survey below and return the insert today to receive 2 FREE BOOKS and 2 FREE GIFTS guaranteed!

◀ DETACH AND MAIL CARD TODAY! ▶

"4 for 4" MINI-SURVEY

1 Is reading one of your favorite hobbies?
☐ YES   ☐ NO

2 Do you prefer to read instead of watch TV?
☐ YES   ☐ NO

3 Do you read newspapers and magazines?
☐ YES   ☐ NO

4 Do you enjoy trying new book series with FREE BOOKS?
☐ YES   ☐ NO

YES! I have completed the above Mini-Survey. Please send me my 4 FREE REWARDS (worth over $20 retail). I understand that I am under no obligation to buy anything, as explained on the back of this card.

❏ I prefer the regular-print edition
105/305 IDL GMYL

❏ I prefer the larger-print edition
122/322 IDL GMYL

FIRST NAME	LAST NAME

ADDRESS

APT.#	CITY

STATE/PROV.   ZIP/POSTAL CODE

Offer limited to one per household and not applicable to series that subscriber is currently receiving.
Your Privacy—The Reader Service is committed to protecting your privacy. Our Privacy Policy is available online at www.ReaderService.com or upon request from the Reader Service. We make a portion of our mailing list available to reputable third parties that offer products we believe may interest you. If you prefer that we not exchange your name with third parties, or if you wish to clarify or modify your communication preferences, please visit us at www.ReaderService.com/consumerschoice or write to us at Reader Service Preference Service, P.O. Box 9062, Buffalo, NY 14240-9062. Include your complete name and address.

LI-218-MS17

© 2017 HARLEQUIN ENTERPRISES LIMITED
® and ™ are trademarks owned and used by the trademark owner and/or its licensee. Printed in the U.S.A.

READER SERVICE—Here's how it works:

Accepting your 2 free Love Inspired® Romance books and 2 free gifts (gifts valued at approximately $10.00 retail) places you under no obligation to buy anything. You may keep the books and gifts and return the shipping statement marked "cancel." If you do not cancel, about a month later we'll send you 6 additional books and bill you just $5.24 each for the regular-print edition or $5.74 each for the larger-print edition in the U.S. or $5.74 each for the regular-print edition or $6.24 each for the larger-print edition in Canada. That is a savings of at least 13% off the cover price. It's quite a bargain! Shipping and handling is just 50¢ per book in the U.S. and 75¢ per book in Canada*. You may cancel at any time, but if you choose to continue, every month we'll send you 6 more books, which you may either purchase at the discount price plus shipping and handling or return to us and cancel your subscription. *Terms and prices subject to change without notice. Prices do not include applicable taxes. Sales tax applicable in N.Y. Canadian residents will be charged applicable taxes. Offer not valid in Quebec. Books received may not be as shown. All orders subject to approval. Credit or debit balances in a customer's account(s) may be offset by any other outstanding balance owed by or to the customer. Please allow 4 to 6 weeks for delivery. Offer available while quantities last.

◄ If offer card is missing write to: Reader Service, P.O. Box 1341, Buffalo, NY 14240-8531 or visit www.ReaderService.com ◄

BUSINESS REPLY MAIL
FIRST-CLASS MAIL   PERMIT NO. 717   BUFFALO, NY

POSTAGE WILL BE PAID BY ADDRESSEE

READER SERVICE
PO BOX 1341
BUFFALO NY 14240-8571

NO POSTAGE
NECESSARY
IF MAILED
IN THE
UNITED STATES

Chapter Seven

Dear Mr. Businessman,

 You asked in your last letter about my dreams for the future. An interesting question. Actually, I've been thinking a lot about dreams lately—so far mine haven't turned out the way I'd hoped. Now I must start over, which sounds like a most daunting task. Where do I go from here? How do I go after the things I want out of life?

 What is your biggest fear? It may sound silly, but mine is that I'll always be merely tolerated. Unfortunately, that is the world in which I grew up. My family loves me, in a perfunctory sort of way, but I yearn to have my thoughts and actions truly valued. So, then, conversely, I suppose my biggest dream is for someone to cherish me, as I cherish him in return. But sometimes I fear that is too much to ask. It is hard enough to find any suitor, let alone a promising one.

 Can I tell you something I haven't told anyone? I confess, I haven't been in Deadwood long, but it's beginning to feel more like home than anywhere else has in a long time. The people I work with, the scenery I've grown to love, will be a part of me forever. I'm not sure how long I'll be here before I embark on my next endeavor, but I'm sure it won't be long enough. Thank you for being a part of my experience in the Black Hills. If only I could stay longer. I'll never forget you or your kindness.

Sincerely yours,

TD

Leaning against a pine, Ewan stared at the letter a few more minutes, brows drawn, before folding it up and slipping it into the envelope. After promising himself he'd never stand in that ridiculously long post office line on mail-delivery day, he'd found himself doing that very thing today, bolstered with hope that one of TD's letters awaited him. He inspected the envelope's sketch, a sprawling field of wildflowers, and recalled the contents of her note. She sounded sad. Or lonely, at the very least. And he believed she feared even more the loneliness that was to come when she left Deadwood behind.

The instant she moved away, their communication would end. At least, he assumed so. They would become less anonymous once they had to actually exchange addresses, and he wasn't so sure she'd be willing to disclose that much identifying personal information. Even more than that, TD would be in the process of rebuilding her life…and had made it clear in this letter that bidding farewell to Deadwood meant bidding farewell to him, too.

He frowned. With every letter they exchanged, he became less and less ready for that day to come.

Pocketing the note, he crossed the worn grass to the Golden Star's side door. As he turned the knob, a voice behind him called his name.

He turned. Marcus Lieberman stood in the stamp mill's door, his voice barely audible above the pounding. It was the start of the new shift. What could the manager need at this hour?

Ewan waved his hand in response and started in the direction of the mill. "What is it, Marcus?"

"The upper platform." The man leaned closer. "Something's wrong with it. I guess it ended up rotten in one spot. Or got wet, or—I don't know. But it gave way under George, and if Ralph hadn't been there to yank him back—"

"It gave way?" Ewan's body went rigid. "Is George all right?"

"Yeah, thankfully." Marcus shook his head, crossing his arms. "I can't figure what happened, though. Seemed fine yesterday."

"I'd better take a look."

Pushing through the door after his manager, Ewan met the scent of dust and the thundering of his stamps unmasked by the building surrounding them. He scanned his two five-stamp batteries, ten stamps in all. Business continued as usual around him. Men fed ore into the batteries, and turning cams caused the stamps to churn up and down, crushing the ore into fine pieces. The fractured dust of quartz and gold filtered through screens to land on long amalgamation tables coated in mercury.

George had been restationed to the ground level,

scraping mercury and amalgamated gold from the tables to be separated.

Ewan breathed a prayer of relief. After checking with George to ensure he was fine, Ewan made his way to the far end of the ground floor, following Marcus as the manager pointed up at the second-level platform's underside. The splintered hole where platform boards had ripped free caused Ewan's brow to tighten.

"See here?" His manager pointed out neighboring V-shaped supports that were still intact and showed no signs of rot. "These sections seem to be fine, but somehow this middle part collapsed."

Ewan inspected the platform and the fallen pieces of wood, now a pile of kindling on the floor. Crouching by the pile, he picked up pieces of the platform and its support posts, turning them over in his hands. "Strange thing is, Marcus, this wood doesn't appear rotten."

Marcus didn't respond right away. When he came closer, he knelt beside Ewan, his mouth firm. "I worried that we'd find as much. Suppose I was being hopeful thinking it could have been something we'd missed."

Hopeful that the support post had rotted? Why would he hope for that? What other possibility could be worse? His words caused Ewan's heart to stall. Slowly, he raised his gaze to meet the manager's. "What are you saying, exactly?"

Drawing in a breath, Marcus set his jaw. "I'm saying, if this damage wasn't done by something natural, then it had to be something unnatural."

Tampered with. His manager didn't have to say the words for them to ring in Ewan's ears.

They continued to haunt him as he climbed the stairs back to his office. When he stepped inside, he found Winifred seated before the safe, where he'd asked her to organize a box of files. She lifted her head at the sound of his entrance, and immediately Ewan noticed the pursed shape of her usually care-free mouth.

The look stopped him just inside the door. "What is it? Did you find something?"

"Well…" She seemed to hesitate, glancing over the papers in her lap as if she wanted to be certain of what she'd say. "I'm finding a lot of extra expenses from the past couple of months."

Was that all? Ewan closed the door. "Yes, I had to make quite a few purchases after those beams col-lapsed in the mine."

Winifred shook her head. "No, other things, too. Before the accident. Repair to Lars Brennan's cart—"

"A broken axle."

"New hammers…"

"A few went missing." Ewan shrugged, making his way to his desk. "Things like that happen from time to time."

But her frown only deepened. "A medical bill for a Mr. Jones after an unexpected dynamite blast, a re-pair to your scaffolding after part of a stope wall caved in…" She flipped through the pages, shaking her head. "There are a lot of mishaps here, Ewan."

Tampered with… The words rang again through his mind, resounding like a gong warning of danger. She was right. There were a lot of mishaps as of late. But no, they couldn't all be related, could they?

"That's the way of the business," he said. "Accidents happen, and sometimes machinery needs to be replaced." He lowered himself into his office chair, that warning gong still clanging through his thoughts. "Mining is a dangerous job by nature."

Ewan picked up his pencil and let the silence hover, its weight heavily pressing down on him, no matter how desperately he wanted to deny the truth. Who was his explanation kidding? Not Winifred, judging by her raised eyebrow. And certainly not himself. "Winifred…the mine is in trouble, isn't it?"

She bit the corner of her mouth and took a breath before launching in. "Well, now, maybe not. We shouldn't jump to conclusions until we've looked more thoroughly at the evidence…"

"I can more or less explain away all of these problems except for the feeling I have that something isn't right." He placed his pencil on the desk and looked up at her. "Something happened at the stamp mill today."

She sat a little straighter, the pile on her lap forgotten for now. "What happened?"

"Part of the platform broke—the floor of it just collapsed into pieces. But it doesn't appear to have rotted." He ran a hand down his mouth, wanting to deny the suspicion Marcus had implied. "Maybe the supports wiggled loose over time."

Winifred blinked. "Doesn't someone inspect everything?"

Yes—on a regular basis. Exhaling, he looked away, hating the hole of suspicion eating through his gut. "Maybe the platform's underside was neglected during inspections."

She glanced at the pile of papers on her lap, then slowly looked back to him. "I've been calculating your books, going back to the beginning to see if I could find a place for you to save money—and I'll be honest, Ewan. You've spent more these past couple of months than you have since you purchased and assembled your stamp mill at the beginning of your operation. Prior to that, you would occasionally have unexpected costs from something breaking or getting lost, but now it's happening over and over again." She grimaced, sympathy glinting in her eyes. "Something's wrong here. This doesn't feel like a fluke."

"You think these repairs, these accidents, are connected?"

"Judging by the evidence, that's what I would guess." Standing, she placed the pile of receipts and records on his desk before him, evidence supporting the theory he didn't want to believe. "I'm certainly no detective, but it does make me wonder if someone is trying to keep your mine from making money."

Winifred filled the lunch pails sitting out for the morning crew. As Granna Cass made sandwiches, bare of all but a thin slice of salted pork—an indicator of the cost-saving measures—Winifred took the opportunity to slip her drawings into the pails.

This would be her fifth day doing so. Sketches of the mine, of the trees, of the rolling horizon, of the town. Whatever she could see, she drew. Sometimes even people, though it was much easier to find those walking by than in the mine itself, since she'd been more or less banned from the stamp mill and knew she'd get lost—not to mention getting in severe trouble with Ewan—if she tried to find miners within the mountain.

Every morning and evening, she slipped the sketches into the lunch pails for the men to enjoy. Wasn't much, but it didn't cost Ewan a thing. And it seemed to help with morale—the men took their lunch pails like usual the first day, not expecting a thing, but the next day they all had something to say about the gift they'd found when sitting down to eat. They eagerly asked if they'd receive more. She hoped the gesture would motivate them to mine with more zeal in their steps.

"Such a fun idea." Granna Cass glanced at Winifred as they worked side by side.

"That's a talent, for sure." Delia set a pot of roasted potatoes on the table for the men's breakfast. With her hair washed and pinned off her face and her facial wounds healed, she was quite a pretty woman. The most beautiful part proved to be the shine reappearing in her eyes.

"Thank you." Winifred grinned as she stuck in each drawing, none the same, each different from the last. Growing up in her uncle's world, which was dominated by numbers and strategies, her artwork had never been appreciated, except by Aunt Mildred. What an honor it was to brighten others' days with her talent.

Just as she slipped the second to last drawing into a pail, she heard the doorknob twist. She looked up as Ewan walked in and stuffed the last drawing behind her back.

Ewan hardly noticed her awkward stance. He nodded a greeting to her and Delia before turning to Granna Cass. "Cassandra, I need my lunch in the office today, please."

"Oh, of course."

"Thank you." With that, he headed back toward the door. As he left, he sent Winifred a smile. She returned it, trying to ignore the flutters swirling in her middle. Things had become cordial between them while working side by side in his office. But all was still held together with an exceedingly tentative thread. At least he didn't glare at her anymore.

Since their discussion concerning his expenses, she could think of little else. Could someone really be sabotaging the mine? Or was it simply her overactive imagination?

He shut the door and Winifred released a puff of air.

"Missy Winnie, are you hiding your artwork from the boss?" Granna Cass eyed her beneath arched brows.

"What he doesn't know won't hurt him." She stuck the last picture into the last pail with a surge of triumph.

Delia shook her head. "A shame to hide your art like that, next to a pork sandwich. Drawings this good should be shown to everybody."

"No…" Winifred crossed to the stove where a cooling sheet of breakfast scones lay. Granna Cass had done wonders with the latest food restriction meant to save money. Somehow, she'd still managed scones. Snagging one and taking a bite, Winifred leaned a hip against the stove. "It's better to keep things like this small and hidden, not drawing much attention. I've been reprimanded by Ewan before for my nontraditional ways."

Delia leaned her hands on the table. "When?"

Granna Cass cackled. "When not?"

Winifred sighed. "I tried to rearrange a few things

in the store, and he'd have none of it. Then I tried going around the property introducing myself to the workers and thanking them for their hard work, but he put a stop to that as well."

One of Granna Cass's eyebrows lifted. "That's because you were standing next to a power wheel in your big fancy gown. He probably saved your life."

Heat tinged Winifred's cheeks. The woman's statement was likely true. "Anyway, Delia, no matter what I do, I tend to make a mess of it without even trying. The bigger the gesture, the bigger the mess. Better to keep things small."

For all the good intentions she had in the world, she probably would be injured—or worse—if Ewan didn't set up perimeters around her. In that way, his rational thought overshadowed her whimsicality. And honestly, she probably needed more of that in her life from time to time.

"I'm heading to the meat market," Granna Cass said, removing her apron and hanging it on a nail near the stove. "Do you need anything while I'm out?"

"No, ma'am," they chorused. The only errand Winifred needed to run in town was to drop off her latest letter to Mr. Businessman. Her insides warmed at the thought of his latest note—his encouragement for sticking things out even when they were tough. Winifred took another bite of the scrumptious scone. "Unless you need more supplies to make these again. They're so good. I can't stop eating them."

Granna Cass laughed on her way out the back door. "You're something else, Miss Winnie. Now watch those pails until the men have picked them up."

"I will do that."

"I'm going to work," Delia announced as she sneaked a scone from behind Winifred. If they weren't careful, there wouldn't be enough scones left for the men, and they'd be stuck with only potatoes.

"The store doesn't open for another hour."

"Yeah, but I want to make sure there's not a speck of dust in that place."

Winifred smiled before taking another bite of her breakfast. That gal certainly had pride in her new job and worked hard at it.

After Delia left, the door opened again and a few men popped inside, ready to start their day of work, dressed in their mining clothes and heavy boots.

"Morning, sunshine," Rogan Scott said to her, eyes dancing.

Since she'd met him nearly two weeks ago, along with his buddies Walter Martin and Adrian Birkeland, she'd grown fond of the trio. Rogan told her yesterday about his wife and children back home in Illinois, how he made enough money for them to live comfortably near his wife's aging parents in Peoria. Walter, a bachelor in his fifties, enjoyed the single life surrounded by his friends and had a penchant for deep, echoing laughter. Adrian, the young blond man who'd called her out for not meeting him when she'd made her rounds, had a mother he supported back home in Minnesota.

Rogan leaned over the table, nose pointed at the stove. "Mmm-mmm. My, but that breakfast smells good."

Walter broke into boisterous laughter. "Much better than what they serve at the boardinghouse, that's for sure." Winifred wondered if that laugh shook the underground tunnels. And what would happen if he sneezed.

"Here." Winifred selected two scones and two plates for their potatoes. "Eat up. I'd hate to see what would happen if these were left entirely in my care."

As she passed over the second plate, she glanced at the young man with blond hair tousled over his forehead who had just walked in. His usual good-natured grin was absent today, replaced by a distracted look in his eyes.

"Ready for breakfast, Mr. Birkeland?" She watched him as she selected another plate.

He looked up from the table as if suddenly waking. "*Ja*, Miss Sattler. Breakfast would be good."

She passed him one of the scones and a plate of potatoes. "Are you feeling all right?"

"Adrian got bad news by telegram last night." Rogan clapped a sympathetic hand on the man's shoulder. "His mum's not doin' so good."

"I'm so sorry to hear that."

Adrian shrugged, though obviously attempting to hide his emotions. "She's been sick awhile. I'll be talking to Mr. Burke after our shift to see if I can go home for a short time to take care of her."

Winifred's heart squeezed. "I understand, though we'll miss you here."

A brief smile warmed his face. "There now, Miss Sattler, I don't mean to make everyone's day worse. My problems are my problems. You know what would make me feel a little better? One of your cheery drawings in my lunch."

He dug his hand inside the pail and pulled out the page as if it were a gold nugget from a gushing spring.

"A tree? Aw, now, come on, Miss Sattler." His eyes began to sparkle as he pinned her with a look. "You can do better than a tree, can't you?"

"I'm running out of things to draw," she admitted.

"Come draw us men in the drifts."

Her brows pinched together. "In the drifts?"

"The tunnels. Drifts. The roads inside the mountain." His grin spread wider. "See, Miss Sattler? You don't even know what a drift is, and you're living at a gold mine. You *have* to come with us now."

"I knew what a drift was," she protested, which made Walter burst into booming laughter. "I just didn't know if that's what you meant to say." It would mean traveling into the mountain.

"'Course it's what I meant." He rested his elbow on the plane of his thigh. "There's a whole world under there you haven't seen. And we can show it to you."

"Oh, no." She shook her head. "I couldn't do that." The last thing she needed was another stamp mill incident. Ewan would make her pack her bags for sure.

"No, it's no trouble at all, Miss Sattler. In fact, if you could draw me a likeness to bring back to my *mor*, that sure would be grand. I'm sure she'd really love to see her boy at work." A depth reflected in his eyes that went deeper than the carefree tone of his voice, touching Winifred's heart. "Please?"

Go into the caves to sketch a portrait for his dying mother? Ewan might disapprove, but how could she say no?

"I'd pay you a day's wage," he prompted.

"A day's wage—are you serious?" Rogan asked, which made Walter guffaw. "How about while she's in there, she sketches one of me, too, to send home to my wife and daughters. Then I'll split the cost with ya."

"Oh, Mr. Birkeland, Mr. Scott, I could never take your money." She thought about it. "All right, as long as I don't get in your way, I'll come down for a few minutes. Just long enough to draw you three, and then I'll need to get out. Does that sound reasonable?"

"Agreed." Adrian's grin stretched wider, if that was a possibility.

Even Rogan looked excited about it. "My lasses will love it, Miss Sattler. Their letters sound like they're missing me something fierce. Makes it hard to stay here so long. But this will be of some comfort, especially coming from you, sunshine. You make everything brighter round here."

"Here's what we'll do," Adrian said around a cheek full of potatoes, his growing excitement for the project obvious. "Just before noon, I'll meet you outside the mine, and you can follow me in. Stick with me till you have what you need, then I'll escort you out. Pure and simple."

"We promise we won't blast while you're in there. Only the safe stuff," Rogan added.

Walter laughed.

All three looked so hopeful, Winifred couldn't help but feel like a greater purpose could be accomplished here. On top of which, if she could enter the mine, maybe she'd be able to glean clues that would help Ewan discover if his increased expenses were indeed the result of sabotage.

"Perfect." Turning, she checked the time and opened the oven to pull out the second batch of scones. The other men would be along soon. "I'll meet you at the tunnel's entrance at lunchtime."

"Adit." Rogan said.

She stopped to face the man. "What?"

"It's called an adit, Miss Sattler. If you're gonna live at a mine, you oughta know what a tunnel's entrance is called."

"Right. Ewa—Mr. Burke told me that during my tour of the mine. I just forgot."

As the men continued their breakfasts, and other workers entered for theirs, Rogan's words echoed in her ears. *Living at the mine.* Fingers of a dream wrapped around her heart. Wouldn't it be fun to live here all the time? With the sweet smell of pine and the rich scent of soil. With Granna Cass, and Delia, and the miners. And Ewan. All those things made the mining life so much richer, and just like when she wrote Mr. Businessman, she knew that all she wanted to do was stay.

But Ewan didn't have room, nor the funds, to keep on a girl like her permanently, and her time here ran short. Her aching heart knew that to be true.

Chapter Eight

Gray clouds overlooked the Black Hills as Ewan wandered back from the post office with his hands in his suit coat pockets. He'd just dropped off another mail-order response letter to a woman calling herself Mrs. M. She showed promise—more than any of the others had. The mother of a couple grade-school-age children, she lived in Lead City, three miles away, and had heard about his advertisement through a sister who lived in Deadwood. Her husband had been killed in a mining accident this summer, and she needed a place to start over.

The notion of bringing children into his precarious situation made him nervous, but Mrs. M said she knew the mining business. Said she knew the Lord, too. And she sounded matter-of-fact and in need of a good home. All things he'd hoped to find in a wife.

So why hadn't she leaped from the page and grabbed his heart?

He'd written back a letter of cautious interest, though not one of commitment. Not yet. He had to get his bearings first.

Instead of going through the office building's side door, he cut right and crossed the worn grass to the stamp mill. He made rounds nearly every day to see the production and talk with Marcus Lieberman about the business. Keeping his hands in the mining process kept him grounded, kept him understanding what was needed and what wasn't necessary.

And now, more than ever, he saw the necessity of making rounds and asking questions. Was it possible that Winifred's suspicion of foul play was true?

The metallic pounding and grinding of rock grew louder as he opened the door. Amazing how his manager could hear at all anymore. Marcus stood in front of the nearest amalgamation table pointing to crushed materials as he shouted over the noise to Frank, the worker beside him.

From the door, Ewan looked over the mill, and thought about all the work he'd put into this place. He remembered buying his first five-stamp battery and placing the structure on this land, exposed to the elements without a building around it for protection. He had refused to continue spending the time and money it required to send his gold to be processed at independently owned stamp mills in the surrounding towns. And when he started that battery up and watched those cams turn for the first time, listening to their clean stomp and feeding his first load of ore through the machine—ah, yes. Now *there* was a few-and-far-between feeling of satisfaction. The satisfaction of success.

Buying his own batteries had been costlier up front but paid off in the long run.

Or would…if he could stop acquiring more bills than he had profit.

He caught his manager's eye then. Marcus excused himself from the worker and met Ewan at the door. "Let's talk outside," Ewan shouted.

Nodding, the manager followed. They shut the door behind them, dulling the noise enough to speak without yelling themselves hoarse.

Ewan leaned against the railing. "How is production today?"

"Good, for the most part. We'll want to make a lot of progress since tomorrow is cleanup day."

Performed on an as-needed basis, clean-up day was the one day his stamp mill would be silent. A day of lost production but necessary to keep the batteries running smoothly. They would strip down the machinery, clearing it of dust and debris caught in the moving parts. With everything fresh, they'd start anew the next day.

Maybe life was like that, too. Maybe some days had to be sacrificed to cleaning out the dust and debris. Maybe this season in his life was that cleanup time. That time of renewal. Soon, things could turn around for the mine and Ewan could start again fresh with long-lasting success.

"You seem lost in thought, boss."

Ewan snapped out of his woolgathering. "My apologies." Sighing, he dug his hands into his pockets again and scanned the horizon. "I guess I had my mind on other things."

A moment of silence passed by. Should he tell his manager about the mail-order situation? It wasn't business related. The man really needed to get back to work. Ewan shouldn't keep him.

But it would be nice to have someone to confide in.

He'd begun to confide in Winifred a little more, now that she worked in his office. But that was usually business-related, too, and frequently consisted of trading ideas on how to help the mine. Her ideas were often bizarre and would never work, but getting things off his chest had proved helpful for his mental state. And she was a great listener. Not what he'd expected from someone who flitted from idea to idea without much pause.

"What's on your mind, boss?"

"Since you asked…" Ewan shot his friend a simple grin. "I'm trying to find a wife through a newspaper advertisement. Did I ever tell you that?"

Marcus crossed his arms. "I think you mentioned it once or twice." He slanted him a glance. "Any replies?"

"A few. Nothing really catching my interest." Then Ewan thought better of his statement. "Actually, the first one was intriguing. She wrote me out of frustration for the mail-order marriage system, saying it didn't show people's true character."

The manager sniffed and shifted his feet. "Probably accurate."

"Anyway, I have also received a second promising one. She seems perfect for the position. Young, straightforward, knows the mining business…"

"You marryin' this gal or hiring her for a job?"

Ewan's ears burned at the manager's chuckle. "Suppose it does sound a little rigid of me. But I need a good business partner as well as a wife. A serious, practical partner."

Marcus shrugged. "I'll tell ya, my wife and I have been together for twenty years. She doesn't know the difference between gold and pyrite, but she makes the best roasted chicken."

"So all I need in a wife is a good cook? Are you saying I should marry Cassandra?" Ewan chuckled at his own joke.

His manager stood stone still, like a mighty tree standing watch. "I'm saying there are some things more important than business know-how to make a marriage work for the long haul."

Catching the man's meaning, Ewan lowered his gaze. "Yes, well, I tried finding a wife for love, and it hasn't worked out."

"So try again."

The man said it like it was the most obvious and logical choice. But was it? Could Ewan let go of his safe restrictions and allow his heart to become vulnerable again? Marilee had cradled it in her hands only to dash it to the floor and trample over it, like ore sacrificed beneath the metal cams in his stamp mill, leaving nothing left.

It had taken him years to get his heart back into place.

"What about that other gal?"

"Which other?"

"The first one you wrote." The man shrugged. "Said yourself she was intriguing."

"She's not interested in pursuing a relationship." Ewan toed a rock with his shoe. "We only write to let off steam."

"How long you been writin' her?"

"A month."

"And she's still talking to you after all that time?" He grunted, his expression sparkling with amusement.

"Sounds to me like you're having a hard time finding a gal to marry because you already found one."

Ewan raised his head. Could that be true?

A thundering sound crashed and ground inside the stamp mill. Shouts filtered through the walls. The two men met eyes before rushing inside.

Shivering, Winifred glanced around. Not that she could see much. "Are you sure this is a good idea?"

"Sure thing, Miss Sattler." Adrian smiled at her over his shoulder as he led the way into a drift. Or, at least she thought he'd smiled—hard to tell in the dim candlelight.

They had left sunlight behind them a while ago. She hadn't been this far into the mountain before, and when the outside light faded behind them, gooseflesh climbed her arms and legs. This time felt different than when Ewan had been with her. It hadn't even crossed her mind to be afraid when he was by her side. Now, though…did the walls feel like they were closing in?

Darkness enveloped her and she hastened to catch up with Adrian, whose candle was the only source of light. Clutching her pad of paper and pencil against her chest, she glanced behind her. She should've paid attention to which way they'd headed. They'd turned left once then branched off the original drift, hadn't they?

"Is there going to be more light where we're going?" Her voice echoed softly off the walls of dirty wood planks and tall, thick support columns. A track ran beneath her feet for the ore cart, and she had to focus on not tripping over it. Somewhere she could hear the sound of water dripping, and the air felt cold and moist against the back of her neck.

"Not much. Rogan and Walt each have a candle, so we take turns using 'em. They wear down fast. But we often blow 'em out at lunchtime to save the wax. Especially now, since we only get two candles a day, each. Used to get three. The Homestake Mine gives their employees three candles a day." She heard him scoff at the injustice.

The Homestake Mine. She remembered someone mentioning that place in passing. It was one of the largest, most lucrative mining establishments up in Lead City.

Adrian swung to walk backward. "Hey—maybe you could convince the boss to give us three candles again instead of two."

They needed a whole chandelier of candles at all times, if she had anything to say about it. Winifred managed a weak smile, though her insides trembled. Why did he think she could change Ewan's mind? He never approved of her ideas. And anyway, considering how much he'd already cut, there hadn't been much else for him to choose besides candles.

"I don't know what it is…" He swiped off his cap and scratched at his haphazard hair. "The boss…he don't like listening to nobody."

"He just wants what's best," she murmured.

Adrian watched her a moment, as if weighing her comment. "I hope you're right," he finally said, turning forward again. "Not long now, ma'am. I reckon you don't wanna be in here any longer than you gotta. Can't blame you there."

Even in the darkness, where no one could see her, she worked to mask her frown. "Mr. Birkeland, you sound a little doubtful. Are you dissatisfied with your job here?"

He shrugged. "Sometimes."

She walked in silence for a few yards, listening to the dripping water and pebbles scraping beneath her shoes. One of the reasons she'd agreed to this outing was so she could try to find out more about possible sabotage. From what she'd learned of him so far, Adrian Birkeland seemed as harmless as a puppy—certainly one of the last people she'd suspect of purposefully hurting the Golden Star, but what else did Winifred have to go on? Maybe he'd seen or heard something that could be useful.

How much information could she get out of him without sounding too suspicious? "Are you mostly dissatisfied with the candle ration?"

He shrugged one shoulder. "And other things. Main problem is not knowing if this operation will stay open much longer."

A similar sentiment to what Mr. Danielson had told her a few weeks ago. "Is there talk of the mine closing?"

"All the time. Surprised you haven't heard the rumors. Watch your step, ma'am." His hand moved backward to steer her away from the left side of the tunnel. Only when he forced her to move did Winifred notice the gaping hole in the ground.

Her eyes flew wide open. "There's a hole there!"

"That's a mine shaft. It leads to another drift."

Continuing forward, she struggled to tear her gaze away from the shaft. "When did these rumors start?"

"A few months ago, when Mr. Burke announced he was going to look for an investor."

"But seeking an investor doesn't mean a business is failing. Sometimes an operation just needs a little more capital to move from well-functioning to thriving. And investors won't put in their money unless they believe their investment will turn a profit. So, really, if he believes he can get an investor to come onboard, it would be a sign of good things for the company, not bad."

Adrian glanced over his shoulder, the dim candle-light catching a playful glint in his eye. "Where'd you learn so much about financial matters?"

"I don't know much, believe me." She smiled, unsure if he could really see her face. "What little I know I picked up from my uncle, who invests in entrepreneurs. Do you think some will quit because of the rumors?"

"Some might. Plenty of the men have families to feed. We need to know our jobs are secure."

"Might some be angry enough with Mr. Burke to do something drastic?"

"Drastic? Like what, Miss Sattler?"

"Like…like…"

As she fumbled for an example that wouldn't immediately suggest sabotage, a faint light around a corner caught her attention. She nearly cried in relief. It was as if they'd been rescued.

"The men are just ahead." Adrian led the way around the corner. More questioning would have to wait. When Winifred followed, she found herself in a small but cavernous room in the presence of several workers eating their lunches. Some she vaguely knew, but Rogan and Walt were also among them.

"Hey." Rogan looked up from his sandwich. "Thought you'd never get here."

"What're you doin', burning a candle?" Adrian stopped beside a spike in the wall and fed one of his unlit candles into it. "I thought we agreed to save yours and just use mine to lead Miss Sattler in."

"We didn't want to scare her by sittin' in the dark," Walt explained, following his sentence with a laugh that echoed off the walls.

Bracing herself against a timber column, Winifred coughed, her lungs squeezing. She looked back the way they'd come and felt sweat collect on her brow. "The air is thin down here, don't you think?" And to be under several tons of mountain, where no sunlight could reach…

"You get used to it." Rogan put his lunch away. "Nice drawing in my pail today. Got a tree, just like Adrian, but at least I'm thankful for mine."

"Aw, quit your foolin'." Adrian puffed his chest. "How 'bout you draw me first, Miss Sattler?"

"Shouldn't she get all of us at once?" Walt questioned around a bite of sandwich.

"What're you numskulls talkin' about?" another miner piped in. "She's drawin' you?"

While the men squabbled about the idea, Winifred leaned to the side, staring down the long tunnel—*drift*. Even with the flames' light thrown that direction, the end of the tunnel looked black. Endlessly black. Displaying an emptiness she had never seen before. Her clammy fingers slicked along her pencil.

"I'll find a place to sit." The statement came out sounding a little breathless. She turned to the back of the stope. Against a slippery wall, she found a flat surface where she could sit. Or, kneel, really. She didn't want to ruin the back of her dress.

As the men finished their meals, they set aside their pails and started their work for the afternoon. And Winifred began to sketch. The dimness of the room had her squinting, but she didn't dare ask for a candle. Knowing these fellas, one would sacrifice the only one he had left for her. Chills ran up the back of Winifred's arms. What would happen if their candles ran out before they finished working?

The men worked as partners, exactly as they had explained to her. Rogan and Walt chiseled holes into the walls near her—one holding the chisel and the other holding the hammer—while others built up the end of the drift where it met the opening of the stope. Vertical columns had been sunk into the ground along either side of the drift to support the low beam ceiling. Behind the columns was the dirt wall of the mountain. Adrian and another miner drove planks of wood behind those columns with wooden mallets, sandwiching the planks between the columns and the dirt wall. Each plank lay side to side up the wall, creating a paneled effect until the dirt was completely hidden.

"See, Miss Sattler?" Rogan's voice traveled from behind her. "We chisel twelve holes into the rock wall in one place. Then we fill them with explosive material and blast."

She whipped her head around. "But you won't do that now, will you?"

"No, 'course not, ma'am. I already told you I wouldn't while you're here. Besides, all blasting happens at the end of our shift, so the dust settles before the next shift starts."

"We promise we'll keep you safe, Miss Sattler." Adrian shot her a grin from across the small stope, candlelight outlining one side of his young, beardless face. "Just make sure you capture me in a strong, hardworking pose. I want *Mor* to be proud, you know."

Another miner snorted. "That'll take some imagination on Miss Sattler's part."

Walt guffawed.

Hammering echoed throughout the room, ringing in her ears worse than the stamp mills did outside. Winifred watched the men work, far enough removed that she could sketch without getting in the way. She tilted her head to one side as she drew Adrian's mallet connecting with the wood. Were those planks used for decoration, or did they serve a purpose?

She opened her mouth to ask, but a rumble interrupted her. A deep rumble that reverberated in her chest. It paused for an instant, then began again. Louder. Her pulse spiked. Something wasn't right. She moved to stand and saw the men turn. Shouts came, and a shower of debris broke forth from the ceiling, raining down, hitting her in the face and along her shoulders. A pelting like hail.

Winifred winced, backed up. More shouts came from farther away. Her scream lit the stope as the candles went out.

Chapter Nine

A broken stamp. Exactly what Ewan didn't need.

Inside the mill, he shook his head, stifling a cough as the dust caked his lungs. He couldn't believe the mess a busted cam could make. When he'd rushed inside, workers had already begun scrambling to stop the machinery before it tore the battery apart completely. In the wake of the breakdown, chunks of quartz and gold lay everywhere, scattered across the floor and shot up atop the stairs and supplies lying around the room's perimeter. Dust mixed with gold on the mercury-coated tables. The mangled machinery had finally been put to rest before it destroyed anything else—though a considerable amount of damage had already been done. Not to mention the drop in production they would see while this equipment was nonoperational.

"We'll have to send for a new part. Maybe a few," Marcus said beside Ewan. "I'll be honest, it probably won't be cheap."

Ewan looked away. "I know."

Thankfully, no one had been hurt. He glanced at

George, who couldn't have heard the disaster happening and might have unknowingly moved in the wrong way at just the wrong time, and Ewan's mind replayed Winifred's worry of sabotage. He hadn't wanted to believe her, but what if she was right? Sabotaging the machinery would be easily accomplished—someone might have loosened a bolt or thrown something into the machine…but who would go to such great lengths to hurt his company—and the people who worked here?

One thing was certain: Ewan couldn't handle another injury to his workers, the people under his care.

"I'll look into buying a part," he replied, though he knew it would be too expensive to purchase right now. Unfortunately, without the repair, he was down to one five-stamp battery. How could he hope to increase his earnings and fix his second machine if his production would now be cut in half? Especially if more unexpected breakdowns popped up around the mine.

The men dotting the room didn't speak, but Ewan could read their thoughts anyway. In their minds, this was one more disaster, one more tick mark, against the Golden Star Mine. And as surely as he stood here, they were losing their faith in their jobs faster than he could restore it.

Lord, how can I turn their faith around? First thing was figuring out why so many problems had arisen in recent months. He clapped one of the workers on the shoulder and turned to leave. "Heading to my office. Thanks for all you do." Maybe it would be enough, but maybe it wouldn't. Winifred's advice had never been so true. *Tell them you care. Encourage them to continue working as hard as you do. You're only as strong as your weakest link, and if you don't change something, weak links will start popping up all over the place.*

He stepped outside and started for the office building.

Shouts caught his attention up the hill. Slowing his walk, Ewan raised his eyes to the mine. Miners dashed in and out of the adit like frantic ants, carrying shovels and rocks, shouting to each other.

"Mr. Burke!"

The voice came from Ewan's left. He flicked his gaze toward the office building, where one of his workers emerged.

"Mr. Burke!" he called again. "I just came from your office, looking for you."

Squaring his shoulders, Ewan faced the young miner, his heartbeat ratcheting up a few notches. "What is it, man?"

"There's been a cave-in."

The news fell with the weight of a thousand pounds of rock. "What?"

"A little one," the man assured him, wheezing as he drew closer, obviously exerting himself. "But some people are trapped inside."

No. Chest tightening, Ewan turned his quickened steps toward the mountain.

"Which men?" He needed to know who to look for. *Lord, this can't be happening. If anything bad befell them...*

"Rogan, Walt, Lloyd, Roger..." The man coughed as he tried to keep up with Ewan's swift gait. "And that girl, I think."

Ewan's eyes shot open wide. He whirled to face the

miner, nearly knocking the man back with his glare. "What girl?"

Before he answered, Ewan knew. Knew at the core of his bone-cold being.

"The talkative one—brown hair? Helps Granna Cass in the kitchen."

Lord, please, no.

Ewan pushed himself even faster toward the mountain. Removing his coat, he crossed the ground with the power of a locomotive. He climbed the outcropping. Rocks scraped against his hands, slipped beneath his shoes. When he reached solid footing, he unbuttoned his wrist cuffs and rolled his sleeves, barreling ever closer to the sight he didn't want—couldn't bear—to see.

A couple men paused in the adit as Ewan approached. "Which drift?" he asked the nearest man before yanking his lantern down from the rock wall.

"Follow me." The miner lit Ewan's lantern, then led him into the darkness. "I don't know what happened," he said over his shoulder. "There weren't many on that excavation."

"What was Miss Sattler doing in here?" He pushed through the tunnel with his heartbeat pumping against his chest. The man answered, but Ewan heard nothing. Thought about nothing. Except saving his men and Winifred.

His powerful light cast dark shadows across the drift. He choked on dust as the air grew hazy from the fallen rocks and soil. Turning a corner, he nearly collided with a crowd of workers clogging the way. The miner with him shouldered a path through the men. As they realized their boss was present, they began to back out of the way on their own. When Ewan finally reached the front, his heart nearly stopped.

Rubble strewed the former opening to a small stope. He lifted his lantern higher. Black soil and rocks rose to the drift's ceiling. Men scrambled to pull debris out of the way, shouting to one another and to those on the other side to see if they were alive and to tell them they were coming. Except no one could listen for their replies because of the ruckus.

"Everyone be quiet!" His voice rang up and down the narrow drift, and in a ripple effect, people silenced. Never had he raised his voice to his workers before, but if these people kept him from properly assessing this situation for one more moment… "I'll give the orders on how to proceed, so everyone better listen closely."

He began doling out responsibilities, sending some men to fetch the doctor. Others to inform the rest of the miners currently working that a cave-in had occurred and that for safekeeping, they needed to evacuate. Still more were asked to help dig out the victims.

The victims. *Oh, Lord, please help.*

Taking his place by the rubble, he helped Adrian Birkeland ease a large rock from the pile. All the while, he tried not to imagine Winifred's face. The man, bleeding and covered in dirt, worked harder than any to remove the rocks. A haunted shadow had fallen across his face and he refused to let anyone guide him away, even as a gash on his arm turned his sleeve red. "I'm so sorry, so sorry."

"It's not your fault." Ewan's throat felt like broken glass.

The young man shook his head, digging faster. "I almost got trapped under all this, too. I should have!

Why'd God spare me? Honest, Mr. Burke, I had no idea this would happen. If I'd known, I never would've asked her to come."

The man's words pinged through Ewan. "You *asked* her to come?"

"God, please forgive me," the man prayed, his voice shaky with a sob. "I had no idea this would happen, really."

With a surge of strength, Ewan heaved more rocks away. His back strained against the weight, his fingers aching as they scraped against the rough edges, but he continued to pull. Rock after rock. Others pitched in alongside him. All the while, he begged God to preserve them. A by-standing woman who had no business being inside the mine was now trapped in their newest stope. Exactly where Ewan had told her *not* to go.

A pile of debris gave way near one side, so he pawed to create an opening. Had they broken through? Blinking to allow his eyes to see through the dust, he lifted his lantern for extra light. Beyond a sliver in the wall of rubble, he spotted a small room—a pocket behind the cave-in. Holding his arm up to signal that no one was to follow him, he began to climb inside, shoving loose rocks and dirt out of his way.

Any minute, the pocket could collapse.

Inside, Walt heaved his shoulder against a boulder, trying to move it while nursing a wounded arm against his chest. As Ewan stepped over a timber support beam snapped in half like a twig, he spotted Rogan hunkered along the opposite wall, a figure lying sickeningly still in his arms.

Winifred.

"God, please, no." His lantern teetered as he set it down, then he crawled to the man beneath the low ceiling. "Is she breathing?"

"Yes. But barely conscious." The man got to his knees with Winifred in his arms and Ewan scooped her up into his.

"Help me get her out of here," he murmured.

Others helped him clear the rubble wall enough to walk through, then the men parted sides as he made his way down the drift toward the opening with her close to his chest. One of his men led the way with Ewan's lantern, while others held up their candles to light his path. Winifred's body was snuggled against him, warm but hardly stirring. He nearly tripped on the railroad ties, stumbling along as if he didn't know this place like the back of his hand.

Emerging into sunlight, he squinted, cradling her closer as he slid down the rocks and shale. Dirt streaked her face, or at least what he could see of it, nuzzled against his shirt. Had he felt her move? He couldn't tell against the rapid pounding of his heart.

Where was that doctor? Straining to fill his lungs with enough air, Ewan called to a miner who followed him, "Tell the doctor I took her to Cassandra's." The man ran with him and opened the office building's side door. Ewan pushed inside and forced his way down the corridor. "God, don't let me lose her," he whispered.

He glanced at Winifred for a better look. Dark hair fell haphazardly across her face, accentuating the cuts and scrapes scattered across her high cheekbones. Had it only been this morning that she had smiled at him from across the kitchen?

Her lashes fluttered slightly at the jounce of movement. "Hang on, Win," he murmured a little louder. "Hang on. Don't leave me."

Winifred heard a voice overhead. Far away at first, then closer. Something heavy covered her. Heavy and soft. Blankets? Something cradled her head, and she could only guess it was a pillow. But when had she gone to bed? She couldn't remember...

The voice came again. Quiet, nearly soundless. Squeezing her eyes farther shut for momentum to open them, she finally found the strength to lift one to a slit.

The room spun a half circle. When it righted, she focused on a blurry figure sitting beside her pallet in Granna Cass's quarters. No, not her pallet—Granna Cass's bed. It was higher off the floor. How did she get here?

She wanted to move, but her limbs wouldn't work. White haze coated everything, and her eyelids grew heavy again.

The figure shifted. White shirt, sleeves rolled to the elbows. Certainly wasn't Granna Cass. Or Delia. The person lifted his head over folded hands, suddenly coming into focus.

Ewan.

But what business did he have sitting at her bedside?

"Please," she heard him whisper. The rest remained inaudible, but evidently he was praying. Hair disheveled, dirt smudging his knuckles, forearms and sleeves—the always-fastidious man looked like he'd been hurled about by a cyclone, but he didn't seem to notice as he was deep in the throes of prayer.

Winifred breathed in. The mine. She remembered now. The rocks falling down around her. The men's shouts. Her scream. Yet somehow she'd made it out alive. How had that happened? Aside from her splitting headache and inability to think clearly, she wouldn't know anything had happened at all if she hadn't seen the aftermath on Ewan's attire and expression.

Had he helped her get out?

Was he praying *for her*?

"Ewan."

Her voice came out scratchier than she'd hoped. He jumped at the sound of his name. Eyes wide, Ewan leaned in and scanned every bit of her face with urgency. "Win?"

He breathed her name like it was precious gold itself. A nickname. *A nickname?*

Leaning closer, he continued to search her face. "Win?"

The sound was like soft kid leather against her skin. Blinking, she managed a nod. "Yes."

"Oh, thank You, Lord." His voice rushed through a breathy whisper. "I thought—I feared that..." He trailed off as his eyes softened into gray pools.

His hand moved to her face, warm against her cheek. Soft and tender, as though he treasured her. Her eyes widened. She didn't have the strength to jump away, but—did she want to?

Just as quickly as his touch set her skin aflame, Ewan pulled his hand away, like he'd been burned, too.

"I—" He swallowed. Blinked. Met her eyes for an instant before glancing away. "I apologize. I didn't mean to—" He stood and looked around, rubbing his hands on his mud-encrusted trousers. "I'll let Cassandra know you're awake." With that, he rushed from the nook.

Beyond the curtain, a door shut, leaving her alone in the silent kitchen. But even lying alone for several minutes, Winifred's heartbeat refused to slow as she remembered the feel of Ewan's hand on her cheek, the look in his eyes, the urgency in his voice—as he called her Win.

This reaction was ten times what she'd felt from touching his hand in the woods. But how, just from a little brush against her face, like butterfly wings? And yet, it'd affected her deeply. What was happening?

Chapter Ten

The cave-in, along with the stamp breakdown, had jarred the entire staff. For the next week, Ewan felt like everyone floated through their work. Sleepwalked, maybe, himself included. All while Winifred lay in bed, healing under Cassandra's skilled guidance.

To find out the source of its collapse, he'd set aside a portion of his salary to hire an expert's analysis. If results came back showing someone had tampered with equipment or weakened the structure within the stope somehow, then the guilty party had better leave town before Ewan found out who he or she was. The whole notion that someone would put his workers, his friends, in harm's way made him sick.

The letters in his suit coat pocket flapped against his torso, one of them reminding him how he'd fallen short. He hated asking Father for funds. It certainly wouldn't impress Mr. Johns. Instead of being as successful as his brother, Ewan had only proved his father right—coming to Deadwood had become a foolhardy mission that would end in heartache.

His other letter to mail? To his pen pal. A light in

his shadowy world. Strangely, he had checked with Sol Star earlier in the week and nothing had arrived for him. They had exchanged letters like clockwork recently. He probably should've waited to write again until he heard from her, but he couldn't help composing another missive. Ever since his manager had pointed it out, Ewan had realized the man was right. He found himself attracted to TD. She intrigued him, comforted him, gave him the friendship and deep conversational connection he craved in a wife. If only she were interested in exploring a romantic relationship.

As he approached the post office, he spotted Winifred coming toward him from the direction of the Golden Star, her gown swishing over the dirt street before she stepped up onto the boardwalk. Without warning, his heartbeat stumbled.

He didn't *want* to have feelings for Winifred Sattler. She was all wrong for him. Lively and fun, often too talkative, and too nosy. She couldn't go a full day without causing some sort of disturbance—or necessitating the occasional rescue.

His stomach tightened at the memory of how that cave-in could easily have taken her life. Of course, that had scared him. But what scared him almost as much were the emotions that had come over him when Winifred woke up. He couldn't believe himself. Touching her face, calling her *Win*? What had he been thinking?

Perhaps he hadn't been thinking at all. Must not have been, if he'd allowed her spunk to creep into his heart and stake a claim. He'd already been down this road with Marilee. How many times did he have to remind himself of that fact? Fun, vibrant women were wrong for him. Why couldn't his traitorous heart enjoy a steady, straightforward woman for once?

And of course, the irony hadn't escaped him that he had feelings for two women. Neither of whom, he could—or should—have.

Looking up as she neared, Winifred spotted him and released a small, reserved smile. Which was so unlike her. Did she feel as awkward about last week's encounter as he did?

Gripping his hands, Ewan forced away the memory of her cheek's warmth and offered his own cordial smile. "Good morning. Feeling better today?"

"I am. Thank you. The ache in my head has finally subsided."

Ewan nodded. Silence stretched between them, and finding himself at a loss for words, he sidestepped to the post office door. "I wish you the best with your downtown errands, then. I'm off to mail a letter."

"That's where I'm heading, too." She lifted the leather valise she carried and stepped toward the door, a slight blush covering her cheeks.

"Oh." Moving back, he opened the door as his mother's teachings flowed through his actions. "After you."

Dipping her chin in a thank-you, she walked inside, her heels clicking across the floor in slow steps. Hanging back by the door, Ewan allowed Winifred to make her way to the counter in privacy. She didn't need him hovering over her like some overprotective chaperone. It didn't matter to him who received her letters. A beau back home, most likely. She'd never mentioned one, but surely someone like her had one—maybe scores of suitors waited for her return.

The postmaster's eyes lit when he looked up from a note he'd scribbled. "Miss Sattler." When his gaze passed her and landed on Ewan, his brows rose for an instant before he masked his...his what? Surprise? Though Ewan didn't know why the man would be surprised to see him here. Since TD had come into his life, Ewan had likely become Star's most frequent patron.

"Morning, Mr. Burke," the man said with a nod.

"Good morning," Ewan replied with a nod of his own.

Winifred cleared her throat. "I have a letter to mail. As well as a telegram." She unhooked the strap on her valise and withdrew an envelope before slipping it across the counter.

Star took the letter and smiled as he passed her a telegram slip. "I have one for you, too. I'll be right back."

As Winifred waited for him to return, she stood with her back as straight as a board, staring forward as she filled out the telegram form.

He couldn't help but watch her, observe her. The silent memory of her too-still frame in the stope still cut him down at the knees. Of all the injuries and disasters he had endured as owner of the Golden Star, this particular scare had terrified him the most. But why? *Why* did the mere idea of this woman in danger have the potential to frighten him senseless?

"Here you are." Star returned from the back room and slid an envelope across the counter.

Winifred snatched it up and stuffed it into her valise without reading who it was from, glancing at Ewan over her shoulder before turning back to Star. "Thank you."

She paid for her telegram, then stepped away from the counter and nodded to Ewan, as if to signal that she'd finished her business. He expected her to walk out as he approached the counter, but she didn't—only lingered near the front door, as he had.

Clearing his throat, Ewan shuffled his envelopes so the one to Father sat on top before passing them both across the counter. Winifred was too far away to see the writing on his envelope to his pen pal, but that didn't mean he wanted to take the risk. One little glimpse would tell her it didn't list a recipient's address. And if she asked, he didn't know how to tell her he had sought a wife through the mail. There were some things that affected a man's pride too much.

Ewan lifted his eyes and caught Star smiling. "What?"

"Nothing." He took Ewan's letters and backed up. "Just happy to say you have mail."

Did he have to sound so obvious? Ewan schooled his features, hoping red didn't climb his neck. "Thank you."

When Star returned with the envelope—so obviously doodled upon—he pushed it across the counter in as concealed of a manner as Ewan had done with his—for which he was thankful.

Pocketing the letter, he thanked Star, who continued to wear an incredibly odd smile, and left the post office. Winifred stepped out first and fell in beside him as they ambled back to the mine. Usually he preferred silence, but today was shaping up to be a strange day.

"So—" he toed a pebble as he walked "—sending a telegram to your family?"

"My aunt and uncle. To let them know I almost have enough fare, and that I'm coming home soon. Though it took a little of my money to send the telegram…" She shrugged, watching her skirt swish over the road. "You?"

"Yes, to my father." Never mind the second letter. "He likes to be updated on my progress from time to time."

"Any good news to share?" She let out a little gasp. "You didn't tell him about the cave-in, did you?"

"No, I left that part out…" He stole a sideways glance at her. "Although, while we're on the subject, I wish you had never gone in there."

"Oh, me too." Winifred glanced at the sky, a little of her usual animated inflection seeping back into her voice. "I was so conflicted the entire time. But they promised I wouldn't be in the way, and besides that, I thought maybe I could find out if someone is trying to hurt your mine."

"Did you find out anything?"

Her shoulders sagged. "Not really."

"Well, at any rate, I'm glad you're safe." Crossing his arms, Ewan watched the road near his feet. "Also, I know about the drawings in the miners' lunch pails."

He'd extensively interviewed the men involved in the cave-in, knew of their innocent yet careless plan to have Winifred draw sketches of them at work to send home to their families. Of all people, those men should've known the dangers they were exposing Winifred to. As punishment, he'd suspended them each a week without pay, hoping it would motivate them to think about what they had done.

"Ewan, I'm so sorry." She clasped his sleeve in her hand, pausing where the Golden Star's walkway met the road. "I never expected my drawings to end up like every other blunder I've made here. Worse, even."

"No." He shook his head. "They weren't a blunder. The sketches were a nice surprise. I didn't even know you liked to draw."

She shrugged. "It's something to do."

He suspected she was being humble. "Well, the men really appreciated the gesture. But may I ask, why did you draw pictures for them in the first place?"

Wide, blue-gray eyes gazed up at him as she seemed to prepare herself for the explanation. "I wanted to give the men a reason to look forward to coming to work each day. A surprise that cost the mine nothing. A spot of sunshine."

The pieces began to click together. "You did this to help the mine?" *To help me?*

With hesitation, she nodded—as if she thought he would be mad. But how could he be? She'd known his frustrations with the mine, his constant effort to cut costs and keep the business afloat. And, without spending a dime of the mine's money, she'd rallied the miners together, boosting their zeal. All with a simple stack of pencil sketches.

"Thank you," he whispered.

Brown hair brushed across her forehead, and her dangling red earrings caught the sunlight. Striking. Everything about Winifred was striking.

Wait. What was he thinking? Blinking, Ewan dipped his chin and took a step back, putting more distance between them. The sketches were simply acts of kindness on Winifred's part. Yes, he was touched, but that didn't negate her carelessness in so many other things. Speaking her mind too boldly, rearranging his store without asking, nearly killing herself in the stamp mill, venturing into the mine without him—

"Thank you for saving me, by the way." Giving him a small, shy smile, she continued up the front walk.

Managing a smile in return, Ewan slanted her a glance. "Of course."

"When I was younger, I fell into a narrow ravine," she said. "I was twirling with my eyes closed, and I didn't see it until my foot slipped. I had to wait hours before my aunt came looking for me. It was one of the scariest experiences of my life until last week." She paused in thought. "It's interesting how our childhood experiences shape our lives."

His shoes scuffed against the wooden walk. "I've seen my share of cave-ins, but this one scared me more than most."

"Oh?"

Listen to him. Entirely too personal, too vulnerable. Time to return to topics of business. "And I didn't tell you, but the day of the cave-in, one of my stamps broke."

"Oh, no. What will you do?"

He shrugged. "Fix it. Somehow."

She frowned. "You don't have the finances to do so."

Ewan pursed his lips. "Yes, thank you for the reminder." He huffed a weak laugh and opened the shop door. "And now I need to fix a drift and a stope, too."

She nudged brown wisps off her neck. "What you

need is to earn money quickly. Like with a fund-raiser or an auction."

"Yes, because gold mines do that sort of thing." Chuckling, he entered after Winifred—but nearly bumped into her as she halted in the doorway.

Two men in suits, hair slicked back beneath their hats, stood at the counter. Ewan's chest tightened.

Delia popped to attention at the sight of him. "These gentlemen are here to see you, Mr. Burke." Her fingers trembled against the countertop. Had these men, the owners of the Sphinx Mine to the north, insulted or intimidated her?

"Mr. Burke." Mac Glouster removed his hat, and his brother, Bradford, followed suit. Their confident smiles only served to irritate him. "We'd like a word with you."

"I don't recall us having an appointment." Ewan looked from one Glouster brother to the other.

"Just the same, we think you'll like what we've come to offer you," Mac replied.

Ewan glanced at Winifred. She hung back by the threshold, as if she didn't know whether she should go up to his office and work, as she normally did this time of day, or stay in the shop. Oddly, he kind of wished for her to accompany him. But that desire didn't make any sense.

"Miss Sattler, can you help Miss Richardson in the store for a few minutes?"

Winifred ran her hands down the front of her skirt panel. Finally, she nodded and slipped behind the counter.

Ewan let a couple of seconds tick by before he gave the men an answer. "All right, follow me, please." With straightened shoulders, he led the way down the corridor and up the winding stairs. *Lord, give me strength to deal with whatever they have to say.*

Winifred continued to watch the door after it shut behind Ewan and his visitors.

"I thought they'd *never* leave." Delia collapsed against the counter as if her stamina had finally given out. "You came at the right time. I had no idea what else to say to them."

"You don't think they'll try to badger Ewan, do you?"

"All I know is I didn't get a good feeling from 'em." Delia seated herself on a stool and sighed. "Mr. Burke isn't the type to be pushed around. He'll be fine."

Of course he'd be fine. Winifred worried too much. She leaned her hip against the counter and crossed her arms, pushing aside thoughts of him upstairs battling those men for his business. "Any sales yet today?"

"A few, but not many." Sighing, Delia leaned her elbows on the counter and surveyed the sales log outstretched before her.

Winifred approached to look as well.

"One man told me we have nice supplies, but he always forgets we're here. You know, being at the end of a long street of other shops." She plopped her chin in her hands and stared at something beyond the sales log. "I think we need to attract more attention in this direction."

"That's probably true. It couldn't hurt, at least." Winifred joined Delia at the counter, also propping up her chin. They both stared out over the customerless store. "We also need to find a way to save the mine."

"What do you mean?"

Winifred shrugged. "It's not doing so well. But most of that is because of recent expenses that have been out of Ewan's control." She glanced at Delia, weighing if she could trust her with more information. "I think someone is trying to harm the mine."

Delia gasped. "Really?"

"I have no proof yet, but when I worked through his expense reports, I saw things I'd consider strange." She shrugged. "I'll keep looking into it. Anyway, in the meantime, I need to find a foolproof way to help the mine make more profit to counterbalance recent, excessive costs. But everything I've tried has gotten me in trouble with Ewan."

"That man is a complete mystery." Delia sighed. "But a handsome mystery, at least."

The statement left Winifred speechless. She simply swung her gaze to meet the store clerk's and raised a brow.

Delia laughed. "Don't worry, I'm not interested in him. I've sworn off men for quite a while."

Weight hung beneath her joking tone. Winifred could hear it even if Delia tried her best to keep her turmoil hidden. She certainly felt proud of how much the spunky woman had blossomed, how well she'd adapted to her new life.

Then Winifred frowned as Delia's words ran back through her mind. "Wait—why are you apologizing to me? Why would I be worried?"

"Because…because I wouldn't want to make you jealous."

"Why would I be jealous?"

"Aren't you two courting?"

Winifred's eyes shot wide open. "What? Me, courting with Ewan Burke?"

The outside door opened. Both girls shot to an upright, standing position. A woman entered and sent them a brief smile before crossing the room to the pyramid of flour sacks. Winifred grinned back in relief that the conversation had been interrupted, pretending her heartbeat hadn't ratcheted higher at Delia's misinformed belief.

She and Ewan—a *couple*?

What worried her was how transparent her growing feelings must have become. A piece of her heart had followed him up the stairs minutes ago. Before she could stop it, of course. Disloyal thing. How could she suddenly feel softer toward Ewan just because he'd saved her from the mine? Or because he'd brushed a finger over her cheek and called her by a nickname?

Or because, somehow, in their mixture of banter and mishaps, they'd developed a friendship she treasured more than she cared to admit?

The woman bought a bag of flour, then exited. Even before the door closed completely, a snicker arose from the store clerk. Delia beamed unabashedly. "I knew it."

Winifred rolled her eyes. "Knew what?"

"You're smitten." Delia's eyes glittered. "I knew it."

"You knew nothing." Then why were her cheeks warm? Fiddlesticks. "Anyway, sales—we were talking about sales, weren't we? Show me the profit from yesterday."

The smile slid from Delia's face. "Profit?"

"Right. How much did the store make?"

The woman blinked. "Um, we had four men come

in." She dropped her gaze to the ledger and pointed at the numbers. "So, that means…"

Understanding blossomed as Winifred watched. "Delia, do you not know how to add?"

She shrugged. "Hardly know how to read, much less how to add or subtract numbers."

The poor dear. Winifred grabbed a pencil from the counter and slid the ledger closer between them. "Here, let me show you. First, do you know how to count?"

"Yep."

"Good. So let's start with an easy one. One plus one." She wrote the equation. "Now, see this pencil?"

Delia looked at her like she'd lost a set of marbles. "Yes."

"How many? Count."

"One."

"Excellent." She glanced around for another pencil. Oh, the one in her valise! She undid the straps and opened the bag for her pad and pencil, then plopped both on the counter. "One pencil. Now, how many pencils am I holding?" She slid the second pencil into place beside the first and held them up.

"Two."

"Great!" Winifred clapped her hands, then used one of the pencils to scribble the equation on the corner of the ledger paper. "See? Adding is simply counting up. One plus one equals two."

Delia blinked a few times, staring at the equation. The wheels turning in her mind were almost visible. "I think I'm starting to get it."

"Good. We'll keep working on it. In the meantime, I can tell by these numbers that we need more sales.

I think we should figure out a way to draw attention to the store."

"Yes. More sales mean more money for Mr. Burke and the mine."

"Indeed, it does." Ideas began to spark. Winifred crossed to the middle of the room, crossing her arms with one hand rubbing her chin. "I was thinking earlier that he needs money quickly—like through a raffle or fund-raiser. Maybe we could combine all these ideas."

"Like a celebration of some kind at the store?" Delia asked.

Winifred snapped her fingers. "Yes. A bazaar at the store! Granna Cass and I could bake cakes and other desserts to sell, and I could help you decorate the store so it looks really inviting." Her words picked up momentum. "Maybe we could even acquire new merchandise."

"You could sell your sketches!"

"And the miners' wives could make up quilts for us to sell. Or baked goods. We could even hold contests and give away door prizes to get people inside."

"Oh, this is very exciting." Delia straightened her spine. "Do you think Mr. Burke will let us?"

A smile spread up Winifred's face. "I think we could convince him."

Ewan ignored the Glouster brothers' nearness as he steeled himself against whatever they would have to say. He'd met with them before, and if their offer was anything like last time, or like the capitalists' offer, it wouldn't take long to show them out.

When the three of them were in his office and the door had shut, Ewan faced the wolves, breathing a silent prayer. "To what do I owe this meeting, gentle-men?"

"We talked with you a few months ago, as I'm sure you recall," Mac said. "We gave you an offer to sell, and now we're back to hear your answer."

"Answer is still no." To the Sphinx, to the capital-ists, to anyone else interested.

They smiled at each other. "We thought as much." Bradford lifted a folded slip of paper from his suit jacket pocket. "We've come with a better deal than before." He handed over the note and spoke as Ewan proceeded to unfold the paper and inspect it. "We are prepared to buy at a hefty sum, including the equip-ment, buildings and mine."

"And the water rights, of course," Mac added. "We would be paying the most for that piece of the equa-tion."

Of course they would. As a growing operation, the Sphinx clearly coveted his water rights and the gold in his portion of the mountain. Not to mention the power of his stamp mill. Currently, they sent their produc-tion off to a mill that worked for hire. But owning their own would pay long-term dividends—and buy-ing a working one would make them money faster than building their own.

Ewan stared at the paper, at the indeed *hefty* sum staring back at him.

"This is valuable land, as I'm sure you're well aware." Mac Glouster tipped his head to one side. "But your personal resources aren't enough to care for—and grow—such a business. Let us take it off your hands at this price, and you'll make more in this deal than you did while mining your claim for a year."

The offer tempted him. Badly. He would finally be rid of the burden of anxiety that followed him wherever he went. And what if his father was right, that this place had been nothing more than a waste of his time? He might be forced to give up the mine soon anyway. Using this money, he could go into another field, like accounting. Maybe go back to school to become a lawyer. Something that would prove more successful than the boom and bust of the gold-mining life.

But what of his mission? He had a whole staff to think about. George. Lars. Cassandra. Delia. If he could find out the reason for all he recent costs—quickly—then maybe he could turn things around.

"I'm sorry, but the answer is still no," he replied. "I just can't accept at this time."

"This is an important deal." Bradford narrowed his eyes. "I would consider it carefully, if I were you."

Folding his hands on his desk, Ewan leaned forward, turning his gaze on the other brother. "Let me ask you something, Mac. If I sold you my land, where would that leave my staff?"

"We would examine the workers and make decisions from there."

Ewan nodded slowly. "In other words, you would only keep them on if you thought it necessary and beneficial to your business."

"Of course, naturally." Bradford chuckled. "That is how you run a solid business, Mr. Burke. You hire the best of the best and terminate those who hold you back."

"But what about their lives? Aren't they worth something?"

"Sure, they're worth something." Mac shrugged. "Just not to the mining company."

"If they're not fit for the dangerous work involved in mining, then they need to apply for positions elsewhere," Bradford agreed.

"Where, for example? Some of my staff have nowhere else to go. No one will hire them."

"Your reputation precedes you around town, Mr. Burke." Mac voice came flat, clearly tiring of the conversation. "And if you want my opinion, it's the root of your problems. You can either run a charity or you can run a business. You cannot do both."

"No, I'm sorry. This mine doesn't leave my possession when so many lives depend on it. Now if you'll please show yourselves out of my office, I would be much obliged."

He didn't look up from his oh-so-important paperwork until he heard the brothers leave the room. As soon as the latch clicked, he tossed his pencil onto the desktop and stood. But before he could take two steps, another small knock sounded on the door.

Ewan gritted his teeth. *Kindness, regardless of affliction.*

The door slid open just enough for Winifred to peek her head inside. A measure of relief hit him at the sight of her.

"Ewan? How are you holding up?"

He grunted as he paced the rug.

She inched into the office. "I heard a little bit of the conversation outside the door." As if formulating her thoughts, she paused. "I thought you handled them very well."

If only. Ewan took another trip along the length of

his rug. "I've tried everything I can think of, Win. I don't know what else to do. Maybe I should just give up."

"Hey, now." In quick fashion, Winifred stepped in front of him and clasped his arms. "Enough of that thinking. We'll figure this out. Delia and I devised a few ideas of our own, some ways to at least help the store produce more income. Maybe that will cover costs until we find out what's causing the mine's suspicious activity."

Ewan expelled a sigh. Sweet Winifred. She tried so hard—her mind never stopped coming up with new ideas. And he had certainly tried everything else. Maybe it was time to put a little faith in the woman standing before him.

"All right." He lifted her hands off his arms and held them in his own. "What would you have us do?"

"Why don't we throw a party of some kind? We could get people to come into the store, perhaps, and spend more money."

As her excitement built, Ewan's began to wane. "A party?"

Winifred continued to smile. "Why not? It would be fun."

He hated to disappoint her. "Because that doesn't make sense. Mines don't do things like that."

"So change the status quo, Ewan." She squeezed his palms in hers. "Be the first mine in history to host a party. A revitalization of your store."

"But, but I'm barely hanging onto my business as it is. I don't have time or resources to play around with changing the status quo. I stick to what works."

"You've tried all that already, and it didn't work

after all." Her smile widened, undeterred by his excuses. "Now, it's time to step out on faith and try something new. You might just be surprised at the results."

Chapter Eleven

"Some of you have been with me since nearly the beginning, when we were nothing but a placer mine beside the creek. Others of you hired on within the last six months, when we started mining the mountain, but I can tell you right now I wouldn't trade a single person here for someone else."

Ewan stood near the counter of the store during shift change for the meeting he had arranged. All eyes turned toward him as he expressed his true sentiments—Winifred's idea—for the people as well as the business. Truthfully, things he should have said long ago.

"Furthermore, I need to be honest with you and put the rumors to rest." He glanced over their faces. "I don't know what the future holds for the Golden Star Mine. But no matter what trials lie ahead, I will fight fiercely for this business to prosper. And by business, I don't simply mean the production of gold."

He spotted Winifred against the wall, near the door that connected the store with the corridor, her blue-gray stare whispering hope. She nodded for him to continue. Lifting his chin a little, he focused again on the others.

"This business is nothing without all of you. I hope you know that." And he hoped, if there was a saboteur in their midst, that the culprit heard, too—and felt pricked to the heart to change. "You make this company great. I firmly believe you have the power to fight for this place and bring it success as much as I do. Production has dwindled a little in the past few days, and a couple of accidents have taken place." He paused. He was veering a little too much on the negative side. This was an encouragement talk, not a production meeting. "So I encourage you to fight for your jobs. Seek the motivation you felt your first week here, and give yourself up to it. Keep this a positive and healthy work environment where you want to come and decide that you will be productive while you're here. You have the power. I have faith you will all do your part in keeping the Golden Star running for years to come."

Ewan couldn't help but glance at Winifred again. This time her eyes shone with tears. *Tears?* She'd been that moved by his words? Soon she began to clap, and everyone joined in.

The pride filling his chest wasn't something he felt often. It was, if for no other reason, because he could tell his workers genuinely appreciated what he'd said. If he'd managed to inspire them all, there was no telling what they could accomplish before Mr. Johns arrived for his second inspection.

He owed it all to Winifred. "Miss Sattler has organized an event I think you all will enjoy. It's not only a way to earn the mine extra revenue, but also to celebrate the accomplishments we've made so far and to look to what is to come in the future." He rubbed his hands together as he spoke, realizing some of Win's excitement had actually inspired him in the last couple of days. "We'll host a grand party at the store. There will be contests and dropped prices for the day. I'll have more information for you as the day grows closer, but until then, I'm asking each of you to plan on supporting the event. Bring your families. In fact, if your wives or children want to make anything for us to sell, we'll split the profits with you. How does that sound?"

Again, applause filled the room. Ewan could have been the president of the United States for how well his employees responded to him at this moment. Gratitude tugged at his chest, and once again, he caught Winifred's eye. He mouthed the words *thank you*.

She only shook her head, laughed and continued clapping.

The workers split up for the day. Ewan hung back as everyone filtered from the store, hoping he could catch a moment with Winifred. But when he scanned the diminishing crowd, she had already disappeared. Oh, well. He pushed down the hint of disappointment he hadn't expected to feel. Surprising how much he'd come to enjoy her presence, her positivity.

And her support. Where would he have been if she had given up on the Golden Star?

Ewan shook his head. He was getting ahead of himself. All her support wouldn't automatically bring in revenue or save the mine. The results would begin to show themselves at the bazaar and then again when Mr. Johns returned.

Cassandra squeezed his shoulder as she passed him,

ambling toward the shop door leading to the corridor. "You did a good thing this morning. I'm proud of you, no matter what happens to the mine."

A smile lifted Ewan's mouth. "Thank you, Cassandra."

"That Miss Winnie is something else, isn't she?"

Her statement caused his smile to widen. "She certainly is."

Now to check the mail before making his morning rounds.

Visiting the post office had nearly become an every-other-day activity. One never knew what surprises awaited. Just thinking about TD put a spring in his step as he pushed open the shop door and stepped onto the walkway.

"Hey, boss? That you?"

Ewan looked up. One of his miners came running toward him. "Yes?"

The man stopped beside him, catching his breath. "Boy, I hoped I'd catch you before you left."

Ewan braced himself for another catastrophe. What was it now? Another cave-in? Another injury?

"We found something," the man said. "In the mine."

Ewan frowned. Just when they'd found fresh zeal to push forward. "What is it?"

"You'll have to come see."

"I thought I wasn't allowed in the mine anymore."

"Yes…but this is different."

Ducking into the shadows of the drift, Winifred followed Ewan, all the while trying to keep her nerves in check. She hadn't come into this place since the cave-in—an experience that still haunted her sleep. Lying half-conscious in that black pocket of the mountain like it was the belly of a dragon...

Winifred shuddered.

On the other hand, she'd developed a strange love for this place. Something about being where the temperature cooled and the air grew moist. The place had begun to sink into her as deeply as if it were a fire in a hearth, instead. Like home.

What a strange thing to think—a mine feeling like home. But it really did, mostly because it was attached to all the other things, and people, that had made the Golden Star home.

"I'll be curious to see why you whisked me out here at dawn," she said through a yawn.

"Trust me, this is worth losing sleep over."

By the light of Ewan's lantern, she saw where the collapsed drift had been barricaded off as they passed by it. A chill ran over her skin. Talk around the supper table was that some men had been put in charge of clearing out the fallen debris and were supposed to fix the broken beams that caused the cave-in in the first place. The expert Ewan hired said the beams had been weakened, or perhaps hadn't been installed correctly. That discovery only served to harden her suspicions. Someone wanted to sabotage the Golden Star, and she'd fallen victim to that person's attacks.

Her thoughts flashed to Mr. Ansell and attacks of another nature—instead of aiming at her life, he'd aimed at her heart. Determined to explode it into a heap of splinters.

"I say, Winnie, wait!"

Her former mail-order prospect had chased after

her all the way back to the stagecoach depot—and had had the gall to use her Christian name.

Might as well have used something entirely intimate, like darling or dear, cookie or muffin. Except she was no one's muffin, least of all Mr. Ansell's.

He had spoken as if he'd had a right to her. As if her very presence in Dakota Territory made her belong to him—and that leaving town only fifteen minutes after meeting him had been the crime… instead of the real problem, his cowardly approach to matrimony.

Tears pricked her eyes. So many dreams had been shattered in those fifteen minutes.

"You said yourself that you've ruined every match you've been given" he'd said. How dare he twist her words? And after she'd poured her heart out to him in her letters! She hadn't ruined *every* prospect. Only three of them. And the last one being a married man was *not* her fault.

"A woman ordered on six separate occasions? No one else will ever want someone like you." He'd pelted her with those words like the stoning of Stephen—and they had haunted her ever since.

This time, *this time* the arrangement should have worked. She'd done everything right, asked the right questions and answered his honestly. She hadn't been so overly eager to make it work that she'd sugarcoated her situation. How had she not seen the catastrophe coming before she'd gone to Spearfish?

Nibbling on her fingernail, she realized the truth stared her in the face as boldly as the sun glared into the eyes of someone exiting a cave. Except, instead of blinding her like the sun, the truth made her see her life for what it really was.

Six times mail ordered. Never once a bride.

Who would ever take a chance on someone like that?

Ewan's hand touched hers, and she jumped. Before she knew what had happened, his fingers encircled hers, clasping tight, as the barricaded tunnel faded into the darkness behind them.

It was almost as if he'd read her mind, sensed the tension rising inside her. Except holding his hand wasn't doing much in the way of calming her down. She needed to turn her mind to something else, lest she fool herself into believing something substantial could bloom from this hand holding.

"So what's this surprise you wanted to show me?"

The lantern light threw their shadows on the wooden walls. She heard him chuckle softly. "Not telling yet."

She fought back a smile. So mean.

As he led her along, she noticed the rare sight of easy roundness in his shoulders instead of his usual rigid corners. He was finally showing signs of peace and happiness—the teasing, the chuckling. Could he have possibly turned a corner in his mood?

She glanced at their hands, unable to ignore the tingle in her stomach. Since he'd saved her from the cave-in, had they turned a corner together, too?

"This drift here," he said, veering left. "It's new, just built this week, so it's not terribly long yet." His voice, holding promise, echoed in the quiet. "It's actually near the edge of our property line, so I'm thankful it isn't a few yards farther to the north."

"Thankful *what* isn't farther to the north?" She

stumbled a bit on a fallen shard of rock, then righted herself.

Ewan paused to catch her against the sturdiness of his arm. "This. Right up here."

His voice came hushed, like a soft touch against her cheeks. Then he lifted his lantern to illuminate an open area, like a small cave. Swirls along the stone, both smooth and jagged, caught her eye. White and gray and…

"Gold!" Winifred's eyes widened. Swirls of glittering gold caught fire, reflecting the lantern light. It shone with elegant beauty unmatched by the most priceless jewelry she could imagine.

"And judging by the quartz deposit here—" Ewan let go of her hand to draw an arch along the wall "—there should be a whole lot more where this gold came from. Patterns like this are called a lead, meaning it'll lead us straight to the mother lode."

Her heart began to patter faster. She stepped close and placed her hand on the cold stone. "I can't believe it. We're saved!"

"Well…" Ewan shrugged a shoulder. "I hope so, but there's no telling exactly how much is in here."

Oh, this realist of a man. Winifred nearly rolled her eyes. "But if it produces the amount you suspect?" she prompted. "Would that be enough to save us?"

"We'd still have to curb our mysterious costs…" In the dim light, his mouth twitched at the corners. "But possibly so, yes."

A thrill shot down her arms. She gripped her hands to keep from clapping, but it only lasted a few seconds before she applauded full force. And squealed. They were saved! The Golden Star could remain open, and everyone could keep their jobs.

She threw her arms around Ewan's torso, jumping up and down. Stiff at first, Ewan moved with her. A laugh surfaced from within him, and she joined in. Thank the Lord, they would get to keep the mine!

As their laughter faded, so did their dance—until they stood motionless in the semidarkness. But even stopped, Winifred couldn't drop her arms. "Can we still have the store's party?" The question sounded more breathless than she'd meant.

His free hand cupped her back. Orange light flickered in his eyes and shadowed a portion of his face as he stared down at her. "Of course. We have more reasons to celebrate now than ever."

The fabric of his suit jacket caressed her fingertips. Did she dare let go? Or worse, did she dare hold on?

Ewan searched her eyes. What did he see there? His chest rose and fell beneath her chin. Flutters moved through her middle. He tilted his face down toward hers.

Distant laughter echoed from the tunnel entrance. Gasping in air, Winifred spun her body away from Ewan's, pretending to stare at the swirls of quartz. More candlelight filled the stope, and as men's voices grew louder, she was thankful the unsteady light would hide her burning cheeks.

"Hey, boss," one said. "Showing off the mother lode, huh?"

Winifred closed her eyes, as if she'd been caught doing something bad. Had she?

"Can't wait to get this stuff to the mill," the other miner piped up. Farther into the stope, he dropped mining supplies with a series of loud clangs—chisels, hammers. Other things. So opposite of the peaceful quiet that had enchanted her earlier. "Pretty amazing, ain't it?"

Winifred threw Ewan a glance. In the few moments since their interruption, he hadn't moved. Like he'd been carved from the very pocket of quartz he'd shown her. The only sign of life was the slight rise and fall of his chest in the light.

"Amazing, yes." He raised his eyes, connecting his gaze with hers, and her breath caught.

It felt exactly like the mysterious emotion that had coursed through her veins when Ewan touched her face and called her Win. A heady joy that stopped up her lungs and nearly brought her to tears. So overwhelming, she ached to run away. What sort of feeling was this? Warm and good, yes, and certainly unlike anything she'd felt before…but was it real and would it last? Did she dare take the time to define it for her heart?

Because if whatever this was betrayed her, she didn't know what she'd do.

They left the mine in silence, moving down the hill as the sun rose over the Black Hills horizon. Though the mountain ranges around Denver were beautiful, there was something quaint and unique about the way these hills dipped, the way the craggy rock faces jutted from the grass and trees. Ewan had never seen anything quite so breathtaking.

Not that he'd truly regained his breath since spending a few moments alone in the dark with Winifred.

As they reached the larger rocks at the base of the

outcropping, he lifted his hand to her. He didn't speak. Thankfully, neither did she. Instead, she simply accepted his help, using his hand to balance her as she climbed to the grass waiting below.

Oranges and reds, yellows and purples splashed across the sky. The clouds suggested rain, or maybe snow. Oh, hopefully not snow. But October had certainly come to the Black Hills. Most of the leaves had fallen from the aspen that intermingled with the ponderosa pine. A crispness bit at the tips of his ears as they crossed the grass toward the store and offices.

Some distance hung between them. Part of him wanted to close that gap, while the sensible part wanted to leave it wide-open, broad enough for a winter gale to rush through. It was dangerous to analyze her further—because of what he might find. If he found a link that connected his heart to hers, he'd be in a world of trouble. For one thing, she surely had enough fare money by now. He wouldn't be surprised one bit if she left after the store's celebration. And if he opened his heart, where would that leave him once she was gone?

"Your mind seems to be full," Winifred murmured.

Ewan dipped his chin. "Sorry about that. I was just…" Just what? Realizing that this woman had come to mean more to him than he'd ever wanted?

Winifred shivered. "Chilly morning, isn't it? Winter is around the corner."

"Yes, it is," he replied, thankful for the change in topic. "And only a couple more months before Mr. Johns comes."

"The mother lode will certainly impress him." She beamed up at him, her smile filling him with unbidden warmth. He managed a small smile, then looked away.

"I've been praying, searching for a solution to keep things running." This lead was necessary to make this place—to make himself—a success, and it'd finally happened. Dared he hope that this was God showing favor on Ewan's endeavors?

TD would be so proud.

Frowning a little, Ewan dropped his gaze to the ground, sidestepping a rock and rubbing his hands down his trousers. He glanced at the woman walking beside him. He had a desire just as strong to share this victory with Winifred as he did with his mystery friend. Alarming, to say the least. Where did that leave him, desiring to share his joy with a pair of women he could never have? The person he *should* be excited to share this news with was his father—a father who didn't yet recognize his son's accomplishments. Maybe this vein of gold would remedy that problem, too.

"Thank you for showing me the gold." Winifred broke into his thoughts.

She smiled, the lines of her mouth soft and kind. Ewan dragged his gaze away from her and opened the door. If it was the last thing he'd do, he would forget the urge he felt to kiss Winifred Sattler. What a close call he'd had in the cave! He had almost succumbed to the desire, and that would have been the worst thing he could have possibly done.

"You are welcome." He allowed her to step in ahead of him. When he shut out the rising sun, the darkened hallway met them, lit only a little by small windows around the corner. "I'll walk you to the kitchen," he murmured, taking a step forward, occupying his hands by crossing his arms.

"You know," she began, "once some of that vein is

processed, you'll likely have the money to fix the broken platform. And the cam."

"And the collapsed drift columns."

"I'm so glad, Ewan." She looked up at him then, touching his bicep with her hand. "And we'll catch whoever is sabotaging the mine. I promise."

Though he couldn't see the full shape of her eyes in the dim light, he knew by the tone of her voice that she stared at him in earnest. Everything she did was with that same sense of urgency and emotion. Which often led to putting the cart before the horse, getting herself in a world of trouble. But even so, her heart always seemed to be in the right place—in helping others reach their potential.

She was different than Marilee in that way. His former fiancée had only cared about herself—that was clear to him now. It was not her vivacious personality that was to blame, but rather her cold and indifferent heart—a fault that could never be ascribed to Winifred Sattler. But he still couldn't allow himself to fall for a woman who flitted around like a hummingbird from flower to flower. Mission to mission. Always busy but not always steady.

And he was coming dangerously close to falling for her anyway.

Had she felt it, too? The pulsing shock to the system when they'd stood in the cave, as close as they stood now? Pushing the moment aside, he reached for the kitchen doorknob. "Have a good day, then."

Hesitating, she finally nodded. "Yes. You, too."

He turned the knob and opened the door, allowing the kitchen's light to fill the corridor. Leaning in, he nodded to the cook, who stirred a pot on the stove.

"I'll breakfast in my office this morning, Cassandra. Thank you." And at home tonight. Surely he could find a crust of bread in his bare cupboards to tide him over.

Leaving the women, Ewan marched down the hall, then stepped back into the morning air and breathed in its crisp bite, praying the late-autumn temperature would break the spell he was under.

Spending time with Winifred lately had made him want to believe. Believe that simply because she wasn't like Marilee, she wouldn't someday hurt him. But logic told him otherwise, and the reminder solidified within him his reasoning for seeking a serious wife. A dependable woman, who cared deeply for loyalty and put her heart in the work of the mine. He didn't care one iota if she was beautiful, or had a warm smile, or even if she enjoyed laughing. Those things wouldn't keep a business fortified. They were only good for breaking hearts.

TD had told him she wasn't interested in pursuing a relationship. But after they'd sent so many letters, would she possibly change her mind?

She seemed stable and consistent. Even helpful and undeniably understanding of Ewan to his core. What would she be like in person? She wished men would consider their actions before pursuing women like a game. Well, he'd stopped and considered the possibility until a chill ran down his spine—and it wasn't from the cold.

He gripped his hands into fists and released them as he mulled over the most exciting, and scary, thought he'd had in years.

What would happen if he asked TD to meet?

Chapter Twelve

Meet Mr. Businessman?

Oh, dear. Winifred's hands trembled as she refolded the letter and shoved it beneath her pillow. This circumstance hadn't even crossed her mind up to now. How could he possibly want to meet, after she told him specifically that she wasn't interested in a relationship?

Which was a lie now, wasn't it? It might have been the truth starting out, but with every new letter, her opinion had shifted. She wanted to meet him more than doing just about anything else. But she hadn't seriously thought it would happen. Could she do it?

Letting out a shaky breath, she left the empty kitchen, tying her sash and listening to her heels clicking down the hallway toward the party starting in the store. This was a decision she'd have to make later. Right now, everyone had congregated with their arriving guests, and she was late.

When she entered, she stopped short at all the patrons flooding the room.

Homemade decorations hung in swags from the windows and shelves. A sign for a guessing contest had been set up in the corner—how many pencils had been stuffed into a jar? The winner would receive five pieces of hard candy for free. Laughter poured from her right and conversation from her left. Granna Cass carried around a tray of gingersnap cookies pulled from the oven an hour ago. Soon Winifred would join her in offering refreshments. A few customers Winifred recognized had come with their spouses. Several others she didn't recognize walked through, though she hoped they'd be frequent customers now.

But who really caught her attention was Ewan. Proud and confident, he stood at the entrance like the host he was, greeting each guest with a smile and a friendly handshake. In the last week, he'd surprised her. Where she thought stood a stern, grumpy business owner was now a passionate, caring man instead— with a hint of humor in his words and a whole lot of heart for people. She had never seen someone work so hard and agonize so deeply over the well-being of others—but all of that had been true from the start. The change now was that the new vein seemed to release his fixation on keeping the mine out of the wrong hands and shift his focus to how to make it grow.

"Isn't this fun?" Delia came alongside Winifred, a cookie in hand. "And your drawings are selling best out of anything."

"Truly?"

"Yep. I guess people like pictures of their town."

In the days leading up to the grand bazaar, Winifred had walked around Deadwood with her sketchbook in hand. Whenever she spotted something worthwhile, she stopped and captured it. Children playing in front of a store. Old miners resting out of the sun, stems of wheat poking from their weathered lips. Well-loved establishments like churches and the post office. Maybe Delia was right about people wanting pictures of where, and with whom, they spent their time.

She looked up as a young family stepped inside. Ewan shook hands with the father before squatting to shake the hand of each small boy. His brows rose as he asked them questions she couldn't hear from this distance. The boys laughed, fully entranced by whatever he had to say. She watched as he slipped from his suit coat pocket two pieces of hard candy. Grins wide, the boys accepted the gifts and popped them straight into their mouths. Then, like lightning, they bolted across the room to the guessing table to cast their votes, apparently in hopes of more of the candy they'd sampled.

Ewan caught her eye. One side of his mouth lifted before he turned back to another arriving guest.

Something about that smile did strange things to her stomach.

"What was that?" Delia questioned.

Winifred blinked several times, pivoting away from the direction of the front door. "What was what?"

"That look you two just exchanged." The woman had her fists on her hips, imitating Granna Cass a little too closely for Winifred's liking.

"There wasn't a look." At least not one that mattered.

But Delia hardly acted convinced. "I saw the same one when you two were hanging the decorations together yesterday. Him hammering string into the wall, and you fightin' fits of giggles at all his jokes."

Winifred lifted her chin. "They were funny."

"Oh, yes, of course. That's the only reason you laughed and carried on."

Was it getting warm in here? "Look, if you're implying what I think you're implying, you needn't worry yourself about it. We're friends. That's all." Regardless of the emotions rushing through her.

"If you say so…" With a wiggle of her brows, Delia spun on her shoe and sauntered off to sneak another cookie from Granna Cass.

Before Winifred could react to that comment, she spotted Ewan coming through the crowd toward her. "Win?"

Would that nickname ever stop melting her insides?

He paused before her. "I just realized I forgot a few of your sketches in my office. I see a lot of people buying them, so I imagine we'll need every last one on display. Would you mind grabbing them for me? I have to watch the front door."

"Of course."

He smiled his thanks and headed back to the door while she spun and fled the store. Her hands shook as she supported herself on the staircase banister. Up and up. Expelling a jagged sigh, she brushed a strand of hair from her forehead. There was no doubt about it. She'd unexpectedly opened herself up to Ewan Burke. Her heart had become warm and soft in his hands, stubborn as he was.

She'd become far too attached for a woman who wouldn't be sticking around. And it was becoming harder and harder to convince herself that going home to Denver, to start her husband search over again, was still the wisest thing to do. But how could she stay? The more time she spent near Ewan, the more she found herself hoping for a relationship that should never be. She must get him out of her head and out of her heart. Sentimental women didn't belong with serious men. Ewan needed to be with someone who shared his stringent outlook on the world. Winifred could never be expected to adopt his way of thinking—over time, it would eventually crush her spirit. Wouldn't it?

Reaching the office, she gave the doorknob a quick turn and went inside. She crossed to the desk, covered with orderly stacks of papers, and ran her fingers along the polished surface. So many memories here. When she left Deadwood, because soon she would, she'd miss so many things. Oh, how she didn't want to go.

She sank into Ewan's cushioned chair and inhaled everything that made up that man. Not just the cologne he wore, but also his determination, his stubborn resolution, his tireless worry over the well-being of his employees and his unstinting kindness toward anyone in need.

Of everything that composed the Golden Star Mine, she would miss Ewan Burke the most.

Enough woolgathering. Now, where were those sketches?

Not on the desk. She glanced toward the desk's top drawer but made no move to reach for it—it was the drawer where he kept his personal papers and it was always locked. Except...right now, it wasn't. In fact, it wasn't fully shut, and through the opening, a shock of color caught her attention.

She inched open the drawer. Corners of pink and red floral paper stuck out from beneath other stacks of paper and envelopes. Strange. The colored paper reminded her an awful lot of her own stationery.

Her brow pinched. "I think it *is* my stationery."

With a quick glance at the open door, Winifred slipped out one of the floral sheets. She nearly dropped it when she recognized her own handwriting.

Dear Mr. Businessman had been scrawled across the top.

Heartbeat rising in her chest, she riffled through the rest of the stationery. "What is going on here?"

Every single letter she'd sent to her secret correspondent was accounted for. Her frown deepened as she plopped back against Ewan's chair. How did he have all of her letters?

Was he...?

Winifred gasped. "No."

Ewan Burke *couldn't* be Mr. Businessman. They were complete opposites. Her companion was tender, attentive and understanding. Ewan was pragmatic, preoccupied and sometimes harsh. Except, when...when he was tender, attentive and understanding.

She covered her face with her hands. Oh, how humiliating. Her boss had seen her deepest worries, her strongest dreams? He knew parts of her heart she hadn't shared with anyone!

Had he written her back as a joke? For all she knew, she'd been duped again—man after man, letter after letter. When would she ever learn not to put her faith in suitors through the mail?

"Except Ewan would be the last person to toy with a woman's emotions," she whispered, lowering her hands.

The pile of papers beneath her letters looked like

correspondence, too. She lifted one and skimmed it. Also addressed to Mr. Businessman, from a woman who lived in Lead City, asking about the living conditions he could provide in Deadwood and about his faith convictions. Another from a woman whose father had owned a mine. Another from a schoolteacher.

She flipped through them faster. These were all addressed to Mr. Businessman—they must be from the women who had seriously answered his advertisement.

Which only confirmed that Ewan hadn't played a practical joke on Winifred. He truly sought a wife.

Winifred stood and slammed the drawer shut. She knew someone who could tell her the truth. Forgetting the sketches for now, she marched from the room and down through the outside door. She didn't stop until she reached the post office.

With clipped steps, she approached the counter. Mr. Star smiled at her, but he must have recognized her sense of urgency, because the smile faded into a look of concern. "Miss Sattler, what is it?"

She placed both hands on the counter's edge, as if clinging to it might keep her from falling off this cliff she dangled from. "I came to find out the truth, Mr. Star."

His brow furrowed. "Truth about what?"

"My mystery correspondent." Her knuckles had already turned white. "Please, sir. Tell me who he is."

Running a hand over his mouth, the postmaster hesitated. "I'm not sure he wants you to know who he is. And you said yourself you didn't want to know."

"I changed my mind. Please." She took the liberty of reaching across the counter and placing her hand on Mr. Star's sleeve cuff. "Will you tell me if I guess correctly?"

He grimaced. "I—"

"Is it Ewan Burke?" Fiddlesticks, she couldn't hide the tremor in her voice anymore. Nor the shaking in her hands. "I found all my letters. He keeps them in a desk drawer in his office."

Mr. Star turned his palms up. "I think you have all the proof you need, ma'am."

She couldn't keep from biting the corner of her lower lip. "But was it real? Was he really writing *me*, or did he play a big charade?"

Squinting, the man cocked his head and shrugged. "I can't tell you his reasons for certain, since he never told me. All I know is he was much more excited to get your letters than mail from any of his other prospects."

Everything began to click together. The numerous trips to the post office, his request for someone practical and not beautiful. He'd written to her about the disapproval of his father, the frustrations of running a business, the loneliness of having no one to confide in. Even when they had annoyed each other in person, they had stolen each other's hearts on the page. Or at least he'd stolen hers.

Oh, dear.

"Miss Sattler?" Mr. Star leaned over the counter. "Are you feeling all right? You're looking a little green."

She rasped in a breath. "I have to go."

Her heels clicked faster on her way back to the party than they had on her way out. Ewan Burke had stolen her heart. The man she'd come to care for on the page—that was *him*. Her boss. Her friend. While she dreamed of Mr. Businessman, he had been upstairs in his office in the flesh *the whole time*.

Laughter met her as she opened the shop door. She looked up into Ewan's eyes as a patron stepped away.

"Win, what are you doing coming in the front?" he said through a chuckle. "Do you have the sketches?"

Why couldn't she stand with her mouth closed, like a normal person? Due to nerves and distraction, she'd entered through the front instead of the side. "I'm sorry, I…got distracted. I'll go get them right away."

She pivoted and marched in the opposite direction back into the street. What was she to do now? She couldn't very well tell him the truth, could she? What would he think of her? And he would know she'd dug in his private desk drawer.

Squeezing her eyes, Winifred shook her head and whirled back toward the store. "Oh, who cares about the desk drawer? I love that man, and I need to tell him before I leave."

Her heart seized. She *loved* Ewan Burke? No, she couldn't…could she? No, she couldn't. She wouldn't allow herself to. They were too different. Sure, they could ignore their differences for a while, but how long would it take before those things drove a wedge between them? Could he ever truly cherish the person she was—his complete opposite?

Besides that, how could she trust her own feelings were real and lasting? She'd thought she loved her other mail-order prospects, but her feelings had fizzled the moment she'd realized the matches were doomed. Wasn't it likely that she was merely in love with the *idea* of Mr. Businessman? If so, that was nothing to build a life around.

Still, finding out the truth had opened her up to the question of *if*. What if they could have a future together?

The question seeped through her veins as she rounded the office and entered through the side door. Gooseflesh climbed her arms, and not just from the autumn air. It would take her a moment to combine the two men in her head, to think of them as one and the same.

Her breath became shaky as she reached Ewan's office. Where were those sketches?

Ah. Stacked on the floor against the wall.

Quickly, she snatched them up. The longer she was gone from the party, the more suspicious Ewan would become. Oh dear, what was she to do now?

She'd spent the better part of five years searching for a husband. Her uncle had sent prospects her way, and she'd found a few on her own. And of course, there were the six mail-order flops. Through all of that, she'd never given up hope that she would find the man of her dreams.

But after Mr. Ansell, she'd begun to lose hope that such a man existed.

Until Mr. Businessman.

Fiddlesticks. This was the biggest mess she'd ever gotten herself into.

She flew down the stairs but paused at the shop door, knowing she'd see him on the other side. Winifred drew in a long breath and shot her gaze to the ceiling.

Who was she kidding? Despite their enormous differences and her efforts to quell her feelings, Ewan had captured her affections. Wholeheartedly. Without warning and without foreknowledge or premeditation.

And she couldn't leave Deadwood without knowing how he felt about her.

It would come as a shock at first, but if he felt even an ounce of the attraction toward Miss Thoroughly Disgruntled that she felt toward Mr. Businessman, then Ewan might just be willing to give Winifred Sattler a try, too.

They could have the beautiful love her parents had shared. Yes, she would tell him. Right after the party. *Lord, please help him hear me.*

"I'm quite certain that was the busiest I've ever seen this store."

Ewan, hanging back to help Winifred count sales and clean up after the last customers had gone, chuckled beneath his breath. "I'm quite certain it's the busiest *I've* ever seen it. Even counting our grand opening."

The buzz that the woman beside him had created around town had worked. Sketching downtown had raised curiosity. Her idea to post an artistically hand-painted sign out front had sparked interest. The flyers she'd drawn up to post inside local businesses had been smart and well received. He hadn't finished totaling the sales yet, but he didn't need his calculations to know the event was a superb success.

"The day went extremely well, Win." He sent her a smile from across the room. "I have you to thank for it."

She looked up from wiping the table that held the pencil-guessing contest—two hundred and forty-seven pencils to be exact. The joy on people's faces had been worth far more than the five pieces of candy. "It wasn't just me. Granna Cass baked almost all the desserts. Delia cleaned the shop. Mr. McAllister's wife made the quilt raffle prize—which went over swimmingly, I might add. So beautiful. I wish I could've been entered to win it myself."

So unassuming, so willing to share the credit with everyone. It made him admire her even more. Ewan pulled another stack of bills from the drawer and began to count. "But if it weren't for you, this would've been an ordinary day. No celebration. No extra sales. No renewed interest in the store. Your creativity shoots higher than I could ever aim for myself, and that is to be commended."

Silence followed his statement. He paused mid–bill swipe and raised his gaze. Winifred stared back at him, the way she did every time he offered her a well-deserved compliment. Did she not receive very many of those? Hesitant surprise hung in her wide eyes, but so did something else. Something warmer, softer. Like vulnerability wrapped up with the need to believe that what he said was true.

"I mean it, Win." He slipped the bills back in the drawer and recorded the amount in the ledger. "You've done excellent work here, and being a temporary employee, that is even more commendable. Most people would've come in, sat at the counter and bided their time until they collected their wages and then left. You never did that, not once. You took a dying store and turned it around. And not just the store. The mine, too. The workers, I mean. The overall mood has heightened because of you. In fact, three men approached me just this week asking if they could work here—"

Winifred's heels clicked across the floor so fast that before Ewan knew what hit him, she had her arms around his neck.

All words left him. Slack jawed, all he could focus on was this woman. And the feelings coursing through him at her closeness.

"Thank you," she murmured against his shirt collar. "No one has ever said such nice things about me."

Pushing through his shock, he embraced her, too. Warm and petite, she fit beautifully in his arms. This, the woman he'd thought about firing at least half a dozen times in the past month and a half. And yet, she was also the woman he'd found himself falling for—deeper than he had ever wanted to.

In his arms, with his thoughts full of all the things she'd done, her behavior suddenly made sense. She bounced from idea to idea because she was so intensely creative. Her well of love for people ran deeper than anyone he'd met before. No doubt she'd throw herself in front of a speeding train if it meant saving someone she cared for—and there was no doubt that she cared for everyone at the mine.

Winifred had the power to change his life. She'd already left her mark on him, and long after she returned to Denver, he would remember her.

Because she would return to Denver. Ewan must remind himself of that fact. He wouldn't ask her to stay. Couldn't. She had a whole life ahead of her, with all those suitable Denver prospects waiting for her return. His heart shouldn't get any closer than it was right now.

"You're welcome," he whispered.

Releasing herself from his hold, she averted her eyes. "I—I suppose I crave affirmation. My uncle is kind, but he's busy and has little interest in feminine pursuits and accomplishments. The only thing I could do to impress him was marry well and I…haven't exactly had the most success in my romantic life." She rubbed a hand up her arm. "You should know I've had six engagements. All resulting from mail-order advertisements. I had thought…well, it wouldn't be like town, would it? Where young men say flattering things to girls but don't mean anything serious by it at all. If a man advertises for a mail-order bride, then he wants to marry. Why else would he do it? I was so hopeful…but they were all flops."

Ewan looked up. "Six?"

Pink colored her cheeks. "A reason existed for each flop—one had an accident and died before we wed. That one couldn't have been helped. But some of the others…"

Frowning, she worked her jaw, staring at her hands. Everything within Ewan urged him to reach out and take her hands in his, to offer some measure of comfort. But he didn't trust himself. Didn't trust his heart to stay neutral.

"I was so set on finding a husband that I didn't take the warning signs in the letters as seriously as I should have. I fell in love—well, infatuation—quickly, and let all the beautiful things they said melt my heart." Propping both hands on the counter, she lifted herself up to sit on its edge. "They always promised great things— elaborate homes, lots of money—promises that were always lies." Startling, she met Ewan's gaze. "Not that I only wanted their wealth. I just knew if they lied about that, then they might've lied about other things."

Ewan fought a smile. "No one would think you

were after their wealth." This, coming from the woman who'd been willing to sit in a drift to draw miners.

"I said all the right things, and so did they." She looked away and sighed, shrugging one shoulder. "I thought I'd learned my lesson and told the whole truth to the last suitor—he knew about the five flops before him, my longing for a husband, my love for art, my family history." She shook her head, like it could deflect her emotions. Didn't work, because a faint sheen had collected over her eyes. "The perfect setup for disaster, I suppose. He was the worst, Ewan. I thought I knew him. But then I found out he was looking for a new wife while deciding if he would divorce his first one. They had children, too, Ewan! Children he planned on abandoning along with his poor wife—the horrible man."

Ewan couldn't help his brows raising, but he quickly regained control of them. Before he realized what he'd done, he joined her on the counter. "That wasn't your fault. He preyed on your willingness to trust."

"But I shouldn't have opened my heart to him."

"Sometimes people take you by surprise, Win. You try your best to be honest and hopeful. You fall in love and want to make a lifetime commitment to that person, and she crushes your dreams. You thought you knew her, but you didn't, and there's nothing to be done about it."

Winifred lifted her head, sniffling. "Her?"

Had he said *her*? Ewan closed his eyes. "I was left at the altar several years ago."

Gasping, Winifred leaned nearer. "Oh, no, I'm so sorry."

He leaned away. Hopefully it didn't appear too obvious, but again, he wasn't sure he trusted himself to keep propriety's boundaries if she came any closer. In fact...

Ewan hopped off the counter and strode across the shop floor. "Marilee was the daughter of my father's colleague. Both of our fathers believed it would have been an advantageous match, but she didn't think so. Not once a better match presented itself."

"Marilee Price? Austin Erikson's daughter?"

Ewan glanced away. "I forgot you know a lot of the same people I do." Which made this conversation all the more humiliating.

Would Winifred defend the woman? He raised his gaze but found her still seated on the counter, tipping her head to one side. Listening. *Of course*, she listened without casting stones—how could he have let his doubts make him forget whom he talked to? She also had a past of embarrassing events. If she trusted him with her most horrendous secret, then he could surely do the same.

He rubbed his cheek as a thought occurred to him. "Was this why—"

"Ewan, there's something—"

They laughed softly at starting sentences simultaneously. "Go ahead," he offered.

Winifred shook her head. "No, I have something to tell you, but you can go first."

"Was that suitor the reason you moved here? Did you plan to marry him?"

Winifred stiffened, clearly not expecting the topic to trail there. Then Ewan remembered his promise. "Oh, no. I'm sorry. I wasn't to ask about Spearfish. Please, you don't have to answer."

She toyed with the hem of her sleeve. "No, I suppose it's fine. Yes, he lives in Spearfish, so I traveled up to marry him."

"And when you found out the truth about him, you didn't have enough money get home." His chest constricted. This woman acted so bravely for everyone else—pushing hard for the benefit of others when she herself had crumbled to pieces. He'd been selfish not to notice, not to spend time understanding her earlier. She deserved every good thing, and it seemed as though time and again she was on the losing side. Yet, somehow, she continued to give.

"Win?"

His voice startled him, came out of nowhere. It must have been the setting sun streaming golden light into the room, illuminating Winifred sitting on the counter, producing a halo of caramel brown around her meticulous curls. The blue in her eyes, their shape framed in long lashes, outshone the gray as she stared back.

Warmth curled around his heart. In three steps, he reached her. Sliding his fingers along her creamy jawline, he let his lips meet hers. Her response came cautiously at first, but soon, her hands trailed up to cover his cheeks and she kissed him back with fervor to match his own. Nothing made sense right now. And yet everything did. The emotions pulsing through his veins, the overwhelming beauty and courage radiating from this woman. He stepped closer to drink her in, but in the last moment, she broke the kiss and leaned back to search his eyes.

"Ewan, wait. What are we doing?"

Dragging in a breath, he brushed his thumb along her cheekbone. "What do you mean?"

She bit the corner of her full lips as she regarded him. Then he saw it—the fear that he would lead her on. Kiss her and then send her back to Denver without another thought. And hadn't he earlier planned on letting her leave? Did he have the right to ask her to stay?

For once, he hadn't denied his heart, and look what he'd done because of it.

"I don't know," he whispered. "I don't know what we're doing."

Hurt flickered in her eyes. Oh, no. She lifted her chin a notch. "I'll be leaving soon, Ewan. You know that, right?"

Traitor heart. Why did it pound harder at her words? "What will you do when you get home?"

"I'll tell Aunt and Uncle I'm sorry for leaving. Then my uncle will likely pick someone for me to marry. He's threatened to do it a couple times." She said it so matter-of-factly, as if she'd told Ewan the sky was blue and the grass was green.

He frowned. "I don't think you want that."

"No?"

"No. You have bigger dreams for yourself than that."

"I don't have a choice. Obviously trying to find a husband on my own hasn't worked out."

"But your uncle choosing one for you? That's not what you want."

"Sometimes it doesn't matter what I want." The brightness in her eyes began to dim. "Sometimes things don't work out the way you dream they will."

Placing a small kiss on her forehead, he couldn't explain why he hated that way of thinking. Maybe he saw himself in her explanation, fighting for the mine all this time in the face of his father's criticism.

Slowly, she slid off the counter, landing on her feet just a step away from him. She peered up into his face with her beautiful mouth slightly open. "Do you know what you want, Ewan? In life?"

He swallowed. Blinked a few times, frowning. "I want the mine."

"Do you want to marry someday?"

"Win—"

"Do you?"

He lifted her hands in his, though he knew he shouldn't. "Yes."

Her eyes searched for an explanation. "But could I ever be such a person?"

"I…" Any words he could've said died on his tongue. Marilee's face flashed through his mind, and doubt arrested his breathing, his limbs, his thoughts.

Her eyes grew watery. "I know where God is leading me, and it's back home. I'll marry someone Uncle chooses, and honestly, that might be the best option for me anyway." A tear slipped down her cheek. "It never fails—I choose the wrong men. I must be searching for something that can't be found."

Conviction gained on him. "I have to be honest with you, Win. I, too, choose the wrong people." He ran his thumbs over her knuckles. "I don't trust myself."

Seeming to understand, Winifred squeezed his hands. "You're a good friend, Ewan. I'm sorry your fiancée left you. You deserve much more than that."

"Thank you."

She glanced to the window, the golden sun lining her profile. "I need time to heal my heart."

Ewan didn't know how to respond. He reached up and touched her cheek. She closed her eyes. Fighting the urge to linger there, he dropped his hand. No use prolonging his avoidance of the truth. He'd promised himself he wouldn't fall for a vibrant, charming, beautiful woman. No matter the cost, he needed to stay true to his belief. Because as steadfast as she seemed today, tomorrow she may change her mind.

"I suppose we'd better say goodnight," he murmured, his voice husky.

Dropping her gaze, she nodded her agreement. "I'll take the pans and plates back to Granna Cass. I'll finish wiping down the counter tomorrow."

"I'll lock the door on my way out."

As if they'd counted to three, they pivoted away from each other, each setting to the task they'd mentioned. Ewan paused at the outside door as Winifred picked up the food trays and headed for the door leading into the corridor, her clicking heels the only sound.

"Good night, Win." He backed out through the door and paused.

Turning, she smiled a little, though her eyes didn't shine. "Good night, Ewan. Today was truly a success."

Had it been? The word thudded against him like a slap to the chest. Finally, he nodded before shutting the door and sticking his key in the lock. He would've agreed with her earlier in the evening, but now, he couldn't help but wonder if he'd just made a huge mistake.

Chapter Thirteen

Winifred slipped the finished letter into an envelope, this one adorned with a sketch of the Black Hills from a distance. One of the first drawings she'd created on her stagecoach ride. She hated to part with it, her first memory of the hills, but at the same time, the man receiving it deserved her best.

Especially when this letter would be her last.

Slipping the note into the pocket of her dress, Winifred left the kitchen and made her way down the hall toward the store. She'd been foolish, really, to correspond with Mr. Businessman—Ewan—so long. Nearly *two* months of delightfully stimulating conversation. To have been swept into a deepening friendship with him, Winifred must've been going mad. No other explanation existed.

But that was all about to change. Last night's encounter with Ewan had reminded her how foolish she'd been to trust her heart. She fell for the wrong men every time—Mr. Businessman wasn't any different. And now she knew Ewan would never accept her as she was.

So in the end, it was better he didn't know the identity of Thoroughly Disgruntled. It would save him from needing to reject her twice.

With what was left of her dignity and her heart, she would go home and heal. Start fresh. Let someone else choose her suitor. This time she wouldn't be so picky about Uncle's choices.

And as for the mine, she'd planned to stay until Mr. Johns came to town next month, but yesterday changed that, too. She had enough money to buy her ticket home. Maybe it was time to do just that.

She pushed through the shop door, spotting Delia seated at the counter, chin propped up by one elbow. When she saw Winifred, her eyes began dancing. Her brows wiggled up and down, as did her shoulders, her grin stretching ever wider.

Winifred narrowed her eyes. "What's got you so excited?"

Delia cocked her head to one side. "You were pretty late coming back from the store last night. We closed at five, but you were here for a couple hours past that." She let her words sink in.

Winifred lifted her chin. "There was a lot to do."

Delia only raised her brows higher. "Were you alone?"

Sneaky. "I do not have to award that question with an answer."

Laughing, Delia slapped the table. "You were with someone. I knew it! You thought you were so clever in hiding it, but you weren't. I figured you out."

"I—" Winifred hesitated. Oh, what was the use? She might as well wear the truth written on her forehead. "All right, yes. I was with someone."

The young woman let out a squeal. "You have to tell me everything." Scooting down, she patted the empty spot at her counter. "You were with Mr. Burke, right? Tell me you were with Mr. Burke."

Her face must've been bright red. "Yes. We were cleaning up the store after everyone left."

"And?"

The pattern of Winifred's heart quickened. "And he kissed me."

If Winifred didn't know better, she would've sworn Delia's eyes grew two complete sizes. Letting loose a laugh, Delia clapped her hands and then shook Winifred's shoulder. "Are you joking with me? Tell me you're not joking with me. He kissed you?"

"I'm not joking. We were talking about our lives and then he kissed me."

"Then what?" She leaned closer as she waited for the answer.

"Then…" Winifred's throat thickened, but she swallowed against it. "Then that was it. We went our separate ways for the night." And her precious news about their correspondence was never shared.

"What? You just left each other? He didn't declare his undying love or ask you to marry him or anything?"

The words stung deep. "No, of course he didn't. He's much too sensible to say or do things he doesn't mean." Although, after last night's kiss, she'd begun to doubt that statement.

A frown diminished Delia's excitement. "What are you talking about? You don't think he loves you?"

"I know he doesn't."

"Are you sure? Do you think he kissed you for self-ish reasons?"

"Well, no. I mean—I don't know." Exhaling, Winifred looked away. He might have kissed her with a passion she'd felt clear to her toes, but… "I know his type, Delia. He's smart and serious, and he'd be better off with a woman exactly like him."

"Haven't you ever heard that opposites attract?"

"Except they don't, not really. I annoy him a lot. And I hardly think he's perfect, either. He's exceedingly stubborn, and he can be harsh when provoked, and—"

"*And* he obviously likes you." Delia shook her head. "Honestly, Winnie. You're too smart to be this dense."

Her eyes began to burn, so she blinked it away. If he loved her, he wouldn't have turned her down. But emotional women weren't meant to be with serious men, and Ewan had been smart enough to recognize it. If only he'd realized it *before* he kissed her.

"Win?"

At the sound of Ewan's voice, Winifred jumped to attention. "Ewan." He stood at the shop door like he'd come from outside. When had that door opened? She stared at him, afraid he'd heard her secret thoughts.

Delia grabbed the broom and began to clean. Winifred focused her attention on the man before her. "What brings you out of the office?"

His gaze searched hers. "I'm on my way back from the post office."

The post office. Their letters. Her last reply waited in her dress pocket, suddenly weighing one hundred pounds.

"I'd hoped to congratulate Delia on yesterday's total

sales on my way back up to my office. I already caught Cassandra."

"Aw, it was none of my doing." Delia elbowed Winifred. "It was all Winnie here."

A blush warmed Winifred's cheeks.

Ewan cleared his throat. "Yes, I—"

His sentence got lost as the door opened behind him. Winifred lifted her eyes to the three visitors and gasped. In the doorway of the shop stood Mr. Richard Johns, a man she didn't know—and Uncle Wilbur, of all people.

Her hand flew to the buttons on her bodice, and her mind rapidly calculated the time Mr. Johns had said he'd allot to Ewan and his business to turn things around before he returned. What was the man doing back so soon?

"Winifred, darling, there you are." Her uncle passed Ewan without so much as a glance. A small man, he yanked Winifred into his thin arms for a hug, then clutched her arms and held her away from him so he could look straight into her eyes. "I demand to know what you're doing in Deadwood. You're supposed to be in Spearfish."

"Um…" She couldn't help but glance over Uncle's shoulder at Ewan. At the sight of Mr. Johns and the other man, Ewan stood stone stiff, as if he'd been etched from the mountainside, his shoulders broad, his chin up.

"Winifred?"

She dragged her gaze away from Ewan. "Uncle, I could ask the same of you. What are you doing here?"

"I've come to collect you, of course." The man huffed, throwing his gaze to the ceiling. "You didn't think you could send me a telegram without me coming to get you, did you?" He removed his hands and crossed his arms. "Now, answer my question."

Across the room, Ewan shook both men's hands. One, then the other, his gaze firm and his mouth resolute. She recognized that expression. He hadn't expected this visit, either.

"Winifred."

"I'm sorry, Uncle." Must pay attention. "I was working here to earn money for the fare home. You told me that my travels to Spearfish needed to come from my own funds, so I didn't feel I could ask you to send the fare. That's all."

"We came as soon as I received your correspondence." Apparently satisfied with her answer, Uncle Wilbur pivoted back toward the men. "And you must be Ewan Burke." Hands behind his back, he approached Ewan like a prosecutor might approach the accused in a courtroom. "Tell me, what were you thinking, holding my niece here against her will?"

Oh, dear. Winifred scurried forward. "I'm not held against my will, Uncle."

The older man narrowed his eyes. "Then why haven't you come home after—however long were you in Spearfish? Another topic about which you have a lot of explaining to do."

Yes, unfortunately only so much fit within a telegram. "I just told you. I first had to earn money for fare."

"Why couldn't this scoundrel show some Christian charity and pay for your way?"

"I say, Dawson," the unfamiliar man piped up, bushy brows low over his eyes. "My son may be foolish about many things, but I won't stand here while you accuse him of being a scoundrel."

His *son*. This man was Mr. Peter Burke?

She saw the resemblance now—the copper-flecked sandy hair, the strong jaw. The senior Mr. Burke took a step toward Uncle, but Ewan placed his arm in the way to silently break up the mounting quarrel.

Her mind began to reel. Mr. Burke, Uncle Wilbur and Mr. Johns were all gathered in Ewan's store. What was happening? Feeling a headache coming on, she moved her fingers to her temples.

"Mr. Johns." Ewan spoke up, his voice considerably calmer than Winifred's would have been. "You're a little early. We agreed upon three months, correct?"

Mr. Johns's squint had a death grip of resolution. "With your father and Miss Sattler's uncle coming up anyway, I figured now was as good a time as any." His hooded eyes scanned the room behind his spectacles, stopping on Winifred. "Ma'am, your uncle has been mighty worried about you."

"And he came running to me as soon as he got your cryptic telegram." Mr. Burke rolled his eyes. "Seemed to think my son had kidnapped you or some other ridiculous notion."

"What was I supposed to think?" Uncle removed his hat, mussing the back of his feathery white hair. "She says she's stuck in Deadwood with Ewan Burke, and I'm supposed to be fine with it? We all know how he left town with the two of you on bad terms—after all the bad publicity with that Erikson girl. For all I know, he's a rascal, running a shady business up here, away from your watchful eye."

"Uncle! What a terrible way to speak of Ewan."

Uncle Wilbur's brows flew upward. "*Ewan?*"

Uh oh. Openmouthed, she searched for some way to reply when Ewan stepped through the circle, clapping Mr. Johns on the back to redirect the conversation as he guided him away.

"Mr. Johns." Ewan cleared his throat. "Over the past couple of months, we've cut costs and raised morale. And there's an impressive vein of ore you will definitely want to see in the mountain. We're just beginning to excavate, but if it's the size we suspect, it should vastly improve the Golden Star's financial situation. If you'll follow me, I'd be happy to show it to you."

Winifred watched them cross the shop. The confidence Ewan exuded as he ushered the older man toward the hallway door…it was breathtaking. How ever could he keep his calm in these dreadful circumstances?

"I'm coming, too," Ewan's father announced, trekking across the floor after the men.

Uncle Wilbur tugged on her sleeve. "While we're looking at gold, you can go pack your bags."

Ewan stiffened. Winifred whirled toward her uncle, hoping he hadn't meant what that had sounded like. "Do what, Uncle?"

"You heard me. Go pack your bags and things."

"Now?"

"Yes, we're leaving tomorrow on the first stage. So don't dally, child."

"But—"

"I can see your obstinate nature has grown since you've been gone." He tucked away his timepiece, his face turning a reddish hue. "I told you I came to fetch you, and that is exactly what I'm doing."

Her mind raced. Yes, she'd planned to leave—soon—but not *tomorrow*. Her time at the Golden Star had slipped through her fingers before she'd known it. Winifred glanced at Delia's worried expression, and at Ewan's back, where he stood motionless at the door.

"Please. Do as you are told." Though still resolute, at least the anger she'd heard moments ago in Uncle's voice had begun to diminish. "You may ask any questions you'd like while we're on the stage, but until then, I'm sure you have much to do to prepare."

Winifred took a step backward, searching to make sense of this situation. To understand why it was happening now, in this way. What about having time to say goodbye without her uncle looking on?

No, she wouldn't get that luxury.

Without another word, she followed Ewan and the others out of the shop and into the hallway. As she headed straight to the kitchen, and they turned right to the side door, Ewan spun toward her.

"W—Miss Sattler?"

She halted. Dragged in a shuddered breath. Slowly, she turned around.

Ewan swallowed, shifting his weight to the other foot. "Your portion of the reopening sales is sitting on the desk in my office. If you happen to…finish packing…before I'm through showing these gentlemen around, you have my permission to go in and pick it up."

That's right. So she could leave without a trace—without even a warm goodbye. After all, she was only a temporary employee.

Her eyes misted. Oh, stupid emotions. She'd known it would come to this, right? Had feared it. Blinking, she pursed her lips and gave a definitive nod. "Thank you, M-Mr. Burke."

Hopefully she turned away quickly enough that he wouldn't catch sight of the tears slipping down her cheeks.

In the cold morning, white puffs of air left Ewan's lungs as he strode toward the mountain. With Mr. Johns, Father and Mr. Dawson flanking him, he forced down the nerves building in his chest. The investor had come a month early. No doubt his inspection would reveal the broken cam and the ruined platform. The cave-ins. Hadn't the man the common courtesy to send a telegram ahead of time, alerting Ewan of the visit?

And his father, seeing the Golden Star for the first time. What would he say about the place?

At the mine's adit, Ewan took his lantern down from the spike. "Follow me, please."

Mr. Johns looked less than pleased to be jaunting off into the mountain, but he followed without complaint. Father and Mr. Dawson seemed a little more interested, if not scrutinizing. Ewan reminded himself that he had nothing to be worried about. All the men needed to see was the vein. Surely that would redeem their opinions of the mine.

The light of Ewan's lantern bounced off the walls ahead as they walked in silence, their scuffing footsteps accompanied by dripping water and far-off echoes of miners' work.

"Will you still return to the Black Hills in a month, Mr. Johns, as originally planned?"

He heard Mr. Johns exhale. "Yes. For a different mine in which I've invested."

Tempted, he wanted to ask which one, but decided it would be considered bad form. "I think you'll like what you'll see in this new stope."

Mr. Johns grunted. "I will be satisfied with numbers on paper."

Somehow Ewan doubted that, what with the stubbornness this man had already shown. It was as if the investor had been against Ewan from the start. But Ewan wouldn't grow disheartened at the man's current indifference. Mr. Johns needed evidence that the Golden Star was worth investing in—and he would soon receive it. "Only a few yards more, and we'll reach the mouth."

God, if there is any way You can see fit to have Mr. Johns approve an investment, please make it happen.

Up ahead at the drift's corner, a light illuminated the far wall. When one of his miners turned the corner and spotted them, he blew out his candle ration, considering Ewan's lantern gave off enough light to fill the space.

"Mr. Burke?" The miner came closer, feet scuffing along rock, and sent a quick glance at the extra men, then back to Ewan. "I was just comin' to fetch ya, boss."

"For what purpose?"

"We, uh, have a situation." The man glanced at the others again. "We found another drift."

A warning ticked through Ewan's ratcheting heartbeat, though he worked to hide it. "*Found* another drift?"

"Leading to our stope. The one with the large vein."

The pit of Ewan's stomach dropped. "Show me where."

Lantern light leading the way, Ewan and the three men followed the miner farther into the mountain. With each step, Ewan's hopes grew darker and darker. He wanted to ask questions, but his thoughts were frozen. When they reached the spot where the vein loomed over them—the place Ewan had envisioned would appear so impressive to Mr. Johns—the miner joined his fellow workers and pointed out a hole in the wall.

Lifting his lantern higher, Ewan stepped closer. The hole, no bigger than a loaf of bread, showed...sure enough, another drift. Empty now, but by the looks of the beams in place to support the tunnel, someone had been working quite diligently.

Palms slicking with sweat, Ewan swung his lantern back in the direction they had come, trying to remember how many steps he'd taken. "Men?" He swiveled toward his workers. "We are still on Golden Star property, correct?"

"Yes, sir," one said. "We checked lots of times."

"And that drift?" He jutted his thumb toward the hole.

The men's faces went grim. "Our property, too."

Ewan closed his eyes. *Not this. Especially not now.* "And the Sphinx property..."

"We've got several yards before we reach them." The miner rubbed his dirty face with a muddy hand. "Sorry, boss."

"The neighboring property undermined you?" Father's voice echoed from behind Ewan, jarring him clear through.

Ewan ignored him for now. There would be plenty of time to hear his opinion on the matter. "How did they find out about this spot?"

The men, wide-eyed, shrugged each in turn. "Don't know, boss," one said. "We talk about it at meals, but not to the public. I ain't even said a word to my wife."

The others shared similar sentiments.

"Well, it sounds like you've got an informant to me," his father responded, followed by a huff. "I'd do a thorough examination if I were you, Ewan. Question everyone. No one can be trusted."

Except acting without trust would be a betrayal of so many of his men who'd seemed genuinely excited by these turn of events. Several had stopped by his office to express how enjoyable their work had been in the past few weeks, not to mention the security they felt now in knowing about the mother lode. None of them would jeopardize the mine by leading their competition straight to the treasure.

Grip tightening on the lantern handle, Ewan forced his thoughts to stay rational. *Someone* had let the word leak to outside sources. Hopefully by accident… though, coupling this incident with all his previous suspicions of sabotage, he highly doubted it.

"Wait—" A miner near the outskirts of the group lifted his head. "I just remembered someone on the night shift mentionin' it over breakfast at our boardinghouse. It was such a simple conversation, really, mixed in with other things. I nearly forgot about it."

"Which night-shift worker?" Ewan lifted his lantern higher.

"Works in the stamp mill. Tall, gangly. Wild hair. Young."

Ewan's muscles solidified, growing rigid all along his neck and arms. He heard his father and the others shift behind him, and heat coursed over Ewan's skin. Why in the world was Charlie Danielson talking publicly about the vein of gold?

Chapter Fourteen

Ewan pushed through the side door of his office building and into the corridor, leaving the older men outside to bicker among themselves. He needed time alone to process what he'd learned. He'd been bludgeoned by the realization that Charlie Danielson had betrayed him.

Earlier, after Ewan and the others left the mine, they'd gone straight to the boardinghouse where Danielson lived and woken him from a dead sleep to find out the truth. Presenting him with all the facts, and bringing up the multiple acts of sabotage, had caused the young man to buckle beneath the pressure. He confessed everything, down to removing the nails beneath the platform in the stamp mill.

Ewan paced the hall, staring at the floor, too agitated to climb the stairs to his office but unsure of where else to go. He'd trusted the man, allowed him access to the mine's resources and permitted him to watch over the well-being of his crew. For the reward of a bonus and a job with the Sphinx, Charlie had willingly put dozens of people in danger.

Soon, he would need to inform his workers. But for now, he only wanted to confide in one person. In—

"Win." Ewan stopped short as he looked up from the floor into the woman's eyes.

Halting in the corridor, Winifred shoved her arms behind her back. "Ewan. I thought you took the men on a tour…is everything all right?"

His gaze traveled over her attire—the kitchen apron over her dress, a smudge of flour on her cheek. "I thought you were packing."

"I was—but since we're not leaving until tomorrow, I thought I'd help Granna Cass with one more batch of biscuits. And then I was going to run an errand."

She took what looked like an envelope from behind her back and shoved it into her apron pocket, so quickly Ewan hardly registered it. He took a few swift steps toward her and grabbed her hands in his, startling her. "I have to tell you something important. It can't wait."

Her grasp tightened around his fingers. "What is it?"

"The Sphinx Mine found out about the mother lode. Their claim being directly next to mine, they drove a neat little drift onto my property and helped themselves."

She gasped. "No."

"Yes."

"When did you find out?"

"Just now, in the mountain."

"Oh, my." She pulled one hand away to cover her cheek as the information processed through her. "Is there any gold left?"

"Some, but who knows how much the Sphinx has

already taken, how much they've already spent? I don't know how much was there to begin with."

Her beautiful brow pinched. "But aren't their actions illegal? They were on your land. Surely there are repercussions."

"There won't be a record of the Sphinx's earnings, and the gold could be anywhere by now. Crushed up and mixed in with theirs. Reporting it won't guarantee I'll see any financial returns." He shrugged, trying to deflect the pain that burned through his chest, when all he really wanted to do was collapse against the wall, defeated. "Besides that, I seriously doubt Mr. Johns will invest in the Golden Star now."

"Don't say that, Ewan. We don't know that for certain."

Her gaze searched his, and for a rare moment, he longed to bask in her naive sunshine. A rare moment that was becoming not so rare, he realized. Ewan's fingers trailed up to cup her soft cheek. Such a precious jewel. She had been here when he'd needed someone the most, and he'd miss her terribly when she left tomorrow.

"Stay longer, Win." The words ached in his heart. "Don't leave so soon."

Her eyes widened, and the beat of his heart jolted.

Oh, no. He'd spoken before thinking. Every word was true—he meant them fully—but by the look on her face, maybe he ought to have kept his wishes to himself.

Nearby, a masculine throat cleared.

Ewan and Winifred jumped apart. Standing on the threshold of the side door, Wilbur Dawson glowered at him, looking as dangerous as a bull caught on the wrong side of the fence. When had he entered? His glare shot spears through Ewan's chest—but before anyone could speak, the door opened again and Mr. Johns entered, followed by Father.

Winifred scurried back toward the kitchen, her plum-colored skirts disappearing through the doorway, and Ewan retreated up the stairs to the safety of his office, though of course, the men followed.

"You've always known I don't approve of your mine, son, but nevertheless, I thought you would be above this sort of thing." Father's voice came from farther down the stairwell.

How many times since they'd left the mine did Father have to state his disappointment? Ewan entered his office and paced near his desk. He'd just asked Winifred to stay longer. For what purpose? Hadn't he told her last night that he chose the wrong girls, implying she was one of them? Dash it to the rocks, but he was confused. He wanted to see if their relationship could blossom, and yet he was afraid to even consider the idea. To top it off, she might see his request as an emotional response to his discovery of the Sphinx's crooked ways, or because of his concerns that Mr. Johns wouldn't invest in his company. The last thing he wanted to do was string her along, to make her feel that he wanted her for nothing more than emotional support.

"I thought sending Richard Johns to finance this place might make it worthwhile, but there's nothing you can do to save it now," Father continued. "Too much damage has been done."

"I've had setbacks, but the mine is still producing

plenty of gold, Father. Now that I've fired Danielson, I can turn things around—"

"I wish that were true, but history will only repeat itself through another offender." Father folded his arms. "A bad apple spoils the whole bushel. I should have known it would end this way. You get your hopes up too high and trust too easily. It's why you shouldn't own a business like this, especially far from home where I can't advise you on whom to depend. You should come back to Denver and work for your brother."

Gritting his teeth, Ewan glanced at Mr. Johns, who hadn't said a word to him since they'd found the secret drift. The investor simply took a seat in the corner, rolling his thumb across his fingertips in a thoughtful manner. Surely he would pull his potential support now. The prospect had only been a glimmer of hope anyway. Ewan straightened his spine and reminded himself that the mine could survive this blow. He still needed an investor to bring his business to a thriving level, but it wouldn't go under now that he'd caught the culprit.

Ewan stopped behind his desk and braced his arms against it. "I'm a grown man, Father. I understand how to run a business."

"Apparently not. What kind of environment is this that one of your own employees would leak information about a mother lode to your neighbor, your competition?"

"The promise of a higher-paying job was worth the exchange to him." Mr. Johns finally spoke up. "Not enough respect existed between employer and employee."

"He told us he thought we'd go under. He acted out of fear."

Ewan's remark caused Father to pin him with a cautionary look. "I don't know why you're defending him. He collapsed your business."

Every muscle in Ewan's body tightened at the notion of failure. "It hasn't collapsed yet."

"Unfortunately, Mr. Burke," Mr. Johns said, leaning forward, "I believe the problems with the Golden Star Mine are inherent and irreversible. Throwing money at this type of hemorrhage will only prolong the bleeding."

Ice seeped through Ewan's veins as he made eye contact with the investor. "What are you saying?"

"I'm saying even your employees don't have faith in this company. Why should I?" He tugged out his pocket square and touched his nose with it. "I won't be investing my money here. You can be certain of that."

The finality of Mr. Johns's decision, his indifferent air and his certainty in Ewan's failure shook through Ewan and destroyed his confidence. Silence rang in his ears. Everything he'd worked so hard for dissolved in front of him. His plans. His future. And if his mine couldn't weather this blow, he'd also lose his home and his ministry. He'd clung to the last thread he had, and with one sentence, Mr. Johns had snipped him loose.

Ewan rubbed the back of his neck, avoiding the men's gazes. "Well. I suppose that settles that." He took a seat at his desk and pulled out his ledger. Might as well start figuring out his next plan of attack since he wouldn't have any help from these men. "I think we're done here, gentlemen. If you'd step out, please? I'd prefer to be alone."

"If I may, Mr. Burke." Wilbur Dawson spoke up, "I'd like to have a private word with you before you get too engrossed in your books."

Winifred shut her trunk. "That's the last of it, I think."

Granna Cass handed off the bag of baked goods she'd packed. "That's it, then."

Winifred accepted the bag and placed it into her stack of luggage, and with it, a piece of her feeble mask dropped off. Ewan had asked her to stay longer. What did it mean? She'd tried her best to remain strong as she filled her final pieces of luggage, but that resolve had worn threadbare.

She should leave tomorrow, right? Shouldn't stay. Not after his rejection last night. But what if he'd had a change of heart? She still hadn't told him they were writing each other.

"Honey child, you know you're welcome here anytime, don't you?" The old woman grappled for Winifred to envelop her in a hug. "This doesn't have to be goodbye forever."

"Thank you." But underneath the sentiment, Winifred could sense that neither of them believed she'd return. When would she ever have a reason to come back to Deadwood? "At least goodbye isn't officially until tomorrow. Right now, I need to pick up my money from Ewan's office and run an errand downtown, but then I'll be back to taste one of those fresh biscuits, all right?"

Granna Cass smiled one of those smiles that filled Winifred with buttery warmth. "Yes, ma'am. I'll be waiting."

Leaving the kitchen and the scent of baking biscuits, Winifred made her way to Ewan's office. In the silence of the hallway, her dizzying thoughts finally came to a head, and Ewan filled her mind again. What should she say to his request? It was all she'd ever wanted from him…except it would mean opening her heart to him again. Could she be so brave?

Maybe, if he was in his office now, she'd wait until he was gone to get her money. Unless, between here and his door, she could decide what she wanted.

Footsteps echoed on the stairs above her, and soon Mr. Johns and Ewan's father appeared. Nodding a cordial greeting, Winifred stepped aside to let the men pass. Where was Uncle? Had he gone to the office with the others? She'd fled the confrontation downstairs so fast she hadn't paid attention to which way everyone went.

Reaching the office, she inhaled and thought to give the door a quick knock. No, listening for voices would be wiser—she didn't want to interrupt. Winifred leaned close to the door.

"What did you want to say to me, Mr. Dawson?" Ewan's voice.

Silence followed for a long, drawn-out moment. As if a storm were about to hit. What were they doing? If only the door had been left ajar. Winifred pressed her ear closer.

"Mr. Burke," Uncle said, his words slow, calculating, "you may not know this, but my darling niece has been entrusted to my care since she was six years old. I don't take that responsibility lightly, if you catch my meaning."

"I do."

Oh, dear. Winifred would rather have sunk into a hole and hidden forever than overhear such a mortifying conversation.

"I would assume you take nearly as much responsibility for the well-being of your company."

"That I do, sir. This place means a great deal to me."

"Hmm…" her uncle mused, and she could almost see him crossing the room slowly, rubbing a hand over his mouth. "Yet it's obvious you also care for my niece."

"I do, sir. Winifred is a special woman."

"Except you know she'd never choose a fledgling gold miner who might lose his business. Especially not when much stronger prospects await her in Denver."

Winifred gasped. Nearly pushed open the door, too, to protest her uncle's accusations, but Ewan's response caused her to wait.

"You underestimate your niece, sir. She may be a dreamer, but she has a head on her shoulders, too. She's driven and won't be persuaded into anything she doesn't want."

Her heart sang Ewan's praises. Maybe she *should* stay, see if anything could become of them together.

"Yes, she is driven. And what about you, Mr. Burke? What drives you through life?" Uncle's voice grew streamlined and on edge. "This land, the water? The desire to be a gold tycoon?"

"I didn't start this business for the money."

"Then why did you start it?"

Ewan seemed to hesitate. Tears pricked Winifred's eyes. The poor man sat in there, vulnerable beneath her uncle's stinging words. Why was Uncle speaking that way?

"It doesn't matter why I started the business," Ewan finally explained, his voice even. "What matters is what I do with it. Right now, it provides work for those who can't find work elsewhere."

"Yes, your father mentioned the charity work. Thus, I have a proposition for you."

Leaning closer, Winifred couldn't help but pin her hope on whatever Uncle might say.

"If you love this mine so much, I'll help you grow it. I'll give you everything you need to make the Golden Star a thriving contender. I'll give you money for more stamps, more employees and more equipment. Your downtrodden workers will never want for another job."

The promise tugged at Winifred's chest. Uncle would do that?

"But?" Ewan prompted.

"But it will come at a price. I'll help your business flourish if you stay away from Winifred."

She gasped, covering her mouth with both hands to muffle the sound. What a horrible thing for her uncle to suggest, paying Ewan like this, as if he was buying her away from the Golden Star. But on the other hand…what an opportunity for Ewan! What a valuable resource her uncle could be for him if he would just agree. And what did he lose by it? He had already shown that she wasn't what he sought in a wife. If he refused the offer, he could lose the mine. If he accepted…he lost nothing that he wished to keep.

"Let me see if I understand," Ewan said, the timbre of his voice unreadable. "You'll keep my workers employed if I promise to let Winifred go back to Denver with you, unattached and free to find a more suitable match?"

"Do you doubt that I can save your mine? I'm a very powerful man, Mr. Burke."

"Yes, but…lose Winifred to gain the mine? What kind of twisted proposition is that?"

Winifred straightened. That foolish man wasn't going to take Uncle's offer! He was actually going to sacrifice the jobs of all those people—Delia, George, Lars—and for what? A matter of principle or honor? No, that could not be. She wouldn't allow it. She couldn't let him throw their lives away like so much rubbish.

Turning the knob, she pushed the office door open.

Uncle stood at the window, Ewan at the corner of his desk. They both flicked their attention to her, the discussion dropping.

"Winifred?" Uncle pivoted. "Did you need something, darling?"

"I was thinking that it'd be best to go home today, on the two o'clock stage." The repercussions of her statement shuddered through her, but she forced her gaze to lock on her uncle's. "Why wait until tomorrow? I'm packed. Besides, I've been missing Aunt Mildred and my life in Denver." Which was all true…even if it broke her heart to leave Deadwood.

And Ewan. But she wouldn't allow her happiness to come at the expense of the mine.

Her gaze sought out the man she'd be leaving behind. The anguished look in his eyes made hers burn. She almost reconsidered. But she blinked the mist away as she stepped back into the hall. No use prolonging the awkward meeting. "Shall we, Uncle? Leave today?"

The older man watched her with hands folded behind his back. A quiet expression gentled his face. "I'll be right down to help with your things."

Winifred nodded and shut the door behind her, then untied her apron strings in haste as she ran down the stairs, her heartbeat suddenly picking up pace. Did she understand the consequences of what she'd just done?

Certainly she did. She was giving Ewan permission to find a steady, serious wife. And saving the mine.

At least, that would be her heart's consolation.

"We're going to miss you, Winnie Sattler."

Tears lodged in Winifred's throat as she stepped into Granna Cass's embrace. How the old woman managed to sound so strong, Winifred didn't know. But she desperately prayed for even an ounce of that strength to rub off on her, too.

"I'm going to miss you even more." Standing on the road outside the store, Winifred lifted her gaze over Granna Cass's shoulder to find Delia lingering in the doorway. If she wasn't mistaken, the young woman's eyes appeared red and puffy. They had said goodbye a couple of times already, and once more seemed impossible.

Behind her, Uncle stood with Mr. Johns and Mr. Burke, ready to walk to the station for their exit on the stagecoach. Thanks to the assistance of a few miners, her luggage already waited there.

She should stop stalling…but there was no sight of Ewan.

Attempting to stifle her sigh, she stepped out of Granna Cass's arms. "I suppose I had better go."

"No tears, now, honey child." The woman swiped

her weathered brown thumbs beneath Winifred's eyes. "Or you'll make the rest of us cry, too."

A soft laugh escaped through a sob. "You have my address, correct? Do you promise to write me?"

"Anything for you, missy." Granna Cass offered a tight-lipped smile. "And even more importantly, I'll be praying for you."

"I'll pray for you, too."

"The stagecoach leaves soon, Winnie." Uncle Wilbur appeared beside her. A hint of tenderness softened his voice, as if he realized the difficulty she had in saying goodbye to these people who had become like family. "Thank you, ma'am, for watching out for my niece."

"She's a special girl." Granna Cass gave Winifred's hand one last squeeze before letting go. "We'll always remember her."

Inhaling, Winifred turned to go.

"Wait! I can't take it." Delia's voice rang out as her shoes clomped down the walkway. "It's not right for you to leave."

"Oh, Delia." Winifred caught her young friend by the shoulders. "Don't you see? I have to go. My life is in Denver."

"No, your life is here, with us." Her hands waved as she spoke. She shook her head frantically, strands of blond hair slipping from her pins. "I can't watch you leave like this and ruin your life."

Despite the lump in her throat, Winifred laughed a little. "Don't be ridiculous. I have a whole life waiting for me back home—and you have amazing opportunities waiting here for you."

Provided that Ewan took Uncle's offer to invest. Oh, how she hoped he would.

"But nothing will be the same here without you."

That familiar burn began behind Winifred's eyes. She threw her arms around Delia for a quick hug. "Be strong. Let God guide you."

Then she tore herself away before her heart convinced her she couldn't leave this place, these people. She had to go. There was no other choice.

But where was Ewan?

Then he appeared at the shop door. Tall, resolute, a tree firmly rooted on the threshold. Her heart wanted to run the other way, to protect herself from the great hurt she'd surely feel at approaching him. But leaving without saying goodbye wasn't an option, either.

She crossed the slatted front walk and stood before the man who'd been both employer and friend. And possibly could have been more, had they been given the chance, but she couldn't allow her mind to trespass there.

A hush fell over them for a moment. "I suppose this is goodbye," she finally murmured.

"I suppose so." Something hard edged his words. She'd wounded him. Her heart couldn't handle this. Stubborn thing, why wouldn't it understand that she and Ewan would never suit? Even if he knew she was his writing companion, he wouldn't be happy with a whimsical woman like her.

Ewan looked away as the silence bore down on them. Winifred stepped back, and a board squeaked beneath her boot. "I'm eternally grateful for all you have done for me." The rasp in her quiet voice ripped through her. "I will never forget your courage and your kindness." The end of the word cut off in a stifled sob.

Ewan squeezed his eyes shut, the muscles working in his jaw.

God, give me strength.

Thankfully, Uncle Wilbur came alongside her and gave her elbow a light tug, signaling that it really was time to go.

With one final, tear-blurred glance, Winifred took in the property as the man led her to the station. Uncle Wilbur slowed until he kept pace beside her, their feet scraping along the dirt road as carts and wagons passed by. "I know you'll miss this place, Winnie, dear, but it's for the best."

Winifred mustered a smile. "Thank you, Uncle."

Exhaling, he took her hand and patted it before placing it on his arm. "When we arrive home and settle you in, I'll do some digging and find you a steady match, all right? Then we can put this whole mess behind us."

Winifred's mind flashed to Ewan. Just the mental image of him helped her world shift back into place—until she remembered she could never see him again.

How could she have been so foolish? For a moment, she had allowed herself to think she'd found the man of her dreams—the one she had foolishly sought through mail-order letters. She had thought try number seven would result in a love everlasting. But the truth stared her in the face—the more she tried to help, the worse she made things become. Always.

And if she stayed to tell him she was his secret

friend, there was the possibility he'd accept her—which would cause him to lose the mine.

So it was best to leave before she caused such damage.

Chapter Fifteen

One more twist, and the cam was secured. "That should do it."

Ewan straightened, grease slicking his hands, and inspected his handiwork. Pride surged through him. The cam itself cost quite a bit of his personal salary, so rather than hire someone else to repair it, he'd studied the mechanical workings and installed the new piece himself. And as far as he could tell, he'd done a pretty good job of it.

Only one way to find out for certain. "Marcus," he called down from the repaired upper platform, "turn her on!"

The manager cleared his throat, and his boots clipped across the wooden floor until Ewan could see him over the platform's edge. "Actually, boss, if you don't mind, there's something else we need to do first."

"What is it?"

"Come down and see."

Curiosity heightened, Ewan took the stairs. What could be more important than this work, which was the only thing that had kept him going these past few days? A week had passed since Danielson was fired and Winifred left for Denver with her uncle. Every time Ewan passed through the store, he tried not to imagine the beautiful woman who used to stand at that counter and drive him mad with her restless habit of rearranging his merchandise. It was hardest when he sat in his office, seeing her graceful hand around the room, where she had organized his files, updated his records and made things run smoother than he could've done on his own.

That's the way she was. Selfless, working tirelessly for others—for the mine. For *him*. And he'd thrown it away the night of the bazaar. That was why she'd left the next day, even when he had asked her to stay. He hadn't known—until he saw her leave for good—what a treasure he'd lost.

"What is it, Lieberman?" Ewan regarded his manager as he approached. The man simply grinned and opened the door.

Outside, a sea of faces looked back at him. Jaw slack, Ewan scanned each one. Workers from the mine, all of them. Both the morning and night crews. But what were they doing here?

"Mr. Burke," Marcus began, stepping out and motioning with a nod for Ewan to follow, "we're all well aware of how much everyone wants this claim. But you've held your ground and developed a sizable business. Not everyone could do that, and you should be proud of your accomplishments."

Ewan blinked. "Well, I—"

"So we've come to offer our gratitude," one of the miners said, stepping forward with a crock in his arms.

"Everyone pitched in what they could. It's to fix the damaged drifts."

A frown overtook Ewan's mouth. What was the man talking about? He accepted the crock from the miner, and when he looked inside, paper money poked out to greet him. And lots of it.

Ewan raised his gaze to the crowd. "Thank you—I really don't know what to say, except that this is far too generous."

"We thought you'd say that," another miner piped up, his comment followed by a wave of light chuckling in the crowd.

"But we've been inspired by Miss Sattler to do all we can for the mine," the first miner added. "She did, even when she barely knew us. It's time for us to follow her example." He nodded toward the crock. "And if that money ain't enough, we all agreed to work rebuilding those drifts for free on our days off until the cost is met."

Heads began to nod, and Ewan's heart ached. *Oh, Win. If you could only see the impact you've had on my men.*

"Thank you." His voice came out scratchy, so he cleared his throat. "I can't say it enough times. This is truly one of the best gifts I've received. And you all are the humblest, most hardworking men I've ever had the privilege to know. I thank God for each of you."

The warmth of their commitment to him and the mine stuck with him as everyone filtered back to work and as Marcus started up the stamp batteries. When the mill thrummed to life, Ewan crossed the yard and made his way inside the office building. His men were right—everything had tried to pull his business away from him, but in the end, he'd held fast. And even though he hadn't secured an investor, he would continue pushing his company until it thrived just the same.

Only problem was…having a successful business didn't seem as important now that he was alone.

The door between the shop and the corridor opened, and Delia poked her head through. "Mr. Burke?"

Ewan paused. "Yes, Miss Richardson?"

"A man and woman are here to see you. They're inside the store."

Visitors for him? Who could they be? Following Delia into the shop, Ewan spotted Sol Star standing near the counter, a woman on his arm.

"Star?" What would the postmaster be doing here in the middle of the day?

His heartbeat rushed for a second at the sight of the woman—until he realized he'd never seen her before in his life. Winifred was gone. He knew that to be true. Why couldn't his heart accept it?

"Burke." Sol offered a polite smile. He motioned to the woman. "This is Jillian Morris. She's come all the way from Lead City to meet you."

To meet him? Ewan's feet stuck to the threshold. His gaze moved from Sol to the woman. Young, she had pinned her dark hair neatly beneath her bonnet and wore a high collar and lace at her cuffs. Though stern faced, her eyes seemed kind and, dare he say, hopeful. What could she possibly want from him?

Suddenly, a couple of small, dark-haired children appeared from behind the folds of her skirts. They stared up at Ewan with large, dark eyes, perfectly mirroring their mother's, and all of the mysterious pieces fell into place.

"Mrs. M." Ewan raised his gaze back to the woman's. "Am I right?"

A twitch on her lips, which must have been a reserved smile, told him he'd guessed correctly. His most promising mail-order bride prospect stood before him in the flesh.

"She appeared at the post office a few minutes ago, asking for you." Sol shrugged. "I apologize, Ewan. I know you didn't want your name known, but she came all the way here for the sole purpose of meeting you."

"I was persistent," Mrs. Morris said. Her voice held authority, similar to her writing. Ewan could easily see the no-nonsense side to the woman's personality. "I confess, I grew tired of writing each other when we lived but a town apart. I determined to meet you and be done with it."

And be done with it. Not exactly the most romantic of sentiments. Not that Mrs. Morris struck him as the romantic type. Though he imagined she had little time for it, even if she had been so inclined. Her husband had passed away this summer, leaving her with children to feed on her own. The woman had to be all about survival, and Ewan suspected the experience had only made her more serious.

His thumb rubbed along the smooth surface of his crock as he watched her. Would her joy return once she'd found security with a new husband? Because she stood there expecting to find out if he could be that man, the one who would marry her and provide for her children. The embarrassing thing was he'd already written up a rejection letter to send her. It lay in his coat pocket now. After nearly losing his mine, and actually losing Winifred, he didn't have the heart to marry just anyone. Especially not someone so serious.

Clearing his throat, Ewan finally found his voice. Stepping into the store, he set his crock on the counter and faced the woman. "It's nice to meet you, Mrs. Morris. I'll be honest with you, it's quite surprising to see you here, so I apologize if my reactions seem stilted or abrupt…but I don't know if we would suit."

At first, she didn't answer. Lifting her brows, she scanned him from shoes to forehead. Her children nestled closer in her dress folds. As her eyes searched his, he thought he recognized doubt flickering in her heart as well.

"Something has come up since I last wrote you," he continued, trying to keep his voice gentle as he prayed for words. "I have fallen for another woman."

"I see." Mrs. Morris inclined her chin, as if she assessed him. "Another mail-order prospect?"

"No, actually, a woman who worked in this very store for a while. But she has since moved home to Denver." He hesitated. "Yet even though she's gone, I can't bring myself to marry anyone else."

She squinted a little. "You love a woman you cannot have."

He tapped his fingers on the legs of his trousers. "Correct."

It would be all wrong to invite her into his situation under these circumstances. There was so little he could offer her—even his heart was not on the list. And truth be told, her serious demeanor, the lack of sparkle in her eyes—the very things he thought he wanted—left him craving vibrancy.

At last, Mrs. Morris nodded, a proud resignation marking her expression. "I think I agree with you, Mr. Burke. And I appreciate your honesty. No matter what, the trip wasn't a loss. I would have wasted several days wondering how you felt, waiting for your letters, when I could have been looking for another husband."

"Thank you for taking the time to visit me." And he truly meant it. Now he knew he'd made the right decision. "I wish you all the best as you search."

Ewan watched Sol Star lead Mrs. Morris and her children away from the store, silently offering up a prayer for the family's well-being. He wasn't the man best suited to be her husband, but he ardently hoped she would find the one who was.

As he turned away, his gaze snagged on Delia. She tipped her head to one side, palms resting on the counter. "Was that true?"

"Was what true?"

"You're in love with Winnie."

At the risk of looking like a fool, he nodded. "Not that it matters now."

Her forehead scrunched. "Why not?"

"Because I figured it out too late. I've missed my opportunity." And that was all he wanted to say on the subject. He gave a brief nod before snatching his crock and crossing to the shop's back door.

"It's never too late," she called after him as he stepped into the corridor.

Poor, sweet Delia. She had no idea. If she'd seen the hurt in Winifred's eyes when he turned her down the night of the reopening, or if she'd experienced the hurt that ripped through his heart when Winifred walked out of his life too early, she wouldn't spout such platitudes.

Ewan started down the hall…he *thought* toward the stairs, but instead, his feet carried him all the way to the kitchen. Cassandra looked up as he entered, cleaning supplies in her arms. "Ewan, honey, I wasn't expecting you for hours. It's nowhere near noon."

Ewan stepped in farther, realizing grease still streaked his hands. "I finished my morning activities and thought I'd come here to wash up—may I?"

"Sure." She motioned to the tub of soapy water perched on the preparation table. "Haven't begun washing dishes yet…it's all yours. I'll get new water when you're done."

"Thank you." He placed the crock on the table before moving to the tub and dipping his hands beneath the watery surface. "Nice and warm."

Maneuvering around him, Cassandra wiped down the table with more vim than her age should allow. "I gather by that crock you're carrying that the men gave you the money."

Ewan smiled. So she'd known about the gift—maybe even donated funds toward it. "Yes. Thank you, Cassandra. I can't express my gratitude enough. I have the best employees in all of Dakota."

"So, I'm guessing, since you accepted the gift, that you don't plan to take your brother up on his offer?"

Ewan huffed, water sliding over his slippery skin as he recalled the telegram he'd received from Samuel yesterday. "I plan to stay with the mine. *My* mine. Not join up with his as a last-ditch effort to appeal to my father's standards."

Honestly, he held nothing against his brother for

asking. Samuel simply wanted to mend family ties, as he'd attempted to do after every argument since they were children. But, for Ewan, it wasn't about having one job over another anymore. It was about upholding the ministry he'd committed to and learning to stand on his own feet.

"I'll write him back to explain why I declined."

"Speaking of writing—" Cassandra bent to run her rag over the chairs "—did you end all correspondence with your prospects, or did you finally pick one?"

"I'm sending off the last of my rejection letters this morning."

Cassandra glanced his direction, her graying brows arched in a grandmotherly manner. "Even to that widowed mother who lost her husband in the accident?"

"I actually just spoke with her in person." Exhaling, he removed his hands from the murky water and reached for a towel. "A shame, since she appeared to be the most likely candidate. And seemed like she needed a husband."

At this, Cassandra pivoted to face him, free hand on her hip. "But…?"

"But, she's not a good match. My heart is elsewhere." He met her coal-black gaze. "Surely you know that already."

"I do."

Ewan half smiled. "After she thought about it, she wasn't interested in marrying me, either." And unfortunately, the mail-order prospect he'd really wanted to meet in person never wrote back after he'd made that suggestion. Perhaps the idea had scared TD away. He should've known—she'd made it perfectly clear she wasn't looking for a husband.

Not to mention, the disappointment plaguing him concerning the woman in the flesh he'd fallen for—too late.

It was a sobering thought. He hung the towel up to dry, then grabbed another rag from Cassandra's bin of cleaning supplies. Swirling it across the table opposite Cassandra, collecting the dust caught in the cracks, seemed to ease some of his nerves. "To be honest, Cassandra, I don't really know what the Lord has in store for me next."

"Whatever it is, it'll be delightful. His plans are designed for you to thrive and prosper."

A wry chuckle climbed his throat. "I have no doubt you're right…except sometimes I think God forgets the prospering part when it comes to me."

"Sure." Cassandra folded her rag in half and scrubbed a stubborn stain. "I can see how you'd think that, if you only define success by your business."

"I'm not. I'm including a wife in there, too." Not a proud moment, laying bare his secret plans to his cook, especially since they hadn't amounted to anything.

"Ewan, honey, let me tell you something. Seems to me like you hang your success on things outside yourself. Your job. A wife. Your father's support. But there is so much more—inside—that makes you who you are."

Finishing his side of the table, Ewan folded his rag and put it back in the bin. "I know."

"No, I don't think you really do, or you wouldn't accuse God of forgetting you." Without warning, Cassandra rounded the table and wrapped him in a fierce hug. "Honey, you are worth more than all the gold in the Black Hills." Freeing him from the hug, she placed her hands on both sides of his face. "It don't matter if you never find a wife. If the mine never becomes a wild success. The fact is, you're God's child, and that is all the success you really need." Stepping back, she poked him in the chest. "Now you just have to believe it."

Gliding back to her rag, the old woman shot him a knowing look—again, a little too grandmotherly. "And while on the subject of success and wives, I know a vivacious brunette in Denver who suits you in every way. That is, if you feel so inclined to chase after her."

His chest tightened. His Win was nothing like the serious, steady person he thought he'd needed in the treacherous waters of his future. Though, if he were honest, she shared his passions. For God. For people. For upstanding principles. On top of which, she'd made his days full of sunshine.

He loved her for it. When had she become so endearing?

Taking Cassandra's supplies back to the pantry for her, Ewan realized she had been correct—sometimes love found people in the strangest places. And love had found Ewan in the throes of a failing business. Winifred was nothing he needed and yet everything he required at the same time. He fully, unabashedly loved her, even when he told himself not to.

Inside the pantry, he stuck the bin in the corner. A crumpled apron lay beside it, so he swiped it up to hang. As he lifted the fabric, an envelope slipped to the floor. He bent to grab it and froze. The back of the unopened envelope faced up, but in the corner, the extension of a penciled sketch curled around from the front.

"Couldn't be." He swiped the envelope from the

ground. But sure enough, it was addressed to Mr. Businessman in the cursive handwriting he loved so much. How had it ended up in the pantry, beneath this apron? Had someone gone to the post office to pick it up? But Sol Star didn't give mail to anyone but the recipient.

Breaking the seal with his thumb, Ewan breathed a grateful prayer. He'd given up hope she would respond. The folded letter slid from the envelope, revealing its beautiful pink and red floral design, and Ewan skimmed the contents like a ravenous man ate at a feast.

She didn't want to meet him.

She had still signed it *Sincerely yours*, as they had each letter before it. But when he read it this time, his heart sank. She would never be his, sincerely or otherwise. His heartbeat stumbled at her words as he read them a second time. It was unfortunate. Months of searching and somehow he'd fallen in love with two women. One he had hurt, and one who'd hurt him. In some ways, they were so similar. But he'd lost both and now he was back at the beginning. Starting over.

God, I don't know where this leaves me. I suppose it's up to You. My entire future is up to You. I have tried to maintain control for too long—which is why I'm in this mess in the first place. Teach me to listen to You. Please guide me.

"Is that—" Cassandra appeared above him and lifted the envelope from his hands. She inspected the drawing. "Yes, I believe it is."

Ewan flicked his gaze up. "It's what?"

"One of Winifred's drawings."

"Oh, no. You're mistaken." Folding up the letter, Ewan stood and plucked the envelope from Cassandra's hands. "See right here—Mr. Businessman? It's one of my mail-order letters. Somehow it ended up in the pantry, of all places."

A frown of confusion twisted Cassandra's face. "That's strange. It sure looks an awful lot like Winnie's work."

He shrugged. "I suppose so." Though he couldn't figure out why it would matter if TD's sketches looked like Win's. They were both excellent artists who made realistic renderings. Of course their work would be similar in some ways.

Cassandra twirled her finger. "Check for her initials hidden in the drawing. Winnie always signed her work with WS."

He turned the envelope to the front and searched. Nothing. When he flipped it over, he nearly jumped as Cassandra pounded her finger against the paper.

"See? Right there."

Below the woman's finger, a neat little WS had been incorporated into the design.

Warning sounded in Ewan's thoughts, but he pushed it back before his imagination could take over. "Do you have anything else with her handwriting?"

Together, they moved across the room to Cassandra's private quarters. She tugged a crate from beneath her bed and withdrew a handful of papers. "A planning list for the store's celebration party should be in here." The woman clucked her tongue as Ewan knelt beside her. "I know I sound crazy, but it really looks like her artwork, honey."

Except it was impossible. Yet his heartbeat spiked all the same. After a little digging, they located the list. He held TD's letter beside it for scrutiny.

Her list was brief. A few words mixed with numbers, but he knew that handwriting. *Knew* it. Even though there was no way he could know it.

"I think it's her." Cassandra shook her head as if no other explanation existed. "I think she's one of your mail-order prospects. She did mail a lot of letters, come to think of it. Seems like they all had sketches on the envelope, too."

Ewan's throat felt coated in sand. Sure, the way her *s*'s curved below her other letters and the slant of her lowercase *y*'s and *g*'s looked identical to those in the letter...but *Winifred* was TD? That couldn't be possible.

"I'll be back." After getting to his feet, he left the kitchen through the side door.

He made his way down the dusty street and didn't stop until he popped into the post office.

"Star, you want to tell me who my mystery correspondent is?"

The postmaster looked up from the woman he was helping at the counter. A look of annoyance crossed the woman's eyes, like Ewan had just interrupted an extremely important appointment. But mailing a letter wasn't as important as this.

Ewan stepped forward. "Well?"

"Have a nice day, Mrs. Granger." Sol Star gave the woman a smile as she turned and left, giving Ewan a glare as she passed. Then the postmaster turned his attention back to Ewan, confusing marking his features. "Which one? I just introduced you to Mrs. M."

"Miss Thoroughly Disgruntled."

He crossed his arms. "I thought you were giving up the search."

"I have. Sort of." He stepped closer to the counter, thankful there were no more loitering customers to hear his words. "But tell me the truth. Do you know who TD is?"

The postmaster nodded, though his eyes didn't shine or dull at the confession. "You all right?"

"I've been better." They had agreed to keep things simple, he and his beloved friend. He didn't know the specifics of her life, and she didn't know his. He had fallen in love with her everyday nothings and the secret longings of her heart. Had she been in his presence every day without his knowledge? "Please, Star. Tell me her real name."

"She didn't tell you?"

"She *knew*?"

"Only at the end." Star turned his head slightly, a knowing look shadowing his gaze. "You know who she is now, don't you?"

The gravity of his question cloaked over Ewan's shoulders. Leaning on the counter, he ran a hand over his mouth. "I think I do."

Leaning his forearms on the counter, too, the postmaster worked the muscles in his mouth, causing his mustache to move. "What will you do now, knowing Miss Sattler was the one you wrote?"

So, it was true. The woman who drove him mad, yet filled so many crevices in his heart, was the same woman whose letters he craved. Why hadn't she told him the truth?

An image of Winifred popped into his mind, that night when they'd cleaned up the store together. She'd had something to tell him, but after their kiss—and his rejection of her—the news was never shared. Just like that, he knew the substance of her news, and it cut him straight through the heart.

He pushed off the counter and nodded a farewell. "Thank you, Star."

Dust coated his lungs as he wove through a jam of carts, but he didn't care. His speed increased the closer he got to the office building, deepening his resolve. He knew what he had to do.

"Cassandra?" Ewan called, pushing into the kitchen. "There's been a change of plans. I'll be going out of town for a while."

Sitting across the tea table from Aunt Mildred felt both refreshing and saddening. On one hand, Winifred was home. Or…at least the familiar place where she had lived with her closest family for years. On the other hand, it meant she had come full circle, that none of her matrimonial pursuits had resulted in actual matrimony. Unfortunately, it also meant the start-up of Uncle's tireless search for her final suitor.

"Don't look so glum, Winifred." Aunt Mildred tipped her head to the side behind her teacup. "I can't be that dull, can I?"

A smile drew up the corners of Winifred's mouth. "No, certainly not." She lifted her teacup and sipped the amber liquid, now lukewarm since she had spent so long staring out the window at the shrubberies. "I don't mean to be so distracted."

"Your uncle will be stopping by later with another gentleman for you."

Winifred couldn't help but wrinkle her nose. But she swallowed her reply with a sip of tea. Her aunt and uncle looked after her without complaint. The least she could do was not complain, either.

So much of her life had been about change. After her adoption, she had traveled with her aunt and uncle for years, from one gold town to another, until they finally settled here on the northern edge of Denver. She had spent her debutante season being introduced to scores of men, all orchestrated by Uncle Wilbur, of course. But she had been wise enough to see the flimsy flatteries the men offered for what they were—an attempt to win their way through her into her uncle's business and fortune—and had declined any proposals she'd received. Call her ridiculous, but she'd wanted someone different when she married. Someone who sent bolts of lightning to her toes. So, with her local options running out, she wrote letter after letter seeking to become someone's mail-order bride.

But the only thing that had done was keep her from clamping down on anything solid and sinking in roots—because she could never be certain where life would take her, where she would find a home. It killed her that the *one* time things could have worked, he had turned her away before she could explain who she was.

"Winnie?" Aunt Mildred's voice cut in. "Dear me, you really must be distracted by something."

"I'm sorry." She straightened to attention, her tea-cup rattling against the saucer she held. "What did you say to me?"

Eyes narrowing, Aunt Mildred watched her. Her dark hair had grayed some in the past few years, but being quite a bit younger than Uncle, and having the means and leisure to take good care of herself, she hardly looked a day over forty. "Before I repeat myself, I have to know what's bothering you. Is it Mr. Burke's son again?"

Just the sound of his name caused her eyes to sting. "Yes." She had explained the entire mess to her aunt and uncle the moment she arrived home. Even her shocking revelation that he and Mr. Businessman were one and the same person. Uncle hadn't said much, which wasn't like him. Aunt seemingly didn't know what to say, either, so she had wrung her hands. But the truth of the matter remained. No matter how much time passed, a piece of her would always cling to the owner of the Golden Star Mine.

Winifred cleared her throat, then forced down more tea. "Now what were you saying, Aunt?"

"I was saying you shouldn't feel so disheartened about lacking a husband. It took me years to find your uncle. For years, I prayed for the right man to come along. Finally, he did." Her pudgy hand reached out to clasp Winifred's, her fingers soft as petals. "Truthfully, I don't know if there's a husband in your future. I hope there is, because your uncle's love for me is a precious gift. But even if no man ever wins your hand, you still have so much to offer the world. And sometimes love waits for the heart to be ready. So prepare your heart, and follow after the Lord. No matter what happens next, you'll never be alone."

Why did her eyes have to sting again? "Thank you," she whispered, not trusting her voice to speak louder. Her heart urged her to say more, but nothing came to mind beyond her gratitude. For once in her life, she had been rendered speechless.

Chapter Sixteen

"It's a surprise to see you in my office, Mr. Burke." Wilbur Dawson leaned back in his large leather chair, hands folded across his lap, and peered over his desk. "What brings you here for this sudden meeting?"

Breathing in, Ewan squared his chest. After over a week of travel, he'd only stopped at his father's house long enough to bathe and shave before coming here, to Reed & Dawson Co., for one of the most important steps of his life. "Mr. Dawson, I want to ask for your niece's hand in marriage."

Silence followed as the older man slowly allowed his chair to cease its rocking. "Is she aware of this intention of yours?"

"No, sir, she is not."

"Then how can you be sure she'll accept your offer?"

Swallowing, Ewan willed himself to show strength. "I cannot be certain, sir. But I am hopeful."

"That's mighty brave of you." Mr. Dawson leaned forward, perching his elbows on his desk's pristine, polished surface. Everything Ewan wanted was at the mercy of this powerful man. "What makes you think I'd be interested in bestowing my blessing on you? How are you better than all the others?"

All the others? How many others were there? Ewan pushed aside the humbling thought. "I'm a trustworthy person in whom she can confide, sir. And we're friends, first and foremost—a solid foundation on which to build a marriage. I keep her dreams grounded in reality. I've seen her heart, and I value it and the person she is." He paused. "But, sir, even more than why I'm good for her is why she's good for me."

"Oh?"

"She softens my hard edges. She encourages me with the way she is steadfast in her principles and loyal to both those she knows and those she doesn't. She expands my mind and makes me believe in the impossible. Everyone who meets her falls in love with her, and my case is no different. I thought I could keep from loving her, but I couldn't help it." Conviction built behind his words. "I know I don't deserve her, Mr. Dawson, but I love Winifred Sattler with everything I am, and I'm hoping you can find it in your heart to grant me permission to ask for her hand."

A half smile settled in the corner of Mr. Dawson's mouth. What did that mean? Winifred's uncle stood from his chair and moved to the window framed in thick burgundy curtains, overlooking his neighboring business district. "Mr. Burke, do you know why I offered you that deal in Deadwood?"

"I assumed to mock me, sir."

That brought forth a chuckle from the man. "It wasn't to mock you. I meant to test you, to see if you valued my niece above your mine. Your affections for one another were easy to see, and I wanted to make sure your intentions were genuine. As you probably know, once my Winifred sets her heart to something, precious little can tear her away from it." He shot Ewan a look similar to the glare he'd sent him in Deadwood when he caught them together in the corridor. "I won't let you break her heart."

"I won't." Never again. He'd acted foolishly once; he wouldn't make that same mistake twice. "If Winifred gives me another chance, I'll never let her go."

Again, the older man fell quiet. His jaw muscles moved as if he considered Ewan's words with all seriousness. Crossing his arms, he turned his face back to the window. "Tell me, before we were interrupted by Winnie, what choice would you have made?"

The idea of an ultimatum still made Ewan's blood boil. "I planned on refusing the offer altogether, sir. I won't be intimidated into picking between two things I value so much." What kind of a man made someone choose between the woman he loved and a ministry anyway?

"Smart man," Mr. Dawson replied, which caught Ewan off guard. He'd half expected him to take offense at Ewan's answer. "I commend you for your confidence. And it's easy to see how much you care for Winifred."

Mr. Dawson seemed to contemplate the issue further, and Ewan held his breath. Speaking up seemed like the wrong thing to do. A silent prayer would be wiser.

"And is the mine holding up?"

"It is, very well. My employees are really showing investment in the place, pitching in where they can to get us back on track after the sabotage debacle." Better to lay everything bare. Ewan would disclose anything if it meant painting a stronger picture for Winifred's uncle. "We're a modest company, but we're making progress."

"Good for you. You have tenacity. I like that." He turned and headed back to his desk. "So, now that you have my blessing to marry my niece, are you also wanting my investment in the mine?"

Blessing? Ewan had to fortify his knees to keep them from giving way. "Mr. Dawson, if you're indeed offering your blessing, then that is more than enough for me."

The older man's eyes sparkled. "Then the money is yours, also."

"Sir?"

"I mean it. I want to reward your efforts to live as God would want you to. Besides, your children will need a legacy left behind, will they not?"

Ewan's grin spread. Stepping closer, he extended his eager hand. "Thank you, Mr. Dawson. Thank you so much."

Mr. Dawson accepted the handshake with a hardy grip that spoke of camaraderie. "So, how will you ask her? I assume an organized man like yourself already has a plan."

At that, Ewan couldn't contain a chuckle. "Yes, sir, I actually do. And I think she'll like it very much."

The firm shut of the front door echoed through the large house, followed by Uncle's footfalls down the hallway. "Winnie?"

Sitting with Aunt in the parlor, Winifred stifled a

sigh. She cast her aunt a look as she rested her hands on her needlework. When her uncle arrived home from work calling her name, it had come to mean he'd brought a suitor. Some overeager businessman from his office building, no doubt. Though she couldn't yet hear a second set of footsteps accompanying him.

Yesterday had been the first day he hadn't brought someone home in the ten days she'd been back. Even on Sunday, a church friend had escorted her home. But yesterday, Uncle had fumbled with some excuse about how the one he'd planned to bring couldn't make it… but something in his voice, and in the sparkle of his eyes, told her he had something else up his sleeve— that today's suitor would really surprise. She wasn't sure if she should be excited or nervous.

Regardless, she'd promised herself to let Uncle help her choose a husband. After the way things ended with Ewan, she couldn't bear searching on her own again. She told herself that all she needed was time for her heart to heal, but if she were honest, she knew there was no recovering from losing someone like Ewan Burke.

But God knew best. Even if Winifred had no idea what the future held, He did. And that would be enough.

Bracing her hands against her knees, she waited for them to enter.

When Uncle stepped into the parlor, he glanced around until he located her on the sofa. "Ah, there you are." Weaving around the other tufted furniture, he carried today's newspaper and some office paperwork, as usual…but no one followed him. Where was the promised gentleman?

Winifred sent the silent question to Aunt Mildred, but the woman only shrugged.

"I wondered if I might find you two here." He stooped to kiss Aunt on the cheek. "Did you have a good day?"

"Wilbur, honey." Aunt Mildred turned her face up toward his, brows pinched above her amused smile. "Where is the caller?"

He paused. "The caller?"

"Yes." She drew the word out for her husband. "You said you were bringing home a gentleman caller tonight for Winnie."

Understanding dawned on his face. "Close," he corrected. "I said I would bring her a prospect, which is a little different than a caller—this time."

Aunt Mildred shifted her glance to Winifred. "I don't follow."

"I don't, either." Winifred turned her attention to her uncle. "Of course, if you didn't bring one, you won't hear me complain."

Uncle returned her teasing smirk. "I think you will like this prospect. Better than my previous choices." He took the newspaper from beneath his arm and handed it to Winifred.

Her brow furrowed as she looked from the paper to her uncle, realization of what he implied sinking into her. "The prospect isn't a physical caller, is he?"

A hint of sympathy flickered in his eyes, no doubt remembering all the times she'd suffered through dinner parties, the numerous hours she'd spent combing newspapers for ads. He took a seat beside her on the sofa. "I've come to realize you will never be truly happy with a husband I choose for you."

Winifred tried to protest, but he held up his hand to stop her.

"You would try, for our sake. Your warm heart wouldn't allow anything less. But since we've been home, I've watched you wander this house like a ship lost at sea, and I understand now that I can't bring myself to force you into a certain life. Please know, all I wanted was your comfort and security—but I see now that those guarantees aren't what will make you happy." When Uncle smiled, small tears glistened in his eyes. "You have become a spirited, brave woman. Your parents would have been proud."

"Oh, Uncle." Winifred lowered the newspaper to her lap, her throat thickening at his touching words. To make her parents proud would be the pinnacle of her life's achievements. She ran a thumb beneath her lashes and drew a breath. "I love you both."

"We love you, too. And you deserve another chance to find a husband of your choosing." Uncle patted Aunt's shoulder as if to signal it was time for them to go. "Now, browse that paper. You never know what you might find." He must have sensed her hesitation because he added, "I think you'll especially be interested in page six."

Shooting her a fatherly wink, Uncle took his wife's arm and together they strolled from the parlor. Winifred watched the open door until she couldn't hear their footsteps anymore. As different as she was from her aunt and uncle, they were a blessing she had often taken for granted. She promised herself to appreciate them more.

Setting aside her needlework, Winifred opened the newspaper and smoothed the paper down. Catching that familiar fresh-ink scent, she fought a hint of nerves. What if her search continued to come up empty? How would she know when to stop looking?

Maybe Aunt Mildred had been right. Sometimes love waits until the heart is ready. And after years of searching, man after man, she knew now her heart ultimately belonged to Someone far greater than any suitor she could find here on earth. And it was up to Him to decide if He would allow it to be loved by another.

No matter what happened, she would never be alone.

She flipped to page six and scanned the advertisements. A sale on shoes, someone with an old shed in need of a new roof…

"Wanted: A Thoroughly Disgruntled Wife."

Winifred inhaled sharply, her hand covering her mouth. Her eyes darted to the parlor doorway. It remained empty. Then back to the ad.

Wanted: A Thoroughly Disgruntled Wife. Exceptionally beautiful, given to rearranging merchandise and offering greetings in precarious places. Needn't be practical nor serious. A joy for life a must. A forgiving heart for a hardheaded businessman much desired.

For a moment, all she could do was stare at the advertisement, mouth hanging open like a codfish. Then, heartbeat dancing a million steps per minute, Winifred tossed the paper aside and hastened from the couch. "Uncle!"

* * *

"Ewan, I'm genuinely excited for you. I can't wait to see where it goes."

Over his cup of coffee, Ewan stared at his twin brother, whose smile couldn't stretch any farther. It made Ewan's grow, too. "I'm glad you think so. Because I'll need my brother by my side, should she say yes."

"Well, I was referring to your new investor, but I suppose winning a woman's heart in the process is good, too."

Unsuccessfully stifling their chuckles, each took a sip of their coffee, mirror images of each other. Seeing his brother was like stepping back in time. Ewan had been back in his parents' house for a total of two days, and upon hearing of his return, Samuel had left his mine to visit him in the city over breakfast. Sitting in this kitchen still felt strange to Ewan—he hadn't done so since he left after Marilee's rejection. The house's turret, stained-glass windows, fancy gables and dentil molding were a far cry from his humble abode back in Deadwood, but the memories of romping around with his brother refreshed him.

Things had gone astray in recent years. Hopefully this short time together would help them right everything. God had a way of working things for the good.

"You know," Ewan said, letting the coffee warm his fingers, "when Marilee ended things and I moved to the Black Hills, I felt like an utter failure."

His brother's features turned serious as he set down his own cup. "What Marilee did to you was wrong. It wasn't your fault."

"I realize that now, but for a long time I thought I

would fail at anything I tried. Especially when compared to you, the perfect brother."

He shot a wry grin, and Samuel scoffed. "Perfect. Right. I have my share of struggles, too, you know." A pained shadow crossed the man's face, and Ewan worried for a moment that he'd said too much. After losing his wife nearly nine years ago, Samuel hadn't been the same.

"Well, our father regards you highly. You've got the nice house, the booming business and a daughter to carry on your legacy... I have none of those things."

"On the contrary—" Samuel held up a finger "—you have a promising business with a solid backer." He shrugged. "Although I wish you'd move back and work with me. It's unfortunate to only see each other every few years."

The thought wrapped around Ewan as he drummed his fingers lightly on the tabletop. "Maybe you should take a chance on a fresh start and come live with me." He winked. "The stagecoach goes both ways, you know."

Samuel's eyes softened. "Touché. So, when are you supposed to hear back from your lady friend?"

Ewan drew small circles over the newspaper lying beside his coffee cup. "I don't know, and really, if I hear anything at all will depend on if she accepts my offer." Wilbur Dawson had promised nothing more than to show her the advertisement. Exhaling, Ewan ran a hand over his hair. He had dressed casually today, the first time in years he'd allowed himself the time to read the morning paper and sip coffee in a leisurely manner. "Everything is in God's hands now."

"Yes." Samuel downed the last of his drink, then

stood. "I'd better be off. I have a meeting with the mining crew in about an hour, which gives me just enough time to stop by the house and kiss my daughter on the way there. She's with her governess." He pointed a finger at Ewan, a grin climbing one corner of his mouth. "I'll see you again before you head home, correct?"

Ewan stood, too. "You can count on it." Arms folded, he followed his brother to the front door. "Greet that little girl for me, will you?"

"Sure thing." Samuel opened the door and paused. Outside, November air skirted snow around the tree trunks and leafless bushes beyond the columns and wraparound porch. "And hey, Ewan? I really am glad you visited. Not just because of your lady friend, but because of us. As brothers. It's about time we figured out how to be a family again."

Ewan nodded, returning the smile. "Most definitely."

Lingering in the entry while Samuel shut the door on his way out, Ewan mulled over his brother's words. Most assuredly, he had been gone too long, had allowed the bitter seeds of jealousy to poison his brotherly affection. Success came from things less tangible than a job. For Ewan's sake, for his family's sake, it had been time to make amends in Denver. And seeing his brother happy, and becoming content with all that he himself had worked hard for, had done wonders for his spirit.

He pivoted away and started for the parlor when a knock at the door stopped him. Raising one brow, he spun back and turned the doorknob. "Really, Sam, you thought your closing sentiment wasn't soft enough, so you came back to feed me more?"

Ewan lifted his eyes and froze.

Samuel didn't stand on the porch. Winifred did. She stared at him, cheeks red from the wind, her brown hair concealed beneath a straw bonnet laced with blue forget-me-nots and tied with a yellow sash, the same one she wore when she first appeared at the mine. Her striking blue-gray gaze glowed with anticipation above gleaming pink lips.

"Good morning, Ewan." Her voice sounded breathless, maybe stolen by the winter gale. She jutted a thumb over her shoulder. "I thought I met you on the front walk, but I quickly realized he was your brother." A little laugh escaped her. "How embarrassing that could have been, am I right?"

He wanted to answer—but he couldn't find his voice. Winifred Sattler really stood on his veranda?

"So, I don't know how to say any of this… I'm just going to say it." Breathing in, she stepped closer. "For the first time in my adult life, I know what I want, and I know what I need. When I lived in Deadwood at the Golden Star Mine, I fell in love with the people there. Granna Cass, Delia, the miners and their wives. I admired their strength, their resolve. Their purpose. I need more of that in my life."

A lump began to form in his throat, but he swallowed against it.

"But most importantly," she continued, "I fell in love with the man who stands behind them all. The man whose dream gave each of those people jobs, gave them a reason to keep moving forward even when life grew impossibly hard." She spoke so fast her voice trembled, as did her gesturing hands. "I fell in love with the man who has become my friend. The man who understands me more than anyone else on this earth, even if he didn't think he would ever figure me out." She laughed softly, wiping her fingers against the corners of her eyes. "Somehow, you must have found out about the mail-order surprise, because I saw your advertisement in the newspaper. I am answering it because I want Mr. Businessman in person. I'm no longer content with a dream behind the handwriting—"

His kiss broke off her words.

The impact stunned him senseless. He kissed her with the same drive he had put into everything else in his life. And she returned it with gusto, wrapping her arms around his neck, tugging him nearer. The sense of her so close righted everything in his world. *This* was how life should be. This was what God intended. Oh, to live in this moment forever.

"Marry me," he whispered in a haggard voice. Foreheads together, he searched her eyes. "Please forgive me for not realizing my love for you earlier."

Winifred's eyes widened. "You love me?"

A soft chuckle left his lips. He placed a light kiss on her nose and rubbed her bonnet sash between his fingers. "This is a strange getup for winter, don't you think?"

She laughed a little, too. "I wore this bonnet because I've worn it every time I answered an ad. Admittedly, it hasn't brought me success yet, but I thought maybe this time it would."

Oh, it had. Mostly assuredly. What a sweet, wonderful woman. He snuggled her into his arms, into the place she'd been intended to fill, as gratefulness bloomed within him. "I don't know how it happened, but it did. I had only planned to help you earn coach fare, but I fell in love with you instead."

She searched his gaze, her expression sobering. "What happened to your mine after the Sphinx stole the gold?"

Ewan shook his head, waving off her concern. "Everything is taken care of. We're picking up the pieces and becoming a business again. Or a family, I should say. You'd be proud of how the miners have risen to the occasion." He visually traced the outline of her face. "I can't wait to bring you back with me. Everyone misses you."

A mist glinted in her eyes. He ran his hands up the back of her scratchy wool coat, guiding her inside and out of the wind. He needed to say a few things more.

"I may be infuriatingly obtuse sometimes, but don't doubt my love for a second. I want the woman whose heart I got to know both in person and on the page. The one whose joy for life overflows and gives wings to those around her." He tucked a loose strand of hair back into her bonnet, delighted by the blush deepening the color of her cheeks. "I want you, Win. More than any mine, more than success in the eyes of others. More than anything else I have ever wanted on earth. This is a real mail-order offer. I want you as my wife. And I don't care how thoroughly disgruntled you are."

She laughed, and the sound of it was pure sunshine. The woman he had fallen for through the mail stood before him in tangible glory. Beautiful, vivacious, passionate Win. She was far too precious for him to lose again, and he prayed he never would.

"Six times ordered but never once a bride," she murmured, shaking her head. Her eyes glittered like the snow swirling outside. "Does this mean my streak is over?"

"I suppose it does." Oh, how he loved this woman. "Seven is a good number, right?"

"Right."

He kissed her again. His soon-to-be *wife*. That was music to his ears. And she loved him, too. Ewan almost couldn't believe it. He might have closed a chapter in his life, but this new one with Winifred would be a grand adventure worth exploring. With God before him, and Win beside him, Ewan Burke would be untouchable.

Listen to him wax poetic. She was rubbing off on him already.

* * * * *

If you enjoyed this mail-order romance,
don't miss these other stories from
Love Inspired Historical!

MAIL-ORDER MARRIAGE PROMISE
by Regina Scott
MISTLETOE MOMMY by Danica Favorite
A MISTAKEN MATCH by Whitney Bailey
SUDDENLY A FRONTIER FATHER by Lyn Cote
MAIL-ORDER BRIDE SWITCH by Dorothy Clark

Find more great reads at www.LoveInspired.com.

Dear Reader,

The idea of a heroine "six times ordered but never a bride" intrigued me, so when I finally got my chance to write her story, I had so much fun! It was a joy visiting the Lead-Deadwood gold mines last summer for research, even if I was experiencing morning sickness while pregnant with my twin boys. My mind came alive as I traveled the damp, dark drifts, imagining Ewan fighting to save the Golden Star...and dealing with Winifred as she jumbled his well-laid life with her unorthodox ways and unending optimism. Two real Deadwood staples are mentioned in the story— Sol Star truly was the postmaster, and the notorious and deplorable Gem Theater really employed women tricked into working there. I always wanted someone like Ewan to give down-on-their-luck people a second chance. I'm thankful to know that with Jesus, we all can have that chance at redemption.

Love,
Janette Foreman

We hope you enjoyed this story from
Love Inspired® Historical.

Love Inspired® Historical is coming to
an end but be sure to discover more
inspirational stories to warm your heart
from **Love Inspired®** and
Love Inspired® Suspense!

Love Inspired stories show that
faith, forgiveness and hope have the power
to lift spirits and change lives—always.

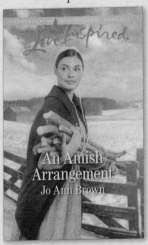
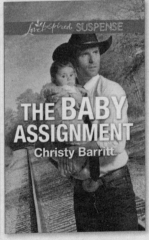

Look for six new romances every month
from **Love Inspired®** and
Love Inspired® Suspense!

www.Harlequin.com

LIHST0318

COMING NEXT MONTH FROM
Love Inspired® Historical

Available June 5, 2018

ROMANCING THE RUNAWAY BRIDE
Return to Cowboy Creek • by Karen Kirst

After years of searching, Pinkerton agent Adam Halloway is finally on the trail of the man who destroyed his family. Then tracking the scoundrel throws him in the path of sweet, lovely Deborah Frazier. Can he trust in love—and in Deborah—when he realizes she's hiding a secret?

A COWBOY OF CONVENIENCE
by Stacy Henrie

Newly widowed Vienna Howe knows nothing about running a ranch, yet now that she's inherited one, she's determined to make it a home for herself and her daughter. Ranch foreman West McCall wants to help—can his plan for a marriage of convenience lead to something more?

ORPHAN TRAIN SWEETHEART
by Mollie Campbell

Orphan train placing agent Simon McKay needs Cecilia Holbrook's help when his partner suddenly quits. The schoolteacher agrees to help him ensure all the orphans have been safely placed with families in town...but keeping her heart safe from Simon won't be so easy.

HANDPICKED FAMILY
by Shannon Farrington

The Civil War is over but the rebuilding in the south has just begun. Newspaperman Peter Carpenter arrives seeking stories to tell...and the widow and child his soldier brother left behind. After pretty Trudy Martin steps in to assist, Peter's search for family takes a turn no one expected.

LOOK FOR THESE AND OTHER LOVE INSPIRED BOOKS WHEREVER BOOKS ARE SOLD, INCLUDING MOST BOOKSTORES, SUPERMARKETS, DISCOUNT STORES AND DRUGSTORES.

LIHCNM0518

Get 4 FREE REWARDS!

We'll send you 2 FREE Books plus 2 FREE Mystery Gifts.

Love Inspired® books feature contemporary inspirational romances with Christian characters facing the challenges of life and love.

FREE Value Over **$20**

YES! Please send me 2 FREE Love Inspired® Romance novels and my 2 FREE mystery gifts (gifts are worth about $10 retail). After receiving them, if I don't wish to receive any more books, I can return the shipping statement marked "cancel." If I don't cancel, I will receive 6 brand-new novels every month and be billed just $5.24 for the regular-print edition or $5.74 each for the larger-print edition in the U.S., or $5.74 each for the regular-print edition or $6.24 each for the larger-print edition in Canada. That's a savings of at least 13% off the cover price. It's quite a bargain! Shipping and handling is just 50¢ per book in the U.S. and 75¢ per book in Canada*. I understand that accepting the 2 free books and gifts places me under no obligation to buy anything. I can always return a shipment and cancel at any time. The free books and gifts are mine to keep no matter what I decide.

Choose one: ☐ **Love Inspired® Romance Regular-Print** (105/305 IDN GMY4)   ☐ **Love Inspired® Romance Larger-Print** (122/322 IDN GMY4)

Name (please print)

Address   Apt. #

City   State/Province   Zip/Postal Code

Mail to the **Reader Service:**
IN U.S.A.: P.O. Box 1341, Buffalo, NY 14240-8531
IN CANADA: P.O. Box 603, Fort Erie, Ontario L2A 5X3

Want to try two free books from another series? Call 1-800-873-8635 or visit www.ReaderService.com.

---

*Terms and prices subject to change without notice. Prices do not include applicable taxes. Sales tax applicable in N.Y. Canadian residents will be charged applicable taxes. Offer not valid in Quebec. This offer is limited to one order per household. Books received may not be as shown. Not valid for current subscribers to Love Inspired Romance books. All orders subject to approval. Credit or debit balances in a customer's account(s) may be offset by any other outstanding balance owed by or to the customer. Please allow 4 to 6 weeks for delivery. Offer available while quantities last.

Your Privacy—The Reader Service is committed to protecting your privacy. Our Privacy Policy is available online at www.ReaderService.com or upon request from the Reader Service. We make a portion of our mailing list available to reputable third parties that offer products we believe may interest you. If you prefer that we not exchange your name with third parties, or if you wish to clarify or modify your communication preferences, please visit us at www.ReaderService.com/consumerschoice or write to us at Reader Service Preference Service, P.O. Box 9062, Buffalo, NY 14240-9062. Include your complete name and address.

LII8

SPECIAL EXCERPT FROM

Love Inspired HISTORICAL

After years of searching, Pinkerton investigator
Adam Halloway is finally on the trail of the man
who destroyed his family. The clues lead him to
Cowboy Creek and a mysterious mail-order bride
named Deborah. She's clearly hiding a secret—could it
be a connection to his longtime enemy?

Read on for a sneak preview of
ROMANCING THE RUNAWAY BRIDE
by *Karen Kirst*
the exciting conclusion of the series,
RETURN TO COWBOY CREEK.

"You're new. A man as picture-perfect as you wouldn't
have gone unnoticed." The second the words were out,
she blushed. "I shouldn't have said that."

Adam couldn't help but be charmed. "I'm Adam
Draper." The false surname left his lips smoothly.
Working for the Pinkerton National Detective Agency,
he'd assumed dozens of personas. This time, he wasn't
doing it for the Pinkertons. He was here for personal
reasons.

She offered a bright smile. "I'm Deborah, a boarder
here."

Her name is Deborah. With a D. The scrap of a note
he'd discovered, the very note that had led him to Kansas,
had been written by someone whose signature began with
a *D.*

He ended the handshake more abruptly than he'd intended. "Do you have a last name, Deborah?"

Her smile faltered. "Frazier."

"Pleased to make your acquaintance, Miss Frazier. Or is it Mrs.?"

She blanched. "I'm not married."

Why would an innocuous question net that reaction?

A breeze, scented with blossoms, wafted through the open windows on their right. In her pretty pastel dress, Deborah Frazier was like a nostalgic summer dream. Adam's thoughts started to drift from his task.

He couldn't recall the last time he'd met a woman who made him think about moonlit strolls and picnics by the water. At eighteen, he'd escaped his family's Missouri ranch—and the devastation wrought by Zane Ogden—to join the Union army. There'd been no chance to think about romance during those long, cruel years. And once he'd hung up his uniform, he'd accepted an offer to join Allan Pinkerton's detective agency. Rooting out criminals and dispensing justice had consumed him, mind, body and soul. He couldn't rest until he put the man who'd destroyed his family behind bars.

That meant no distractions.

Don't miss
ROMANCING THE RUNAWAY BRIDE by Karen Kirst,
available June 2018 wherever
Love Inspired® Historical books and ebooks are sold.

www.LoveInspired.com

Copyright © 2018 by Harlequin Books S.A.

LIHEXP0518

Inspirational Romance to Warm Your Heart and Soul

Join our social communities to connect with other readers who share your love!

Sign up for the Love Inspired newsletter at **www.LoveInspired.com** to be the first to find out about upcoming titles, special promotions and exclusive content.

CONNECT WITH US AT:

Harlequin.com/Community

 Facebook.com/LoveInspiredBooks

 Twitter.com/LoveInspiredBks

LISOCIAL2017